CONSPIRACY THEORY

CONSPIRACY THEORY

A QUINCY HARKER, DEMON HUNTER NOVEL

JOHN G. HARTNESS

Charlotte, NC

FALSTAFF
BOOKS
WWW.FALSTAFFBOOKS.COM

This book is dedicated to Justin LaFrancois, Queen City Nerve, and journalists everywhere who have put themselves in danger to bring us the truth.

I stood on my balcony, Irish coffee in my hands, looking at the lightening sky. My apartment faced south, so I never had the sun streaming directly in, especially not first thing in the morning, but on the rare occasions that I wanted to watch the sunrise, I missed it a little. I sipped at my coffee and grimaced. I'd stood there long enough for it to get cold, or lukewarm, rather, since there's not a drink in the world that will go from hot to cold when left unattended in June in North Carolina, no matter what time of day or night. Still, lukewarm Irish coffee just feels like you're making excuses to drink and should sack the fuck up and take a drink.

So that's what I did. I poured the coffee out, safe in the knowledge that if I doused anyone on the ground twenty floors below me that at least they wouldn't be scalded in addition to wet. There was a bottle of Dead Rabbit Whiskey on a table behind me, and I turned to fill my cup, stopping at the sight of a woman standing there.

It wasn't so much that a woman was standing on my balcony at sunrise that surprised me. I do, after all, live with a woman. But I don't live with *this* woman, and that was the source of my raised eyebrow.

"Morning, Cassie," I said to the diminutive Black woman standing on my balcony in a white fuzzy robe that looked like it had been stolen from an expensive hotel. Although in her gown and bedroom slippers, Cassandra Skyler Harrison, seventy-five years old and razor-tongued, her white hair pulled back in a neat bun, looked like she was there to give me a lecture on the evils of drink. I knew better.

"Want some? You know where the cups are." I poured a healthy slug of whiskey into my mug and turned back to the rail, hoping Cassie would get the hint.

"I didn't come here to drink, Quincy," she said, standing next to me at the railing.

I didn't ask. I didn't want to know why she was here. I knew why she was here, and I didn't want to know why she was here. "Why are you here, then? It's too early for guessing games."

"You still not sleeping?"

"I just wanted to come up and see the sun rise. Is that so strange?"

Cassie laughed, a sharp, irony-tinged laugh that both made me smile and warned me what was coming next. "Boy, the only person I know who hates being up at dawn more than you is your Uncle Luke, and he catches fire if he sees the sun. Don't lie to old ladies, Harker. It ain't polite."

I opened my mouth to say something snarky, and probably profane, and very much Quincy Harker, but I didn't. I didn't say anything for a long moment. I just stood there, my elbows resting on the safety railing around the balcony, feeling the chilly metal spread cold up and down my bare forearms. I needed to get my tattoos redone. I didn't remember draining the power I stored there, but it probably happened some time during my recent torture at the hands of Josef Mengele. Being electrocuted by Nazis that are supposed to be dead tends to take it out of a person.

There was a second where it almost came all pouring out of me, just like cold coffee poured from a balcony, but then I got hold of myself and deflected, like a reasonable person. "What are you doing up at this ungodly hour, Cassie? I'm sure Luke had you up until the wee hours."

Serving as my uncle's current Renfield had some drawbacks, and the bizarre schedule was just one of them. Dealing with working for the world's most famous vampire was another.

She laughed again. I noticed we laughed more with her around. She was something, I thought, this wiry old woman. Like a steel spring found in a junkyard. A coat of rust on her, maybe, but she could snap back from just about anything. "I'm old, boy. Real-people old, not this live forever bullshit kind of old like you and Lucas. I'll be dead soon. Get plenty of sleep then. Besides, when you get to be my age, you got to get up every two or three hours to pee anyway. After the second time, you know somebody's going to be firing up a vacuum cleaner or some other silliness next door soon enough, so you might as well just stay up."

I chuckled. "Nice robe."

She beamed, the Cassie kind of smile that illuminated the balcony more than the off-axis sunrise. "Thank you, Quincy. Your friend Gabriella brought it back for me from an assignment the Council sent her on a few months back."

Well, that answered that. The robe was most definitely stolen. Gabby Van Helsing was a lot of things, most of them complicated, but an inveterate stealer of nice hotel towels and bathrobes was absolutely one of those things. I'd overheard Luke yelling at her over the phone more than once about charges that showed up on his credit card for things she swiped. Part of me thought she was trying to goad Luke into coming after her, just so she could keep the old family tradition of Dracula-staking alive. No matter how many times I told her that her great-grandfather Abraham had ended up good friends with Luke by his death, there was always a little glint in her eyes when she looked at him, like Ahab taking note of a whale's spout off his starboard bow.

"You want to tell me about them?" Cassandra pulled one of the heavy metal chairs away from the patio table with a loud scrape. I winced a little but felt along our mental link that Becks was still sound asleep inside.

"She can sleep through a hurricane, boy. I ain't going to wake that child up moving a chair. Now sit down and tell Aunt Cassie all about your bad dreams." She patted the arm of the chair to her left.

I sprawled out in the chair, grateful for her choice of seats. This let us both look out over the edge of the balcony, pretending to watch the sun come up over the city when really I just didn't want to look her in the eye. "You know I'm not much of one for talking about my feelings," I said.

"I am well aware." The line of her mouth was flat, but I could hear the tiniest bit of smirk in her words. "Except for anger. You have no problem expressing that, fluidly and creatively."

"Rage-swearing gives me an excuse to practice the more colorful parts of all the languages I speak," I replied.

"How many is that, by the way?"

I thought for a few seconds. "I'm pretty conversational in all the Romance languages—Spanish, French, Italian, Portuguese, because I learned Latin young and still use it. My German is good enough to get me by if the other person is patient. I can manage to order food and find the bathroom in Mandarin, Korean, and Tagalog, and I curse fluently in Hebrew, Arabic, Turkish, Persian, and Hopi. I guess with a week or two of practice, my Khmer would probably come back, but that's one I'd rather not revisit. Cambodia wasn't good for me. Or for a lot of people."

"That's a lot of languages."

"I've lived a lot of places, and I don't like tourist food."

"You left out Enochian and any of the divine languages."

"Humans can't really *speak* Enochian. We can't hear the right range of sounds to get the pronunciation right, or at least that's what I've been told. And I'm nowhere near fluent in it. I can recognize it, but I have to translate it most of the time. I have a few chains of symbols memorized, mostly for bindings, but anything past that, I'm gonna need a few hours, a book, and four Ibuprofen. Looking at that shit too long makes my head hurt."

"So, what are you dreaming about?" And there's Cassie. She would have made a great interrogator. Get the subject talking about something, anything, really, as long as they're talking, and then once you've got their defenses down, you hit them with the real question.

I leaned my head back and stared at the sky for a good half a minute, then straightened up and finished my whiskey. I reached for the bottle, but an age-mottled hand slid it away from me. "Talk, Quincy. I don't need you drunk before the sun's up good."

"I might need me drunk to talk about it," I grumbled, but leaned back in my chair. I didn't look at her. I did that thing where you pretend that there's no one else in the room, or in this case on the balcony, and you just talk, like nobody can hear you. It never works, but sometimes it can get me out of my own way.

"It's the fucking dreams, Cass. I'm pretty much okay while I'm awake, as okay as I get, at least. But when I dream…"

"You go back there," she finished.

"No, not even that. If I just went back to being in the moment, I could handle that. I was out of my fucking mind with rage, everything was red, everything was anger, everything was pain and I just wanted to burn the world down and laugh while I watched. But I mean, fuck, that's the normal part of it, right? I thought Becks was *dead*. I thought the woman I love, the woman I love *more than anyone I've ever known*, was gone. Forever. And I knew I'd never see her again.

"I *know* what happens after we die. And I sure as fuck know what's going to happen to me. That means there is less than zero chance of me ever seeing Rebecca again after we're dead and gone. Lucifer's made it clear as glass that he's got big fucking plans for me and they involve my guts and a spinning wheel and making a new blankie out of Harker intestines every fucking day for the first millennia he's got his hands on me, and then he plans to get fucking creative.

"So, rage? Rage makes sense. Losing myself completely in the moment makes sense. Nobody in their right mind could keep their shit together with all that on them. No, it's not the fury that scares me. I don't have nightmares about losing control again." I stopped talking. That torrent of words was more than I'd spoken to anyone about what happened a month ago when I thought Flynn was dead, and it didn't feel good getting it out. Not like everyone said it should. No, I felt raw and scraped from the inside, like I'd puked up battery acid and it scarred me from my trachea to my soul. I was breathing heavy, and I felt the sweat making the hairs on the back of my neck stick to the skin.

"Then what do you dream of, Quincy?" Cassie's voice was soft, easy like the surface of a pond on a spring morning. It calmed me, let me step it back down enough to speak again.

"In my dreams I'm not out of control, Cass. In my dreams, I do all of those horrible things to Mengele and his goons, and I'm there for all of it. I torture that guard. I burn him, I freeze him, and I electrocute him all at the same time, and I watch myself do it. Not from outside myself, like you sometimes do in dreams, where you're observing yourself but not a part of it. No, I'm *there*. I feel Mengele's skin beneath my fingertips. I feel the resistance as I pull his arms off, *feel* the skin tear, hear the bones crack, feel the spatter of blood on my face.

"I'm not afraid of losing control. I'm afraid of doing something like that again and knowing exactly what I'm doing."

She took in a breath, but I held up one finger. "Yes, I could. I appreciate you wanting to tell me I couldn't do that, but we both know it's bullshit. I am perfectly capable of being that monster. And every night, when I close my eyes, I am. That's why I can't fucking sleep, Cassandra. Because when I'm asleep, I can't lie to myself about being the goddamned hero anymore." I stood up, leaned over the table to the whiskey bottle, drained the last few ounces of warm liquid into my throat, and walked inside to take a shower and try to scald or drown my truth for a few minutes at least.

2

Becks was waiting for me when I got out of the shower, sitting cross-legged in the middle of the bed, hair pulled back in a messy ponytail, a CMPD t-shirt on and her legs still under the covers. I leaned over, kissed her, and rubbed my hair dry as I pulled clothes out of the dresser. One thing about Luke getting a new Renfield—my laundry got done a lot more regularly. It wasn't part of Cassie's job to clean up after me, but since our apartment was the de facto headquarters of what existed of the Shadow Council nowadays, she kinda just absorbed our place into her cleaning routine. I wasn't going to complain if it kept me in clean underpants.

"Nice ass, Harker," Becks said, and I could hear the smile in her voice. I thought again how much I loved that woman and felt a rush of warmth over the mental link we shared.

"Thanks, babe. You're not so bad yourself."

"How would you know? I'm covered up."

"You weren't when I got up this morning," I said. "I might own up to checking you out while you sleep sometimes."

"That would be creepy if we weren't engaged." She wrinkled her forehead. "Might still be. I'll get back to you on that. Oh, and I'm calling bullshit, by the way."

I turned to face her and could see from the look on her face that all the joking was over. She had her serious face on, which either meant we were going to have a "discussion," or she was going to shoot me. And since her service pistol was behind me on the dresser, I was safe from getting shot for the moment.

"I might need you to be a little more specific, darlin'," I said. "Exactly what are you calling bullshit on this time? There are a lot of choices."

"She's probably calling bullshit on the word 'morning,' Harker," Glory said, walking in from the living room with two cups of coffee in her hands. She passed one to Flynn and sat on the edge of the bed next to her.

They made almost perfect mirror images, Glory's blond hair contrasting with Becks' dark curly ponytail. Glory's fair skin and blue eyes against Flynn's dark brown skin and brown eyes. Glory's scowl beside the concerned look on Becks' face. "What is this?" I asked. "An intervention?"

"Exactly," Glory said. "And put some pants on. You're distracting Rebecca."

Becks' cheeks darkened ever so slightly, but I felt the flush in her mind, so I pulled jeans on over my boxer briefs and slipped on the black Yellowrock Investigations t-shirt I'd pulled out of the drawer. "Okay, I'm all covered up. Now what exactly are you intervening about? I quit doing good drugs a long time before I met either of you, and I don't drink *that* much."

That was one hundred percent bullshit, but it would be pretty accurate if I said I didn't drink that much for me. It takes a lot to get me drunk, so while I consumed enough booze most nights to kill three ordinary men, it barely was enough to get me to sleep for a few hours.

"You don't drink that little, either, Harker," came a new voice. I turned to see Keya Pravesh standing in my doorway, her arms folded across her chest.

"Oh, for fuck's sake," I exclaimed. "You too? Did you get a nice show out of it, Pravesh?"

"You're not my type, Harker," she said. "But you're right," she said to Glory. "He does have a nice butt."

"For a human, he's well-shaped," my guardian angel replied.

"If you're done objectifying me, can we move this to the den where we can all sit down without reenacting a bad scene from a mediocre sitcom?" I didn't wait to see if they followed me, just shooed Pravesh in front of me and walked into the apartment's living room.

We took out the dividing wall between the den and the dining area as soon as we decided to centralize our operations in my building. That also coincided with Luke's house getting blown to toothpicks, so he lived next door. The entire floor was our people, with a couple of spare furnished apartments in case we needed some place for allies to crash. It had come in handy when we were operating Uncle Quincy's Home for Wayward Archangels the better part of a year ago.

I grabbed an armchair and dragged it over in front of the fireplace, at the end of the two sofas that faced each other across a large glass coffee table I didn't remember buying. I didn't say anything when I noticed new furniture, though. Part of the cost of running away for half a year was you didn't get to say a goddamned thing about what the people you left behind did with your living room.

Becks sat closest to me, and Glory took a spot across from her, leaving Pravesh to take one of the far seats on the couch nearest the balcony. "Are we waiting for somebody else, or is this all?" I asked, not doing a good job of keeping the snark out of my voice. I knew they were worried about me. Hell, I was worried about me, but talking about my feelings had never been useful to me. Explosions and bloodshed, yes, but talking? Not so much.

"No, this is everyone," Pravesh said. "Frankly, I am only here as a favor to Detective Flynn. I am only interested in your psychological wellbeing as it pertains to your ability to carry out our mission to dismantle DEMON and purge any rogue personnel from within Homeland Security." She was a cold-blooded one, our Keya. Literally, too. She was a lamia, one of a race of all-female human-snake hybrids thought to be extinct. I'd read in the Council's Archives about one that operated in the United States in the early part of the twentieth century, but she'd been thought to be the last.

Pravesh only disclosed her paranormal nature when she got shot in the head and had to basically shed her human form. She was also the Regional Director for the Department of Homeland Security's Paranormal Division, and a pretty good shot. She and I were never going to be friends, but there was a growing level of mutual respect between us. I respected her forthright nature, and she respected the sheer amount of devastation I could wreak in a very short time.

"Good to know you're consistent, Director," I said. "And you two?" I looked between Glory and my fiancée, waiting for one of them to start trying to fix whatever they thought was broken.

"You're fucked up, Harker," Glory said. I am pretty sure I will never get used to my guardian angel dropping f-bombs like commas, but she spent some time stuck as a human, and it fundamentally changed her. She had her wings back, and all her angelic powers, but I'm not completely certain she was still divine. I wasn't going to tell her that, though.

"Succinct, but correct," Pravesh said.

"We're worried about you," Becks said. She glanced at Pravesh and shrugged. "Well, most of us are, anyway. You haven't slept through the night since you got home from Memphis, and I'm pretty sure it's not the lack of bar funk and blues music that's keeping you awake. Talk to us. Shit, talk to *me*, if nothing else." *I hate this as much as you do,* she whispered to me mentally. *But you won't sit still long enough for me to talk to you about it, so I had to call in reinforcements.*

I sighed and leaned forward, putting my elbows on my knees and bending forward until my fingers tangled in my messy hair. "I'm not much for the 'talk it out' stuff, but here goes. I died." I held up a finger as they all started to speak. "Not metaphorically. When the medusa turned me to stone, she didn't encase me in stone. She *turned* me to stone. I was dead. Way dead. Real dead. I saw Lucifer again, and he was way too happy to see me. I cashed in my favor with Uriel and got back, but that was a one-time only offer. Then I got kidnapped by a psycho Nazi, tortured to within an inch of my life, fought my uncle almost to the death, and *then* thought that the woman I love was murdered. I lost my shit. I went full dark, no stars on those mother-fuckers, and part of me wasn't just awake for it, he was having a *really* good time."

"You were traumatized, Harker," Glory said. "It was worse than when Anna died, and your fugue state when that happened is the kind of stuff they use to train Guardians about what can go wrong with powerful charges like you."

"That's just it, Glory," I said, locking eyes with her. "It wasn't anything like when Anna died, because back then, there was nothing of me left. This time, I was still aware. A big part of me knew what I was doing, and that part was having a damn good time. I'd already decided I was in Hell, and if I was going to walk through the valley of the shadow of death, I was going to be the baddest motherfucker in the valley."

"But you came back," Flynn said. "You came back, and we saved Luke, and I wasn't dead."

"I was," Pravesh said. "But I got better. It happens." Fucking lamiae.

"I did," I said. "But not all the way. Or maybe I'm back, but I brought something nasty back out of the dark places in my soul with me. Because I can *feel* it lurking there, this part of me that revels in the slaughter, and the blood, and the pain. He's sitting there, waiting for it to all go sideways again, because he wants to watch the world burn and he knows if he just lets me go blindly after Shaw and her cronies, that I'll eventually light the match."

"That's the demon talking," Glory said. I opened my mouth, and it was her turn to hold up a finger for silence. "Trust me. I can't tell you everything I know about Skyffrax, the demon that lives inside Luke, and has a derivative in you, but I can tell you that those thoughts aren't actually a part of you. They're infernal in origin, and while they're a part of you, they're not necessarily a bad thing. No, hear me out." This time the finger went toward Becks, and she obediently closed her mouth.

"Harker's had this thing inside him his entire life, and it's been gaining strength for over a century, but it's always remained hidden, at least until now." She turned back to me.

"The past few years have certainly been the most stressful you've lived through, but instead of giving in to the demon's control, you've gotten stronger. You're actually a better person than you were when we met, Harker."

Glory paused and gave me a little smirk. "I take no small amount of credit for that, by the way. The truth is, the shard of Skyffrax that lives in you has grown in power, too. But you keep him in check, Harker. You haven't gone on some rampage and stormed the Gates of Heaven with a horde of demons at your back or burned entire continents to the dirt. You haven't even engaged in mass murder."

"Staggering property damage, yes. Mass murder, no." That Pravesh, always putting the best light on things.

"So yeah, it's been a rough year. A rough couple of years. And the next few months look like they might get worse before it gets better. But you've gotten stronger the more fucked up things have gotten, and you've got people around you to bring you back down to earth if you start to slip. Like Becks did in that warehouse." Glory and my fiancée shared a warm look, but I read as much relief in Glory's posture as anything. That's when it clicked for me.

"Holy fucking shit," I said.

Everyone turned to look at me, and when I locked eyes with Glory, she looked like something tasted really bad, and I knew I was right. "You're my Guardian, but you're not here to guard me, are you?"

Flynn's head whipped back and forth between me and Glory. "What the actual fuck are you talking about, Harker?"

"Answer me, Glory," I said. My voice was low, and level, and despite the emotions roiling within me, I managed to keep a lid on everything going on inside me. A lot of assumptions were about to get flipped on their head, and I wasn't sure who was going to be standing when the dust cleared from the bomb I was about to drop.

"No, that's right. You're my assignment, but guarding you is only a part of the job." Glory met my eyes, and for the first time in the decade we'd been together, I saw a hint of the cold distance I'd always seen in every divine creature I'd ever encountered.

"What's the job, Glory?" I asked. "They deserve to know the truth. *She* deserves to know."

The angel on my couch sat in silence for a long time, then she looked at Flynn. "I'm sorry."

She turned back to me. "I do care about you, you know." It wasn't a question. It also wasn't a lie, but it wasn't the whole truth, either.

"I know. Now tell her."

Glory took a deep breath, then let it out slow and looked Rebecca in the eye. "I'm Harker's Guardian, and I am tasked with keeping him alive and safe. But he's right. That's not the whole job. It's not even the main job. My primary task is guarding the world *from* Harker. He is unique in human history, a human born with a shred of demon essence, but not a Cambion. There has never been anything like him before, and Heaven doesn't know what would happen if he ever completely lost control or embraced the demon inside himself."

"I...don't understand," Becks said, but I could see the lie written in her eyes, her jaw, the set of her shoulders. Every inch of her screamed that she was full of shit but really, really wanted to be telling the truth.

"I'm here to make sure that if Harker ever goes dark, that the damage to the world is kept to a minimum. I'm here to keep the loss of innocent life as low as possible."

"She's not here to keep me alive, babe," I said. "She's here to kill me."

3

———————————————

That revelation went over about as well as you would expect, and after some threats, and a wealth of profanity including some words I didn't even know my fiancée *knew*, she threw her coffee cup at Glory's head and stormed off into the bedroom to get ready for work. Pravesh had slipped out of the room as the first epithets were hurled, so that left me and Glory sitting in the living room together in the uneasy silence to end *all* uneasy silences.

"So..." I started, but ran out of words after that.

"Yeah."

"That's a thing."

"Oh yeah. It's totally a thing."

"What are we going to do about it?" I asked.

Glory sat silent for a long time. I watched her think, mulling over for the first time the level of power wrapped in the guise of a gorgeous blond woman. She was, to put it mildly, built like a brick shithouse, with a cover-girl face and long curls that always managed to look both messy and perfectly arranged. She was one of the most beautiful women I'd ever seen, and I wondered now if she chose that form to hide the threat she presented.

We sat in silence long enough for the sun to rise past the level of my floor-to-ceiling windows, so I got up to open the blinds. As long as I'm pretty sure nobody is going to come crashing through the glass, I try to keep them open as much as I can. I paid a lot for the view, might as well enjoy it. Glory took a deep breath as I walked back over and sat in the chair again.

"I don't really know, Harker," she admitted. "Like I said, you're unique. There's never been anyone or any*thing* quite like you. Normal rules don't apply."

"What are the normal rules?" I asked.

"Normally we never interact directly with our charges. Normally they only believe we're real if they're already religious, and we just keep them safe. That was never going to work with you. Aside from your raw power, you already knew too much for me to stay hidden. So…"

"So you let me see you," I finished.

"Yeah."

"Why tell me now?" I asked.

Glory didn't meet my eyes. "What?"

"Why tell me this now? We've been working together for a long time, and at any time you could have told me that your primary job was keeping me from burning the world down around us. But you didn't. So why now?" I leaned forward, elbows on my knees, my stare boring holes in the top of her head as she sat there, eyes downcast.

"I need your help." The words were soft, almost inaudible even to me, but I knew they were coming.

I leaned back in the chair, never taking my eyes off her. "Okay. Whatever you need."

Now she met my gaze. Her head snapped up like it was on a spring, and she looked as stunned as if somebody hit her with a two by four. "What?"

"Okay," I repeated. "I'll help you with whatever you need."

"You're not even going to ask what it is?"

"No," I said, then stood up. I walked to the sliding patio door and pulled it open. "If I took a swan dive off this patio right now, what would you do?"

"First I would dive after you to catch you, then halfway down I'd probably remember just how hard it is to kill you, and I'd let you smash into the ground just for being a dick and scaring me. Now come back inside."

"But your first move," I said, hopping up onto the four-inch strip of concrete that marked the edge of my balcony, "would be to dive after me."

"Not if you do it now, because I've thought it through and I'm almost certain the fall wouldn't kill you."

"I've lived through worse," I said, remembering a time when an angry wizard tossed me from an office building at least twice as high as my place.

"I remember. Now get back in here."

I hopped down and walked back inside. "That's why I just said yes."

"I still don't get it."

"I don't either," Becks said from the doorway to our bedroom. She had showered and dressed in record time, pulling her hair back and taming it somehow and throwing on a charcoal gray pantsuit with a scarlet scoop-neck t-shirt under the jacket. The only part of her outfit that wouldn't look perfectly at home in a normal office was the Sig Sauer .40 service pistol on her right hip. "Why are you agreeing to do anything for her after what you just figured out?"

"She gave up her wings for me, Becks. When Barachiel was about to cleave me into little Harker chunks, she got in between us, even though the price for that was her wings."

"And you literally went to Hell to get them back," Flynn shot back. She was right, of course. She has an annoying tendency of being right almost all the time. But it didn't matter.

"I got her wings back, but we don't know if I got her divinity back. Do we, Glory?" I turned to look at the angel, and there was that stunned look again. I was getting pretty good at surprising my Guardian today.

"What...how did you..."

"You never said 'fuck' before you lost your wings, but you never stopped after you got them back," I replied.

"Swearing, or lack thereof, is not an indicator of sanctity," Glory said, a little primly.

"But I'm right, aren't I? Something changed in you in that moment, and it's never changed back."

It was Glory's turn to pace and run her fingers through her hair, again leaving it perfectly messy and arranged. If she wasn't still divine, she definitely still had some of the mojo. "No, it hasn't. I...I can't communicate with the rest of the Host."

"They aren't answering your calls on the Angel phone?" Becks asked. The snark was strong in this one today.

"Before...for all eternity, I have been part of something larger than myself. I have been connected with every angel in every plane of existence. Every member of the Host in Heaven, every Guardian on Earth, even the Sentries posted to watch the entrances to Heaven in case Lucifer tries to invade again. We have always been connected, more of an Angel-net than a phone system. If I thought about it, I just needed to reach out to any angel anywhere, and they would hear me. But since I lost my wings..."

"Radio silence," I offered.

"Yes. I thought getting my wings back would just plug me back in, like a reboot. But not so much."

"And what do you expect Harker to do about it?" Becks asked. I noticed she didn't use the word "us" anywhere in there. She had a wall up between our minds, but I could feel the anger and hurt coming off her in waves. She felt betrayed, and let down, and I didn't begrudge her any of that. I felt a little of that, too, but it didn't touch me as deeply as it did Becks. I was a *lot* older, and maybe that gave me a little perspective. Or maybe I just inherently thought most people sucked, so when one proved me right, it bothered me less. One of those.

"I need to talk to Michael," Glory said simply.

I let out a breath. Michael, the lead dog in the Archangel sled team. The guy who threw Adam and Eve out of the Garden of Eden, flaming sword and all. I hadn't seen him since we came back from Hell, and frankly hoped I never would again. He was kind of a dick. "How am I supposed to get in touch with Michael? It's not like we're Facebook friends. I mean, he doesn't even follow my Instagram."

"You don't have an Instagram," Glory said.

"I'm not even sure what it is," I replied. Technology has never been my strong suit. One of the difficulties in being born in the nineteenth century was a childhood without the internet. Or electric lights. Or penicillin. "But I'm pretty sure there are no angels following it."

"You call angels just like you call demons, Harker," Glory said, and the casual tone she used rocked me on my heels mentally. "We're the same thing, remember? The Fallen started off as angels, and the lesser demons are just their creations. We're two sides of the same coin, so any spell you can use to summon a demon will summon Michael. Now, he probably won't *like* it, but it should work."

I was still processing all this when Becks came over and kissed me on the cheek. "I've gotta go to work. Please don't do anything apocalyptically stupid in the next nine hours."

"No promises," I said. *Especially if I try to* summon *the boss of the fucking Archangels*, I said over our mental link.

She looked at Glory, and I could see her hand twitching like she really wanted to be touching her gun but was restraining herself with serious effort. "You and I are going to have a long conversation about trust, and secrets, but not today. Today I'm going to go to work and hopefully only have to keep my city safe from human threats. But tonight...let's just say you'd better be prepared to find out if an angel can get drunk, because the chat we're going to have is going to require a lot of whisky. Expensive whisky."

I made the executive decision to have someplace else to be when she got home from work and watched her walk out the door. Like the old saying goes, I hate to see her go, but I love to watch her leave. With Becks gone, I turned my attention back to Glory. "You know I can't summon Michael without his true name."

"I know."

"I don't *know* Michael's true name."

"I know."

"Did you have a solution in mind?"

18

"I do, but I'm still trying to decide how terrible an idea it is," Glory said. Her expression was pensive, with a furrowed brow. She was chewing on her bottom lip and took a very long time before she finally said, "I know it."

"You know Michael's true name?" True names of angels and demons are a big deal. Having a demon's true name meant that with the right incantation, you could summon it anytime, and with the right binding spells, you could *force* the demon to do your bidding. Trying to force a demon to do anything was generally a really bad idea, even worse than summoning it in the first place. Demons didn't get to Hell by being tractable, agreeable sorts; they're contrary by nature, and most of them are pissed off about everything. All the time.

Summoning one isn't the problem. Most demons actually like getting out of Hell once in a while. They get to cause havoc in a new place, meet interesting people, devour their souls, sow discord, wreak devastation—all the demony kind of stuff. But you try and order one around and you're taking your life and your soul into your hands. I'd done it a few times. It...often didn't end well.

I figured that trying to summon Michael and force him to do my bidding would be even more difficult, and even more dangerous. That danger was exacerbated by the fact that unlike demons, angels and Archangels can come to our plane of existence whenever they want, so if I tried to force Michael to be my lapdog, the second the spell ended, he'd just come back and shove a flaming sword all the way up my ass.

No, we were going to have to do this the hard way. I was going to have to ask nicely.

4

Y ou want to *what?*" Sister Lucia's voice climbed an octave, and her eyes got as wide as dinner plates. She stared back at me from my tablet screen, through the marvels of video calling. Lucia was a nun, and if she wasn't near as old as me, I'd eat my hat, but she had an encyclopedic knowledge of things mystical and sacred, and if anybody I was on speaking terms with knew how to call an angel, it would be her.

"We need to call Archangel Michael," I said again. "Glory needs to talk to him, and her connection to the Angel Internet is on the fritz."

"Well, then, call him," Lucia said. "You were with him for the better part of two years, running around collecting Archangels like Poké-mon, then taking every last one of them to Hell like the idiot you are."

"What?!? It's not like I had many other ways to keep Lucifer from taking over Uriel and waltzing into an unguarded Heaven."

"I didn't say it was the wrong thing to do. I just said it was idiotic." She smiled then, all the lines around her dark brown eyes crinkling. Lucia leaned back in her chair, away from her computer, and for the first time, I realized how thin she'd gotten.

"Lucia, are you okay?" I asked. "You've lost a lot of weight." It had been about a year since the last time I saw her, when I was hunting Raphael in New York, but she was down a good thirty or forty pounds since then.

"No, Quincy, I'm not okay. I'm old. Bad old. Not as old as you, but also completely human. Well, maybe a little bit upgraded. But still human. It's coming up on my time, and as soon as I can get this baby nun sitting over here gawking at me trained up, I'm gonna lay these old bones down and get some rest. I got a lot of people I want to see that I ain't seen in a while, and that boy from Mississippi promised me a private concert when I get upstairs."

I took another long look at her. People dying of old age was out of my realm of experience. I hadn't ever really known anyone who didn't die before their time. My parents were both relatively young when they died, Mother in an accident and Father from what we assume was a heart attack. Both my brothers were killed by the flu, and most of the people I've known as an adult died violently. Looking at Lucia on video was the first time I'd really *seen* someone who was staring their mortality in the face. Having known her as long as I did, it was no surprise that she stared down Death with the same placid exterior she wore when facing demons. Sister Lucia was a badass, no doubt about it. But I could see the weariness, how it wore on her. She had done the work of two lifetimes in one, and she was tired.

"Well, there's a lot of us down here who'll miss you, even if you are a grumpy old bat," I said, teasing.

"It's a good thing you ain't up here, boy, or I would split your knuckles with a ruler. And don't think I can't still tear you up, even at a hundred and three."

I froze, my mouth dropping open. "Did you just say—"

"Yes, Quincy, I am a hundred and three years old. Don't look like you just sat in something cold, boy. You knew I was old. You just never knew how old."

"How…"

"I told you there were some upgrades. Me and the Lord had a talk some years back, when the Sister who was supposed to take my place here got killed by a taxi driven by a demon. There ain't that many people with the knowledge I have, and it isn't something that can be acquired in a weekend. Add to that the need for my replacement to be someone with at least a little bit of power, and no close family ties, and not a whole lot of interest in running around chasing men. Or women. Add all that together, and it's a pretty narrow pool of people to draw from. Sister Dorothea is the first one they could find and get trained up, and it's been a minute to get her knowing everything she's got to know to sit in this chair."

That was the most Lucia had ever told me about her role within the Church, which apparently was a lot more than her work as a mystical librarian and archivist that I knew about. I'd always known Lucia to be an expert on all things holy and profane, which made her very useful to me in my work. And I knew she had at least the Sight, but had never seen her do any real workings. So to get bombarded with the idea that she had some greater purpose, that she was kept alive by God Himself to carry out that purpose until her replacement could be found, and that now she had found that replacement and was ready to lay her burden down...it was almost enough to make me miss the really stunning revelation in her words.

"Lucia..." I spoke very slowly, giving her every opportunity to cut me off or shut down my question if I moved into territory I shouldn't be mucking around in. This kind of truth was like a feral cat, just as likely to tear you to ribbons as run away from you. "Did you say you communicated directly with God?"

"Of course I did."

"Lucia, every angel in Heaven has been trying to get a direct line to Him since the end of the War on Heaven. How did you talk to Him?"

"Well, it wasn't a burning bush, Quincy, but it is the Lord Almighty. He wants to talk to me, He's gonna find me. Although, I reckon 'They' is more appropriate. God doesn't really do the binary thing."

I thought about that for a few seconds. Not the singular "they." That just made sense. But the fact that God had been speaking to humans and ignoring the Host. What did that mean? Why would They leave the angels alone to flounder for literally millennia? "So, this wasn't just you praying and random things happening, this was—"

"Quincy, darlin', either you're going to believe I talk to God on the regular, or you ain't. It don't matter to me. I am on my tenth Pope, son. Your opinion does not carry much weight with me, no matter how much I like you."

"Well, when you put it that way." I kept looking hard at the screen. Lucia looked old, but she looked maybe eighty, tops. But two decades and change more? I gave myself a little mental shake and brought my attention back to the question at hand. "Will you help us find the ritual we need?"

"I don't know if there is one, Quincy. When I talk to God, I just get down on my knees, which ain't as easy as it once was. I've never needed to call an angel. Have you tried a typical summoning? I wouldn't suggest trying to *bind* Michael—"

"No, we already decided that would make Harker's Top Five Worst Ideas List, and that's a tough list to get on," Glory said.

"Well, good. That's one smart thing you've done. I'm going to assume that was your call, Glory," Lucia said. "The fact is, Quincy, I don't know how to contact Michael. But if I wanted to do that, I'd cast a summoning ritual without the binding, and I'd try to do it on consecrated ground. If you can find a church that will let you cross the threshold."

She grinned at me, so I knew she was mostly joking. "There are a few around here that I don't think bar the doors against me just yet. Thanks, Lucia. We'll give that a shot." I reached out to end the call, then paused. "Hey, um…is there a good time for me to maybe come up there and…meet your replacement?"

"You mean say goodbye?" Lucia was never one to pull punches. "We've never been that kind of friends, Quincy. Sentimental bullshit isn't what we do. If you want to come visit me one more time, you should make sure that happens before summer's over. I am *not* putting up with another winter in New York City. Bring Scotch. The good stuff."

I felt an unexpected tear leap to my eye. "You got it, old woman."

"Still kick your ass, heathen." She leaned forward and cut the call before I could.

"So…what now?" Glory asked.

"I do some research on summoning rituals," I said, walking over to one of the bookcases that lined a wall of my apartment. "You figure out what you're going to say to Michael when we drag him back to Earth in the middle of a North Carolina summer."

"You want to do this today?" Glory suddenly looked terrified.

"Yeah," I said. "You got a reason for waiting?"

"No, I just…"

Before I could find out what she "just," we were interrupted by the entrance of perhaps the unlikeliest pair of my allies, even more than my uncle Dracula and Pravesh the snake woman government agent. Jack Watson, attorney, veteran, and great-grandson of *that* Watson, walked in, gold-tipped cane in hand, dressed in jeans and a polo shirt. He looked like a lawyer even in casual clothes. Something about the stick wedged up his ass, I guess. He was accompanied by a being with jet-black skin dressed in a screaming loud yellow Hawaiian shirt, cargo shorts, and flip flops.

"This looks like the worst episode of *My Two Dads* ever," I said.

"Watson said we should dress casually and comfortably for whatever we're doing today. I'm casual, comfortable, and *stylish*," said Faustus, the demon master negotiator who had proven himself to be remarkably trustworthy and not evil. Self-absorbed, arrogant, vain, and always working his own angle, yes, but not evil. He'd bailed me out on more than one occasion, so I held my normal reflexive killing of any demon I saw in check.

"We have different definitions of both casual and stylish, apparently," Watson said. "Regardless, I have faith that Mr. Faustus will be able to find something more suitable once you inform us of our mission."

"It's just 'Faustus,'" said the demon. "No 'Mr.' That crap's for humans. Don't want anyone to get confused."

Every eye in the room turned to stare at the ebon-skinned creature with a completely smooth pate, slightly pointed ears, yellow eyes, and canines that would give Luke a run for his money. "I think you're safe on that front," Glory said after a moment.

"You two are doing research," I said.

"Oh, joy," Faustus replied, his shoulders sagging.

"Don't worry, you may get to kill someone, or even multiple someones," I added.

"Now you're talking my language," the demon said, his grin returning.

"How are we going to end up killing people while doing research?" Watson asked.

"Because the research you're doing is on this mysterious Director Shaw person, and the best place to start that kind of research is Mort's." Director Shaw was the shadowy figure currently sitting atop the food chain at DEMON, one of the government agencies tasked with dealing with supernatural threats. Since taking over the organization, Shaw had turned their prime directive from "keep humans safe" to "kill any nonhuman you can find." This led to her masterminding a kidnapping of my uncle, my torture, Pravesh getting shot in the head, and me ripping Josef Mengele to pieces in front of my fiancée before Shaw and her stormtroopers attacked us. Faustus and Watson bailed us out of that mess, but we hadn't seen Shaw since. It was time to stop waiting for her next move and hunt her down.

Mort's was a demon bar, a place of Sanctuary for all in Charlotte, and the best place to dig up information on anything underhanded going down in the paranormal world. I couldn't really show my face in there anymore, because the place had a tendency to get destroyed whenever I was there, so I was sending the Wonder Twins.

"Mort's?" Faustus exclaimed. "Fantastic! I'll get changed." He waved a hand in front of himself, and a human visage came into view to mask his demonic appearance. He could look as monstrous as he wanted inside the bar, nobody would care, but looking like a low-rent Nightcrawler on the drive over would make things challenging. I noticed that he made no effort to transmute his clothing, but that was not a fight I was getting into before lunch. Some things just aren't worth the effort.

"I shall return in a moment," Watson said, heading for the door. "If we are heading into a demonic establishment, I believe I shall bring a brimstone-proof windbreaker." As he walked off to properly accessorize, I had no doubt that he actually owned such a thing.

5

D id you set aside an entire apartment for ritual magic, Harker?" Glory asked, looking around at the wards drawn on the walls of the living room. We were in an apartment down the hall from mine and separated from everyone else who lived on that floor by another vacant apartment on one side and the elevator on the other. I picked this place specifically because it didn't share a wall with anyone's living space, just in case my spells, my wards, and my bullets all failed me. Sometimes the things I have to deal with are pretty nasty, so I wanted to make sure there was some kind of buffer between anything that got loose and my friends. Although, let's be real, if it kicked my ass and escaped, it probably wasn't going to be stopped by an extra couple of layers of drywall.

This was a one-bedroom apartment, identical in layout to the one where Luke lived, although where Luke's place was basically set up as a massive library and sitting room with a light-tight bedroom, this place was stripped to the walls. I had all the carpet pulled up, and all the hanging light fixtures replaced with ones that were tight to the ceiling. There was no furniture, just a small shelf along one wall with some ritual supplies—candles, chalk, salt, that kind of thing. I didn't even keep holy water in that apartment. If I needed it for a casting, I brought it with me.

I knelt on the concrete floor and started to draw a circle with a piece of chalk I picked up from the shelf. It was thick sidewalk chalk in neon pink, and Glory raised an eyebrow. "You're summoning the Archangel Michael with neon pink Crayola sidewalk chalk?"

"I've literally never had anyone complain about the color of chalk I used to summon them."

"Have you ever tried to summon anyone as pompous as Michael?" Glory just stood there looking at me, her arms folded across her chest. I sighed, because she was right. Damn angels. They're almost always right. I scrubbed out the quarter of the circle I'd drawn and scrounged a piece of white chalk. It was small, and crumbled every time I used too much pressure, but eventually I had a decent circle, if a bit uneven.

The circle didn't quite meet and close perfectly, and I made it a point to stand up and step directly on the chalk line as I walked over to my other tools. That smeared the circle further but made it less apparent visually that the circle was incomplete.

"What are you doing, Q?" Glory asked. "You need to finish the circle."

"No, I need to make it *look* like a circle, so Mikey thinks he's getting one over on the dumb human when he senses it isn't complete. He'll know he isn't bound in the circle, but he won't know I planned it to be that way."

"So, he'll underestimate you and be easier to deal with. That's a little bit brilliant, Harker."

"I have my moments." I got a piece of dark blue chalk, held it up for Glory's approval, and started drawing symbols in Enochian around the exterior of the circle. This was intended to look as though it was a summoning and binding circle that was trying to trap Michael inside. It wasn't, of course. It was mostly a device to focus my energy and get his attention. Shouting his true name across the entire universe wouldn't be the best idea, but using it inside a summoning circle would narrow the focus to where only he would hear the call. At least, that's the theory. I've never been summoned, so I don't know for sure.

"Okay, do we need anything else for the ritual?" I asked Glory.

"Did you bring the virgin?"

"I thought you were bringing the virgin."

"I brought the virgin last time."

"Yeah, but that was a Memphis prom, and trust me, there was not a virgin to be found in that place," I said. "But seriously, is this it? Now I just recite the normal incantation for summoning, say Michael's true name, and he pops in for a visit?"

"Mostly. Maybe phrase it as a question, though? More like a 'please come visit' than a 'get your angelic ass down here'?"

"My Latin's good, but I don't know that it's gonna be *that* good." I looked over the circle. All my symbols seemed right. If I was right, it only kinda mattered, since it was the name that was going to make the connection. But better safe than sorry. I turned to Glory. "Okay, what's the name?"

Her eyes went wide. "I can't tell you! You're human. It could kill you just hearing it."

"Then how am I supposed to cast the spell?"

Her face fell. "Shit. I might not have thought this through as well as I should have."

I came really close to poking at her for it, but she looked so despondent I didn't have the heart. "Okay, let's go back to my place and look through some of Luke's old texts. Maybe there's something in there to tell us how to call an angel."

"Why not just pray?" Michael said from where he leaned against the wall leading into the apartment's lone bedroom.

"It's like Steve Earle said, Mikey-boy. 'Prayer's too much like begging, I don't need no charity.' We'll figure—wait a... You're such a dick."

"Why haven't you answered me, Michael?" Glory stomped across the room and got right up in his angelic face.

He didn't wear the form of the cage fighter Jo had found in Phoenix with no idea of his true nature, but he couldn't wander around Earth in his Archangel suit without burning out eyeballs, so he was in disguise. This disguise looked a lot like Thor, but not the fat *Big*

Lebowski Thor. The muscle-bound blond Norse god Thor. I felt myself unconsciously standing up straighter and thought, *This is how Star Lord felt.*

"It's complicated, Glory," Michael said. "Why don't we adjourn to your apartment, Quincy? I can explain things better there. And you're probably going to want a drink."

"It's a little early for me," I lied, heading for the door.

"I was talking to Glory," he replied, and I was pretty glad he couldn't see my face when he said that, and even happier I couldn't see Glory's.

"W hat's the deal?" Glory asked as soon as we were all seated in my den. Well, Michael and I were sitting, one on each couch. Glory was pacing in front of the big windows and staring daggers at Michael. "Why isn't anyone talking to me since I got back from Hell? I felt more connected to the Host as a human than I do since I've gotten my wings back!"

This was news to me. Glory had been with me pretty much every day since then, through my trip to Memphis, my return, even up to and after my kidnapping and escape. She'd never mentioned feeling cut off by the rest of the angels. "But you've had contact with angels since we got back," I said. "There was that Guardian in Nashville that called us about the murder, and you've been in contact with—"

"They were all here, Q," she said, turning her stricken face to me. "Everyone I've talked to has been Earthbound. I haven't heard a peep out of Heaven since I returned."

"And you won't," Michael said. "Not until we figure some things out."

"Figure things out," I said. That didn't sound good. Any time somebody with a lot of power has to stop and evaluate an unfamiliar event, whoever caused that event usually ends up having a bad time. "What is there to figure out? She got her wings back. You bunch gave them to her, right there in the ninth friggin' circle." I remembered the scene vividly. Lucifer tried to kill me, and Glory, somehow restored by the same magic that allowed Uriel to be reborn or reconstituted or whatever angels re-do, took a Hell-blast right in the chest for me. But in the midst of all that, she got her wings back.

"She did indeed have her wings restored. We just...don't know how." Michael had a look on his face I didn't know the arrogant prick could even make. He looked *embarrassed*. "We didn't restore Glory's divinity. The fact is, we couldn't have if we wanted to. If she had stepped in to take on the mantle of Uriel, she could have done that by taking up his Implement and absorbing his essence, like your friend Dennis did."

"How come it sounds dirty when you say it, Mikey?" I asked, grinning at the stuffy Archangel.

"I honestly have no idea what you're talking about, Quincy," he replied. It's no fun making double entendres with people who are oblivious.

"So, if you didn't restore my wings, who did?" Glory asked. She looked scared, like she knew the answer and knew she wasn't going to like it. I didn't blame her. Her wings came back in the Ninth Circle of Hell, not a place known for granting awesome gifts upon visitors. Unless that gift is "eternal torment in face-melting flames."

"We have no idea," Michael said. "We didn't do it. We're fairly certain Lucifer didn't do it, and none of the other demons have the ability to do it. That only leaves..."

"The absentee Father to end all absentee fathers," I said. I didn't mention the fact that He'd apparently been speaking to a crotchety nun in Manhattan on a regular basis. That didn't seem like the kind of thing to just drop on an immensely powerful celestial being in your living room.

"Exactly," Michael replied.

"Okay, then." I clapped my hands together. "Problem solved. Now start taking Glory's calls and stop being a douche. Okay, that last bit might be *really* hard for you. Just concentrate on letting her know that she's back in good with the Host, and Daddy made it all better."

"But He didn't," Michael said with a frown. "Or we don't know if

He did. We can't *know* the cause of Glory's wings returning, not with certainty. So, she must remain, unfortunately, excommunicated from Heaven." He looked at Glory. "I am sorry, Glory. You have served us well for a very long time, but you cannot rejoin the Host until we know for sure."

"What's to know?" I asked, getting to my feet. "You said yourself that only Archangels, Lucifer, or God could do that. You've eliminated the Archangels and Lucifer, so Occam's Razor says it must have been God!"

"There are stranger things on Heaven and Earth than are dreamt of in our philosophy," Michael quoted. His expression was placidly irritating, giving him the kind of face that looks so much better with a fist bouncing off it.

"Okay, first—my philosophy has some seriously fucked up dreams, so you'd better pray to…I don't know, yourself, that you're wrong. And second—the whole quoting Shakespeare wasn't your shtick. Don't steal somebody else's gimmick. And third—fuck you, Michael. I'm really starting to want to shove that flaming sword up your ass."

"You are welcome to try, Quincy," Michael said, manifesting the sword in question with the wave of a hand. He stood up, smiling at me.

"Would you put that thing away, Michael," Glory said. "Jesus fucking Christ, even when neuters that are pseudo-male get around males, somebody's always whipping something out."

Michael had the good grace to look abashed as his sword vanished. I barely saw that out of the corner of my eye. Something in what Glory said caught my ear and directed my eyes downward. No lump. Looked like she wasn't joking.

"So, unless God Themself comes back and tells you They gave Glory her wings back, she's cut off from the AngelNet, is that the deal?" I asked.

"Yes," Michael replied.

"What can we—" I paused and held a finger up to Michael while reaching for the vibrating phone in my pocket. It was Watson. "Hold that thought."

I swiped my finger across the screen to answer the phone and said, "Yeah?"

"Harker, you'd better get down here." Watson's normally priggish voice was rushed, and he was out of breath. I heard the sound of screeching tires and breaking glass in the background.

"What's going on?" I asked, but before Watson could reply, Becks' mental "voice" crashed into me. *Harker! You need to get to Mort's! DEMON is raiding the bar, and the inhabitants are fighting back! I'll meet you there!* "Never mind, Jack," I said into the phone. "We're on our way."

I looked at Michael, who stood in my apartment with a placid smile on his too-handsome-for-Earth face. "You should fuck off now. But we're not done."

He raised an eyebrow at me, and I swear he had a better eyebrow than The Rock. I hated him a little more just then. "For your sake, Harker, I hope that's not true." Then he was gone.

I looked at Glory. "We gotta go. Flynn's headed to Mort's. Jack and Faustus are in trouble."

"What did they do?"

"It's not on them this time," I said, going to the closet and grabbing my pistol. "DEMON's raiding the place, and it sounds like all-out war between the government's cryptid hunters and Charlotte's number one demon bar."

"Which ones are we supposed to help, and which ones are we supposed to slaughter?" she asked as we headed for the elevator.

"Check the calendar," I said. "It's the only way I can keep track of who's the Asshole of the Day."

6

_____

The situation got even more confusing when we actually pulled up in front of Mort's, because there were half a dozen unmarked black armored vehicles out front, a bunch of Suburbans with tinted windows, and about two dozen men in almost identical black tactical gear standing in two rows facing off against each other in what looked like the strangest line dance ever.

"I'm guessing the guys in front of the Suburbans are the DEMON guys, and the ones with the miniature tanks are the police," Glory said. "Why do your police officers have armored vehicles?"

"There's money to be made selling them, and there's always somebody somewhere who wants a bigger gun to make up lack of size somewhere else," I replied. I focused on Becks, and felt her drawing near at the same time I heard her car roar into the parking lot. She pulled right in between the lines of armed men and got out.

She didn't draw her gun, she didn't pull an assault rifle out of the car, she didn't even mind-link me to tell me what she was planning. She just glared at both groups, then shouted at the CMPD officers. "Stand down! I'll deal with you in a minute."

The riot cops started, like they weren't used to anyone yelling at them, but they lowered the barrels of their guns. Becks stalked over to the line of DEMON troops and got up in the face of one with more stripes on his shoulder than the rest. "Are you in charge here?" she asked, if by "asked" you mean yelled in the guy's face from three inches away.

He backed up and nodded. "Then tell your men to stand down," Becks said, still loud but no longer actually yelling.

"Be ready in case this goes sideways," Glory muttered.

"How much more sideways can it get?"

"Faustus is inside."

"Good point," I replied, calling power up and coalescing energy around my hands. I could shape it into a shield or a blast depending on what the situation called for.

The DEMON leader opened his mouth, but Flynn put her hand up in his face in a "talk to the hand" gesture. "You don't speak to me. You tell your men to put down their goddamned weapons and then you go get your boss on the line. *They* can explain to me why a government agency is conducting operations in my city without any coordination from local law enforcement. But you don't get to talk. You just do as you're told."

I could see the guy turning red, but Becks didn't back down an inch. After a long staring contest, he broke first, turning to the nearest Suburban and opening the passenger door. The line of men all lowered their weapons, and the police across the asphalt did the same. You could tell from their posture that nobody wanted to shoot anybody, and they were relieved it looked like they wouldn't have to.

Except then the door to Mort's flew open and a werewolf charged out into the parking lot, all claws, fur, and attitude.

"Well, fuck," I muttered as a tide of demons, witches, and cryptids of all flavors poured out into the summer sun after the werewolf. It was the middle of the day on a Wednesday, didn't these beasties have jobs? "Okay, Glory. Time to go to work."

And with that, we were off. Glory manifested her wings and streaked up into the air, zooming back down like an arrow to grab Becks under her arms and get her out of the crossfire. I called up shields on each arm and started toward the door, hoping to get inside and haul Faustus and Watson out before they either got hurt or decided to join the party. The half-shifted werewolf met me halfway to the door, claws out and fangs slavering for flesh.

"Bad guys are that way, Fluffy." I pointed to my left, toward the DEMON agents, and he (and it was exceedingly apparent this was a male werewolf) sprang in that direction. I kept walking toward the door, punching out a nebbishy little wizard with thick horn-rimmed glasses who'd run out with Fluffy and now was desperately trying to call up a fireball. His concentration wasn't great when he realized what he'd stepped into, and it got worse when I bloodied his nose. I'd almost made it inside when the agents opened fire on Fluffy, and the cops, thinking they were being fired upon, responded in kind.

Fuck. Becks, stay back. They're using some heavy shit. The AR-15s the cops carried rattled in the formerly quiet afternoon sun, and the sound of bullets pinging off the asphalt and the vehicles was a testament to how truly shitty the marksmanship on both sides was. I expanded my shields to cover me head to toe and pushed on, but I was getting slammed on both sides with 5.56 rounds, and while they weren't penetrating my shields, the kinetic energy was passing right through. I took probably a dozen rounds to my shields before one ricocheted off the pavement in front of me and shattered, sending a shard of hot metal searing along the side of my face. I felt the shrapnel carve a furrow down my cheekbone, and even the little bit of concentration I was dedicating to my shields was blown.

I dropped to my knees, pulling my jacket over my head while I worked to restore some cover. More bullets slammed into my back and shoulders, beating the shit out of me but not getting through the reinforced leather duster. The damn thing was heavy as fuck and miserably hot in the midday summer heat, but it turned what would have at least been near-lethal wounds into bruises. I still didn't want to take too many rounds to the back and sides, even if they weren't getting through the leather.

I ran through half a dozen possible escapes in a couple of seconds, but then lit on one that might actually get these idiots to stop turning my hometown into a war zone. I pressed my palms flat to the ground, called up energy, and channeled pure power straight down into the asphalt. I'm pretty solid, some might even say muscular, but I'm not a huge guy. So, when I jammed all the power I could channel straight down, Newton's laws went into effect and I shot into the air like a cork out of a champagne bottle. Since this was exactly what I'd hoped for, I kept channeling power through myself, but I didn't restrict it to my hands, instead letting it surround me like a nimbus of blue, red, and purple sparks. I looked like a giant Roman candle popping off into the air, sending streams of light out in every direction.

I turned a backflip in midair, then cut off the juice and dropped to the ground, one knee and one fist on the ground in the perfect super-hero landing. I stood up, held my hands straight out to the sides, and cut loose a blast of pure kinetic force, knocking anyone who wasn't holding onto something flat on their ass.

"Now cut that shit out!" I bellowed, using the last little bits of energy I'd called up to amplify my voice. "Detective Flynn, deal with these morons." I pointed toward the cops. I turned to the DEMON agents, but apparently I hadn't been clear enough in my instructions because one downy-cheeked agent with a helmet that looked like he had to stuff a shirt inside it to get the thing to stay on his head managed to haul himself up to one knee and grab his rifle. He pointed the gun at me, and I started to manifest a shield, but before he could even think about pulling the trigger, a blazing white sword slashed down and cut his gun in half.

"Stop that," Glory said, standing over the stunned young agent in her full angel regalia. She looked like every teenaged boy's D&D fantasy: glowing white wings, gleaming silver breastplate shaped more like a lingerie maker's dummy than anything designed to actu-ally protect her, and a split chainmail skirt that left her legs bare up the majority of her long, long thigh.

Down boy, Becks said in my skull, and I felt the chuckle in her words. Glory was smoking hot, but I never looked at her like that. It was more of a protective thing, like she was my hot sister and I needed to protect her from guys. Because that's exactly how it was supposed to go—I needed to protect my guardian angel from lecherous government agents, instead of her protecting me from getting shot. Yeah, that made sense.

The agent, for his part, just kinda rocked back and sat flat on his ass in the parking lot, staring up at the hottie Xena cosplayer with wings that materialized in front of him. "Thanks, Glory," I said, walking past her. "Who's in charge here?"

The Asian guy Becks had yelled at earlier stepped forward. "Special Agent Won. You are interfering with the execution of a lawful—"

It's funny how fast people stop talking when you lift them into the air one-handed. Special Agent Won was no exception. Right about the time he realized that he was leaving the ground and there wasn't a damn thing he could do about it, he shut right the fuck up.

"I'm talking now, Special Agent Won," I said. "Do you know who I am?"

He nodded. "Very good," I said. "No talking. Good call. Now here's what you're going to do. You're going to take your men, you're going to load up into what's left of your SUVs, and you're going to get the fuck out of my city. You're going to leave your guns, and you're going to leave all your comms gear, and when you get wherever you came from, I'd strongly suggest that you look into early retirement. But either way, you're never going to set foot in Charlotte again. Or I'm going to get angry. You just saw what I can do when I'm a little irritated. Do you really want to see me angry? I don't think you'd like me very much."

He nodded, and I set him down. "Now put your gun on the ground." He did, and I had a moment to actually believe I was going to get out of this without anyone dying, then he pulled the backup piece from his ankle holster and shot me in the chest.

I looked down at the smoking edge of my duster, and then at the hole in my shirt and the slowly spreading bloodstain there. "Ouch." I didn't hurt enough to have been *really* shot, just a little shot. My best guess was that the bullet deflected off my jacket and grazed my side. Not lethal, but it was going to bleed a lot, and it was the second new scar I'd picked up in the last five minutes. And I liked that shirt. I was really annoyed now.

I backhanded Won into next week and found myself staring at a dozen agents with assault rifles and bad attitudes staring back at me. *Fuck.* I leapt into the air before the first one opened fire, but the second I moved, they all cut loose, which meant that the CMPD officers cut loose. *Double fuck.* And of course, there was a whole bar full of monsters looking for either an escape route or an excuse to cause mayhem. So a couple dozen more monsters, demons, and spellslingers came pouring out of Mort's with blood in their eyes and murder in their hearts.

Triple fuck.

7

Glory snatched me out of the air and deposited me behind one of the CMPD armored vehicles, then darted out to drag Becks to safety. Seconds later, all three of us were taking cover behind what was basically an armored personnel carrier with eight or nine cops.

"What's the plan?" I asked Becks.

She gaped at me. "What the fuck makes you think I've got a plan?!?"

"You're the one that gets trained for this shit, aren't you? I just make things up as I go along."

"I got trained how to write traffic tickets, arrest drunk and disorderlies, take down suspects bigger than me, dust for fingerprints, shoot for center mass, and eventually investigate murders. I did *not* get trained in how to fight a three-front battle between police, federal agents, and B-movie monsters!"

She had a point. But plan or no, we couldn't stay where we were. There wasn't enough cover for everyone, and what cover we had wasn't great. I already had two cuts bleeding from ricochets and bullet fragments, and I was a lot hardier than Becks or the rest of the cops.

And their body armor wasn't going to do shit against a demon's claws, or teeth for that matter.

"Okay, here's what we're going to do," I said, but snapped my head up as the vehicle rocked under a sudden weight.

"Die!" screeched the demon crouching above me as it reached down with a clawed hand aimed at my face. It was a Reaver, usually not a huge problem as far as demons go, but he'd gotten too close for me to blast without hurting Becks, so now I had to go hand to hand.

I jerked my head out of the way and latched on to the bastard's wrist. One good yank, and the demon, already off balance, toppled to the ground, landing in a heap right in front of the cops taking shelter. This one was a nasty variation of Reaver, with elongated arms and hooked talons at the ends of its spindly fingers. Its knees were double-jointed, so it sprang up from the awkward landing like it was a walk in the park, then it turned and screamed right in my face.

I was gonna *have* to talk to Mort about the breakfast menu, because even as demons go, this thing had some evil breath. Its howl blew my hair back, and it sounded like the scream of a jet engine in agony was five feet from my nose, the fucker was so loud. I dropped to one knee and saw that all the cops had dropped their guns and clapped hands to their ears. Becks was down on the ground, curled up in a little ball, and Glory had thrown herself over Flynn's body to protect her from errant bullets.

"Shut the fuck up!" I shouted and punched the demon in the throat. Problem with magical creatures—they don't obey natural laws. This thing's scream was apparently some kind of mystical attack, not a sound it was making through its lungs. Which meant cutting off its air didn't shut off the sound. I tried to concentrate through the ear-splitting noise but couldn't focus enough to call up my soul blade. So I did the next best thing.

I drew the Glock from the back waistband of my jeans and shot the motherfucker six times in the face. You can't *kill* a demon with regular bullets. Not with any kind of permanence, anyway. What happens when you shoot a demon depends entirely on the ammunition used, the location of the wound, and the type and strength of demon. This was a Reaver, which could normally be dispatched with mundane bullets, but it was stronger than normal, augmented somehow. So I didn't expect to kill its mortal form and send it back to Hell just by shooting it.

But I'd underestimated the efficacy of a bullet in the eye from less than two meters. The screaming cut off like I'd unplugged Steve Perry's microphone, and the demon flopped back onto the asphalt, its flesh suit already starting to dissolve into black sludge. "Huh," I said, although I couldn't hear anything over the ringing in my ears. "That went better than expected." I looked around, and Glory was crouched over an unconscious Flynn, but as I caught her eye, she gave me a nod, so I knew Becks was going to be all right. That kind of noise at that proximity probably just short-circuited her a little, but she wouldn't suffer any lasting injuries. A hell of a hangover, though.

Emboldened by my success with that demon, I thought this might be a good time to see about taking down a DEMON of a different kind, so I stepped out from behind the vehicle and froze in my tracks at the carnage before me.

The scene in the parking lot wasn't completely unfamiliar, but it was pretty much the biggest mess I'd ever seen that I wasn't the primary cause of. There were DEMON agents down everywhere. There were little agent-bits strewn across the ground, smears of agent splattered across the hoods of Suburbans, a vaguely human-shaped outline smashed flat into the front wall of the bar, and pieces of what used to be human beings strewn around like the world's biggest land mine had gone off in the middle of a mosh pit. There was a lot of black body armor in evidence, and none of it had done a bit of good.

The agents weren't the only casualties, though. I saw a skinny wizard in a vest and honest-to-God top hat lying on his back staring up at the sky through smoking holes where his eyes used to be. A naked woman that I assumed was a were-something lay in three pieces on the ground, her legs literally blown off at both knees. And there were two dead CMPD cops slumped over the hood of a patrol car. One had his throat ripped out, probably by claws, and the other had one neat round hole in her face, just under the lip of her helmet. She wasn't killed by a monster; she died from a DEMON bullet.

There were two more Reavers huddled around the bulk of the dead DEMON agents, picking up arms and legs, peeling the clothes back, and taking big bites out of the muscles. My stomach roiled as I saw one bite a chunk out of one leg, lick its lips in appreciation, and pass the leg over to the other demon for a taste.

I started to call up power to end those nasty fucks once and for all when enough of my hearing came back for me to hear a strange whistling sound. Or maybe I felt the shift in air pressure as something huge fell from the sky. Either way, I looked up just in time to see two massive objects tumble out the open doors of a helicopter, and the chopper turn and speed away from the carnage. At a height of just a couple hundred feet, it took barely two seconds for the gargantuan *things* to slam into the parking lot with enough force to make all the vehicles bounce. I barely kept my feet, and a demon that had been licking bloody person bits off the roof of an SUV lost its balance and smacked into the asphalt.

The pair of huge objects slowly resolved into a humanoid shape as the creatures unfolded themselves from the relatively compact five-foot balls they'd been compressed into. As they stretched and rose to their feet, I could see exactly what these things were. And I was *not* happy to see them. Less than ten seconds after I saw the chopper, a pair of ten-foot-tall creatures that looked like the love child of Andre the Giant and a gargoyle stood in the parking lot. They were huge and thickly muscled, and their massive fists were larger than my head. One of them saw me, and it smiled. That big, cruel grin showed a row of blocky, squared-off gray teeth between darker gray lips. Its beady black eyes locked onto me, and with a booming *thud*, the creature started for me.

Well, this is going to be new and exciting, I thought to myself.

This creature was a new one on me—a stone giant. I'd never fought a stone giant before, and neither had Luke. I found an obscure reference in one of the Shadow Council Archives one time about somebody fighting one, but I couldn't remember if it was Crowley, or

Adam, or Norton, or who. Hell, it might not have even been a giant. It could have been an ogre, a troll, or even a yeti for all I could remember. But what was standing in front of me with a stupid grin on his massive face was definitely a giant.

"You are interfering with an official DEMON operation. We are authorized to detain any and all persons or creatures on these premises. If you are a human, and you leave now, we will pursue no further action against you. If you do not move toward your vehicles, immediately, we will destroy you." The giant was…eloquent? I should have known better, since I spent time around Adam, but I frequently found myself expecting really big creatures to also be really stupid. Or maybe it was just wishful thinking, because there was no way I was a physical match for those monstrosities, so I really needed to believe I could outsmart them.

The giant facing me looked over to the cops, who had come out from behind their armored vehicle. Some of them were checking on their fallen comrades while the rest aimed their weapons at the giants. I could have told them those weren't going to do any good, but it didn't matter. Those guns were what they had, and with two of their own dead, no way in hell were those officers leaving without a fight.

A couple of DEMON agents crawled out from under a Suburban and picked up their weapons, training the barrels on the creatures that killed their cohorts. The monsters gave not a single fuck about the agents anymore; their attention, like mine, was dominated by the behemoths in front of us. Glory stepped up to stand beside me, sword glowing in her hands, and said, "How do you want to handle this, Q?"

"Is running away and hiding under my bed an option?"

"Probably not."

"Then let's see if we can get all the cops and the critters to focus on one giant, and we focus on the other."

"What about the agents?" she asked.

"Not at the top of my list right now."

"But they have guns."

I turned a blast of energy on the pair of DEMON agents and slammed them into the side of their SUV. Their faces bounced off the side of the vehicle, and they collapsed to the ground, limp. "Not anymore."

That was all the reply the giants needed to their demands, and the one nearest me moved forward, closing the twenty feet between us in two long strides. The other one turned with surprising agility and sprang at the pair of Reavers picking their teeth with agent shinbones. The CMPD officers opened fire, and the shit hit the fan.

"Glory, get high!" I yelled, sprinting away from the giant as fast as I could. I'm quick, but the giant was no slowpoke either, and had nearly double my stride. He stayed with me as I hauled ass across the mostly empty parking lot, trying to create some separation from his partner so the cops would focus on the one I left behind. I figured that Glory and I could probably take down one giant without too much trouble.

I'm a complete moron sometimes.

8

So there I was, running hellbent for leather across an empty parking lot, pursued by a giant. Not how I envisioned my day going, to say the very least. I sprinted for a parked Jeep, pushed off from the ground, and vaulted over the SUV. I dropped to the ground behind the vehicle, hoping against all the evidence to the contrary that this giant was at least as stupid as some of the stories made them out to be, and he wouldn't have any sense of object permanence. Cut me a little slack, some people believe in the Tooth Fairy, too. Admittedly, those people are seven years old, but blind, idiotic hope was all I had.

That hope was dashed about four seconds after I crouched down behind the Jeep's back tire, because the whole vehicle lifted up into the air, courtesy of the pissed off behemoth lifting it over its head. With the giant standing there holding a couple tons of SUV up in the air, I saw an opening, and like the dirty-fighting bastard I am, I took it. I drew my pistol and emptied the rest of the magazine right into the center of the giant's midsection. My Glock clicked empty after six rounds, but it could have been sixteen for all the good I did. The bullets didn't even penetrate the giant's thick hide, just slammed into the thing and *plinked* down to the pavement.

The giant grinned at me and said, in a remarkably clear voice, "Nice try, little man. Time to die now," and slammed the Jeep down on top of me. Or at least, on top of where I would have been if I were a normal person. To paraphrase the great Boyd Crowder, I've been called many things in my life, but "normal" has never been one of them. Despite every instinct screaming at me to somersault backward, I dropped my pistol, tucked my head, and rolled forward inside the arc of the descending Jeep and between the giant's legs.

I came to my feet behind the giant, manifested my soulblade, and sliced a deep line across the back of the creature's knee. The giant bellowed and staggered, clutching at its ruined hamstring. It flailed around, torn between clutching its bleeding leg and trying to squish my head like a grape. I danced under its outstretched arm and slashed downward with the blazing magical sword. The blade of energy sliced through the back of the giant's ankle, and I could have sworn I actually *heard* the damn thing's Achilles tendon snap. This time the giant went down, flopping onto its back and sending cracks spiderwebbing out across the asphalt from the impact.

I reversed grip on my sword, raised it high above my head, and buried it in the center of the monster's chest. Not being sure exactly where its heart was, I just kinda slashed around in there for a few seconds until it stopped moving. Then I looked up to see where Glory was, and to see how the cops were dealing with the other giant.

In a word, they weren't. The giant was dealing with them pretty damn well, however. Glory had interposed herself between the giant and the remaining cops and was managing to fend off the creature with her flaming blade. The giant had uprooted a light pole and broken it down to size, so it was trying to batter through Glory's defenses and smash the cops into peanut butter. There were two down, and I couldn't tell how badly they were hurt from where I stood, but they weren't moving.

I let my soulblade dissipate and called up power as I ran back toward them. When I got about ten feet from the giant, I planted my feet and yelled, *"Infiernus!"* A tight stream of nearly white-hot flame streaked out from my upraised palms and slammed into the giant's side. It let out a howl and turned to face me, shifting my blast to the center of its chest and giving Glory a brief respite from the onslaught.

"Get those cops out of here!" I yelled as the giant started lumbering toward me. It was fully bathed in fire now, its tattered shirt and pants completely ablaze. But the thing was still coming, and it still had that damn light pole in its hands. You know what happens when you set a giant on fire in the middle of a fight? You get to fight a flaming giant.

One more step, and the giant was looming over me with the pole sweeping up in a big arc that would pulp my skull if it connected. I cut off the stream of flame and dodged out of the way, noting to my chagrin that the giant's flesh didn't seem to be blistered even a little bit. Apparently giant skin is bulletproof and fireproof. If I didn't get squished in the next thirty seconds, I was pretty sure I knew what I wanted my next duster to be made out of.

The giant struck with its light pole club, which was good for me, because no matter how strong the thing was, it couldn't recover its swing with that enormous thing quickly, so as it *whooshed* by, I was able to blast the lumbering asshat with pure energy, which seemed to have better effect than the fire. Another swing, this one going for my knees, and I leapt over it, focusing all my energy in a glowing purple orb no bigger than a shooter marble. I crammed as much power into that sphere as I could, then I jammed in a little more just for good measure. As the giant lifted its massive club into the sky for another crushing blow, I flicked the energy ball at its head, driving it forward with all the kinetic force I could channel into it.

The sphere of purple magic slammed into the giant's forehead like a bullet. Actually, it was a *lot* more effective than a bullet, because the magic orb actually did something. It seared a hole right between the giant's eyes, and I watched two things happen simultaneously: any hint of intelligence or life went out of the creature's eyes, and a huge cloud of bone and brain exploded out of the back of its skull. The light pole dropped from its senseless fingers to clatter to the pavement, and the giant dropped like a stone, first to its knees, then sprawled on its face, no more alive than the asphalt it lay on.

I spared a glance for Glory, who knelt by one of the downed officers. She saw my look and shook her head. There was no question the other cop was dead, too. No human can have their head at that angle and live through the experience. I looked over at the DEMON agents, but they were gone. They hadn't left, they were just…gone. Most of them looked to have been devoured by actual demons, but at least one Suburban had vanished, so maybe a couple of them did escape the bloodbath.

None of the monsters from Mort's were visible, so either they were dead, they'd run off while I was dealing with the giants that literally fell from the sky, or they'd gone back inside. I knew where I figured at least a few of them were, and I needed some information. I also really, *really* wanted a drink. I was covered in giant blood, and it was truly nasty.

I started walking toward the door, fatigue slowing my stride, and drew up short when a cop in riot gear stepped out in front of me with an AR-15 leveled at my chest. "Get on the ground!" he shouted, his voice high and thready with adrenaline.

I looked at the kid, because that's what he was, really. He might have been twenty-five, and he was pale, sweating like he'd just run a marathon, and I was pretty sure there was a little bit of vomit on his collar. His hands were shaking so hard he could barely keep his rifle trained on me, and his trigger discipline was fucked, because he was definitely ready to fire on me.

I raised my hands. "Put the gun down, kid. I'm on your team."

"I said get on the fucking ground!" He took a step forward, jabbing the barrel of the rifle in my direction, and that was all she wrote.

I was tired. I hadn't had a whole lot of sleep in about three years, my girlfriend wanted to kill my guardian angel, who I'd just discovered was really guarding the world from me, not the other way around. I'd just fought a three-front battle against two sets of armed men with more ammo than sense and a bunch of monsters who saw the scrap as a license to chow down on a human buffet. Then to top it all off, I'd just taken out not one but two giants, the last of which was trying to kill this kid and his fellow officers.

I'll own it. I wasn't at my best. And I'm kind of a dick when I *am* at my best, so when Officer Dingleberry aimed his assault rifle at me, I snapped, just a little bit. I stepped to my left, putting my body out of the cop's line of fire, and I reached out with my right hand to snatch the gun away from him. My intent was to grab the barrel of the rifle and just fling it away behind me. Unfortunately, he had the rifle on a sling that went over his head and one shoulder, thus when I pulled the rifle, he came with it.

I heard the *snap* as his trigger finger broke, and the rifle pulled free from his grip, but didn't come away from him entirely. I saw what was happening, dropped the gun, which swung back and smacked into the officer's chest, then I punched him in the face. Looking back on it, that last punch was probably a little out of line, but in my experience having a gun pointed at me is often a precursor to me getting shot, and I really don't like getting shot.

The cop's eyes rolled back in his head and he toppled over onto his back. I was really glad he had a helmet on when his head smacked into the parking lot, because he was already out cold and couldn't do a damn thing to keep himself from splitting his head open. As it was, I laid him out and resumed my march for the door. Which was more a stagger than a march, but whatever.

"Halt!" another cop yelled from behind me, and I just stuck my middle finger up in the air over my shoulder. I was going to get a drink, and if that meant he needed to shoot me in the back, then he was just going to have to shoot me. In retrospect, I probably wouldn't have made that same decision without a bulletproof coat, because I'm pretty sure he *really* wanted to shoot me right then.

Harker? I felt Flynn's mind touch mine. Her thoughts were unsteady, but she was conscious. Sorta.

You okay, babe?

Not even a little bit. You?

Beat up, bloody, and a little bit shot, but nothing critical. You probably want to stay behind the armored car. It's a goddamn mess out here.

How many dead?

I...I can't tell. Most of the DEMON agents, a bunch of monsters, I think all the demons, and a couple of cops are down. That last one of those is my fault.

Becks took a long time to reply, and there was a sense of real fear when she finally did. *The last what is your fault, Harker?*

I stopped cold in the doorway to Mort's. Holy shit, she thought I killed a cop. *The one that's unconscious is my fault. For fuck's sake, Becks! I don't kill good guys.*

But if you thought a cop was a bad guy, you wouldn't hesitate.

She was right. I'd done it before, putting a bullet into Detective Rich Sponholz, who turned out to be a cambion. *Yeah, but not a human one. Give me a little credit. I didn't kill any humans. I just knocked the shit out of one. And probably broke his trigger finger.*

I could almost hear her sigh. *Goddammit, Harker, what else am I gonna have to clean up?*

A lot, I replied. *Tell the crime scene techs to bring the shop vac. And a squeegee. Maybe a couple squeegees.*

9

I was on my third Jameson's by the time Becks got the crime scene crew started, which was more a testament to how fast I was throwing back whiskeys than to their slow response time. Mort was behind the bar, but the place was otherwise empty. I wasn't sure if all his customers had run out and joined the fracas or if some of them bolted out the back door, and it wasn't really my job to ask. I just wanted to get a little fortification in me before the yelling started.

Mort was wearing a new suit, female this time, a middle-aged Latina with work-worn hands and tendrils of silver shot through her dark hair. "You want another, señor Harker?" the hitchhiker demon asked.

"It seems a little low-key racist for you to speak Spanish to me just because you're wearing a Latinx woman's body," I replied. "And yes, but I'm going to hold off until Becks gets here. She'll need at least one herself."

"Harker, I'm a demon. Racism is the least of my sins. Besides, sometimes when I jump into these bodies, there's enough of the owner left over to influence me. Remember when I wore that quarterback for a while? You should have seen the weird shit I ended up wearing. That dude has a fucked-up fashion sense. Speaking of ridealongs, when you gonna give up the driver's seat on your meat suit for a weekend? You owe me, remember?"

I remembered, but I was really hoping he'd forgotten. I promised Mort he could run around in my body from sundown Friday to sunrise Monday in exchange for helping me out of a tough spot a while back, and I hadn't let him cash in that marker yet. I should know better. In the decades I've known Mort, I've never known him to forget a debt. "It might be a while, Mort. I've been consorting with Archangels again, and you know you don't want to be anywhere near them."

"Uriel's okay, but the rest of them are uptight asshats. Fine, but as soon as you're done with whatever you're working on, I'm driving your bus for two days and three nights, buddy!"

"Can't wait," I said, my tone making it perfectly clear that I was more than happy to wait. Forever, if at all possible.

I was saved from any further discussion of debts I owed to demons by the door to the bar slamming open and Becks walking in, accompanied by her boss, Captain Herr, and two other people in uniforms I didn't know. I guessed from all the gold bullshit on their sleeves and shoulders that this pair were higher on the CMPD food chain than Becks and Herr, but they weren't anybody I'd dealt with before.

"Harker!" Herr bellowed from across the room. "What the actual fuck is going on here?"

I didn't get up, just spun around on my stool and leaned back with my elbows on the bar. "I'm having a drink and waiting for you guys to show up. Y'all want one? Mort's got a brand-new bottle of Jameson's he opened just for me."

What are you doing? Becks asked me silently.

Winding your bosses up so they get pissed off. If any of them are in league with DEMON, they'll let something slip if I make them angry enough.

Looks like you learned something from all those times I interrogated you.

I might not learn fast, but I do eventually learn.

"Are you Quincy Harker?" one of the big high muckety-mucks asked. She was a Black woman, about five-eight, slim but with broad shoulders and an athletic step. She had fewer stars on her collar than her male counterpart, but less shifty eyes, so I liked her better. I really prefer to be the least trustworthy person in any conversation. Makes things simpler for me.

"I am," I replied.

"John Abraham Quincy Holmwood Harker, son of Jonathan Harker and Mina Murray Harker?"

"That, too."

"British citizen, born…" She pulled out a notepad and looked at it, then looked at it again.

"November, 1896," I supplied. It wasn't like she had to dig too hard for that one.

Another glance down at her notepad. "Emigrated to the United States in 1967?"

"One of the times, yes."

"Currently in the employ of the United States Department of Homeland Security as a…special consultant."

"Sure." I had no idea what my job title with Homeland was, I just knew I had a badge that got me through crime scene tape, and that Pravesh cleaned up some of my messes. Speaking of which, this was looking like a good time for her to make an appearance. I wasn't sure what this cop was looking for with these questions, but I expected them to become a lot less pleasant pretty quickly, if the scowls on all four of their faces were any indicator.

"Then I am here to place you under arrest for assaulting a police officer, resisting arrest, and suspicion of four counts of second-degree murder. Please stand up and put your hands behind your back. Detective Flynn, if I may have your handcuffs?" She didn't look at Becks, just held out a hand.

"No," I said. Might as well not lead her on.

"Excuse me?" she asked.

"I said no. I'm not under arrest, and you're not going to handcuff me, so let's sit down and come up with a plausible story that you can tell the media about why four of your officers are lying dead in a parking lot that looks more like an abattoir than a place to stash a

Camry for a few hours. Would you prefer a table, or you want to sit at the bar? Mort, any chance we could get some lunch?"

Careful, Harker, Becks warned. *I don't know what game she's playing at, but this is not the plan they told me in the car.*

Who is this lady? I asked. *Should I know her?*

She's Deputy Chief Alanna Stephens. She heads up the whole Patrol Services Group.

Who's the guy? He looks familiar.

He should. He's the chief of police. Darick Putnam. You've seen him give press conferences?

I don't watch those things. But I guess I've seen his picture.

It is hanging in every precinct in the city, and I know you've seen the inside of more than one of those.

Deputy Chief Stephens stepped forward, again reaching out for Flynn's cuffs. Becks gave them to her, and she walked right up to me. "Get up and put your hands behind your back. I will not ask you again."

"Okay, Alanna," Chief Putnam said, walking up beside his deputy chief. "Let's step it down a notch. Mr. Harker has been...of use to the department in the past, so I'm sure he will be more than willing to explain what went on outside. I think sitting down at a table sounds like a great idea." He walked over to a round table in the middle of the room and pulled out a chair. "Shall we?"

Okay, so it's "good cop, bad cop." I would have thought they could be a little less obvious. It's almost like they aren't even trying. I'm a little insulted.

Suck it up, Harker. These two don't screw around, and there are four dead officers in that parking lot, not to mention the wounded. Their sense of humor is going to be nonexistent.

Point taken. I walked over and sat across from Chief Putnam. He was a slim Black man with close-cropped hair and a strong jaw. He sat with a military bearing, and looked to be in pretty good shape, even though he had to be past sixty. The only hints at his stress were the little muscle jumping in the side of his jaw and the slight lightening of his knuckles when he clasped his hands in front of him on the table. Deputy Chief Stephens looked a little relieved to get the stand down order. Either she was a reasonable person, or she knew enough about me not to want to poke the bear too much. I didn't care which.

"Okay, Chief," I said as the other three sat down. Flynn and Herr took the seats closest to me while Stephens tucked herself right up against her boss. Pretty easy to guess which side she was on, and I had no doubts as to Becks' loyalty. I didn't know where Herr was going to come down on this mess. He'd always struck me as pretty solid, but if he bucked up against whatever his chief decided, it could mean that he never made it past captain. "What can I help you with?"

"Let's start with you explaining exactly what happened here." Putnam leaned forward, elbows on the table, his relaxed posture belied by the tension in his shoulders. I'm sure if Luke had been there, he'd have been able to hear the chief's pulse pounding through his veins like a runaway freight train. I didn't have Luke's senses, but I didn't need to be able to hear his heart rate to know this man was on the edge.

"I don't know how things started," I said. "I got the call from two of my associates that DEMON had shown up, and I hauled ass to try and keep the bloodshed to a minimum. When I got here, there were two groups of armed men in black twenty yards apart in the parking lot, doing everything but whipping out the rulers to figure out which team had the bigger dick."

"What the—" Stephens leaned forward with fire in her eyes, but Putnam held up a hand.

"Calm down, Deputy Chief. We've heard about Mr. Harker's... colorful phrasing. I'm sure that's all this is."

"Sure, whatever you wanna tell yourself," I replied. "Between Becks...Detective Flynn and myself, we got things almost calmed down when the lead fed decided to shoot me in the gut. That set off a chain reaction of fucked up that led to a giant firefight in the middle of the city. Then the monsters came to play." I paused and looked around the table. "You're all up to speed on the whole 'monsters are real' bit, right? Because I don't want to have to waste time convincing you that everything you've ever read in a fairy tale or seen in a horror movie really exists."

"We know all about the supernatural element, and your role within it, Mr. Harker," Chief Putnam said.

Bloody well doubt that, I thought to Becks. But Putnam struck me as the kind of arrogant prick who reacted poorly to being called on his bullshit, so I let it go. As long as he knew monsters were real, the explanation was pretty simple. "So the federal agent assholes opened up on me, I got out of the way, and your guys opened up on them. At some point in that fracas, two of your officers went down. I didn't see how it happened, but it looked like one took a bullet to the face and the other might have died from a demon attack or a werewolf. I'm not really sure."

"Then what?" Putnam said. No visible reaction to me telling him how his people died, but he may have done his yelling on the drive over.

"Then someone, I'm assuming DEMON, dropped a pair of stone giants into the middle of the parking lot, and shit went even further down the road to Fuckedville than they'd already been. Glory and I managed to kill both the giants, but not before they took out two more of your people."

"Who's Glory?" Stephens asked. "The Tooth Fairy?"

The sneer fell off her face when I said, "No, my Guardian Angel. Tall, leggy blonde with a magic sword, six-foot wings, and an ass you could bounce a quarter off of." Becks smacked my arm at the last bit.

Pig

It's true!

Still a pig.

Also true, I admitted. "That's the *Reader's Digest* Condensed version. Rogue federal agents killed at least one of your officers, and monsters killed either two or three others. I'm sorry I couldn't keep them all alive." I meant that, too. Those cops didn't know what they were rolling up to, and they were *not* equipped to deal with the kind of shit I face every day. They really shouldn't have been there at all, but I wasn't the one who had to live with that decision. That was Putnam's cross to bear.

The chief stood up, and everybody else followed suit. "Thank you,

Mr. Harker. We will of course conduct our own investigation into this tragedy, but for now the public story will be a shootout with…gun runners. That will explain the firepower. We may have more questions for you. Please don't leave town." With that, he turned on his heel and headed for the door.

Stephens grabbed his arm and pulled him to a halt. "What the fuck, Chief? You're just going to let him go? You can't believe all that shit he's spewing. There's no way he's not a part of all this!"

Chief Putnam reached down and removed her hand from his arm, then leaned in close. If I were a normal human, I wouldn't have been able to hear him whisper to her, "This isn't over, Alanna. We're not through with Harker and his band of freaks, but this isn't the time, and we don't have the manpower. Let it go. I have a plan."

Then he continued toward the door with Stephens and Herr in tow. Becks gave me a worried look. "Did I hear that right?"

"If you were listening in through me, yeah. He's not done with me, and he thinks I had something to do with this other than trying to keep people alive."

"That's…not good," she replied.

"No, I think having a revenge-hungry chief of police hunting me through my home city, on top of a bunch of asshole secret agents trying to kill every non-human in the country, definitely falls into the category of 'not good.'" It was a serious understatement, of course. Putnam's words, and the look on his face as he spoke to Stephens when he thought I couldn't hear him, told me that there would be more blood on the streets before this was over. It felt an awful lot like the Charlotte-Mecklenburg Police Department had just declared war on me and mine.

10

I sat there for a couple minutes after the cops left, just thinking through the morning, but eventually I couldn't put it off any longer. "Okay, you two," I called. "Get out here."

Faustus and Watson emerged from Mort's back room, and I was mightily thrilled that they hadn't been sitting at the table with me when Putnam and his bad cop deputy chief arrived. Aside from having literally jet-black skin and yellow eyes, with pointed ears and fangs that protruded just slightly past his bottom lip, Faustus just carried a look of guilt with him everywhere, like some people carry a security blanket. And Watson, well, he had that permanently rumpled look that only tenured professors and the truly brilliant can pull off. Watson was neither.

Jack limped over to the bar, grabbed two glasses and a fresh bottle from Mort, and made his way over to sit down opposite me. Faustus was already there, and he held out his hand for the second glass when Watson took the chair beside him. "Your leg bothering you?" I asked.

"The stump is chafing a little today. The humidity in my apartment is low, and I think my skin is particularly dry from it, so there's a little more irritation than normal. Nothing I haven't dealt with before," he said. Watson lost a leg below the knee in an IED attack when he was serving with British Army Intelligence. I looked up the reports when we first started working together. He was the only survivor from Land Rovers that were destroyed. Seven men lost their lives, and Watson lost a leg.

That's going to make him even grumpier than normal, I said to Becks.

Be nice. We need him.

Remind me why, exactly.

I'll get back to you. I smothered a smile. Becks didn't like Jack any more than I did, but he was grandfathered into the Shadow Council because of his familial connections to the more famous Doctor Watson, who had some experiences with Luke and other supernatural elements in England back in the day. He also was useful whenever we needed someone to look and sound like an attorney, since he was one.

"What the fuck happened?" I asked. "You two were supposed to come here, quietly poke around to see if anyone had any information about this Director Shaw, or *any* of the Director Shaws. Not start a damn war in the middle of Charlotte."

"It wasn't our fault, Quincy," Faustus started, but my upraised hand cut him off.

"Faustus, you're literally the last person I'm going to believe. Your name is synonymous with shitty deals and obfuscation."

He opened his mouth to protest, took a look at my face, and thought better of it. I looked back at Watson. "So what the fuck, Jack? How did DEMON show up?"

He looked outraged. "Well, I didn't call them, Harker! Dammit, man, I don't have any contacts with anyone from that bunch of jack-booted thugs. We were asking questions, meandering through the crowd looking for people who seemed likely to share information with us, when Mort's bartender suddenly set off an alarm."

I looked over to Mort. "Where's your bartender, Mort? And do I know this one?"

"No," he said. "You don't. I've purposefully kept them away from you. You've got a bad habit of getting my bartenders killed."

Ouch. He was right, though. His daughter Christy tended bar for him until a demon took her out to get my attention. Then the next bartender of his I met here was a half-dragon that tried to kill me, so I killed him first. I'm pretty sure those are the only two I was responsible for, but to his mind, that was plenty. He had a decent point. "Where is he? Or she. Or they. That's better. Where are they, Mort? I need to ask them some questions."

"*She* is gone," Mort said, stressing the pronoun so I knew I was dealing with a woman. Or a female demon or cryptid with enough capacity for human speech to take drink orders, give change, and break up a fight. Whatever.

"Where did she go?" I asked, feeling my temper start to slip. It was barely noon, and it had already been a long damn day. Which was preceded by a string of long damn days. I was pretty fried and didn't look to be getting a break until Director Shaw, all of them, were in the ground. Permanently.

"I don't know," Mort said. At the dark look on my face, he held up both hands. "Scout's honor, Harker, I don't know. I don't know where she lives, I don't know who she associates with when she's not here, I don't even know her middle name. That's completely intentional, by the way, and all your fault. I pay her cash under the table and try not to know anything about her, so that you can ask me questions like this as much as you like, and I don't know anything to tell you. So tough shit, Mr. Demon Hunter. I don't have anything for you."

It's really hard to tell when a hitchhiker demon is lying. Because they don't own the body they're riding around in, they don't have the usual tics most people have when they're trying to hide something. All I had to go on were Mort's words, which were pretty doubtful, and the logic behind them, which was actually pretty sound. His bartender probably was safer if she was far away from me, especially the way my year was going.

"Okay," I said. "But when she comes back, call me. I want to know if she tipped DEMON off to Faustus and Watson asking around about them."

"Why do you think they were here for us?" Watson asked. "This is a popular place with exactly the type of creatures that DEMON seems hellbent on eradicating."

"Hey!" Faustus protested. "Let's be careful slinging around words like 'creature.' A little respect, if you don't mind."

"Yeah," I agreed. "Get the terminology right. Faustus isn't a creature. He's a legendary asshole, swindler, and turncoat." I smiled at the demon, who gave me the finger. "To answer your question, it's timing. Those bastards have been in town for months, but they finally get up the balls to raid this joint on the day you two are here poking around, and I'm supposed to think it's a coincidence? Not fucking likely."

"Okay, that's a pretty good point," Watson said. "But why come after us if their beef is with you?"

"I guess their Director Shaw is under the mistaken impression that I give a shit what happens to you, Jack," I said. "Or maybe she thought that just causing some mayhem at one of the very few Sanctuaries in the city would be enough to draw me into a confrontation. Hell, maybe she wanted to get Becks out here because she knows that whenever something spooky happens in Charlotte, Becks is on the front lines. Shaw has certainly shown a willingness to go after people I care about."

"Something still doesn't track," Becks said. "I can't put my finger on it, but something feels off about this whole thing. Like we're being set up, but it's not by Shaw." She shook her head. "I don't know. Something about this whole thing is hinky."

"More than hinky," I said. "You're right that something else is going on here, but we won't figure it out by sitting around drinking Mort's liquor and staring at each other. You go on back to work and see what you can find out at the station. Jack and Faustus can poke around a little more at the seedy underbelly of the city, see if they can shake something loose that will tell us where Shaw and her goons are holed up. There aren't that many places to house a small army in a city the size of Charlotte, and even fewer that won't ask questions about where the rent money is coming from."

"How are we supposed to do that?" Watson asked. "I don't know if you noticed, but we don't exactly blend in around here. I am unmistakably 'not from around here,' and Faustus is, well, *Faustus*."

"Ah don't knew wut you're talking about," Faustus said in a thick

Southern drawl. Watson turned to the demon and started at his altered appearance. Where a jet-black bald demon with yellow eyes and fangs had been moments before, now sat a shifty-looking skinny man with bad teeth, a patchy beard, and a trucker cap with "Leather & Lace" in cursive script on it. He looked like an advertisement for cut-rate meth, or maybe incest, or both. But the crude tattoos creeping up out of the neck of his Toby Keith t-shirt marked him as someone who either was too cheap to pay a real artist, or more likely got his ink done while a guest of the state somewhere. I thought the "88" tattooed right under his Adam's apple was a convincing, if disgusting, touch.

"Okay, you and Neo-Nazi Barbie here go poke around. You can be the guy from out of town here to stir up shit among the rednecks. Faustus can be your first redneck."

"What are you planning to do, Harker?" Becks asked.

"Me and Glory are gonna go a-hunting."

"Hunting what?"

"I told your chief that monsters, plural, killed most of the dead cops in the parking lot. That wasn't exactly correct."

"I wondered when you were going to get around to that," Glory said.

"Yeah." I nodded at her. "This one's ours." Turning my attention back to Flynn, I said, "Most of the folks pouring out of Mort's to tangle with the cops were either Reavers or cryptids. Not a huge deal, really. Reavers are bad news in groups, but they're really stupid and not likely to cause too much havoc on their own. One of the cops was killed by one of these Reavers."

"Who subsequently fell to my blade," Glory said with a grim smile.

"Yeah, that," I went on. "But the other two that didn't die to DEMON bullets were killed by the same beastie, and it's a bad one."

"A demon?" Flynn asked.

I shook my head. "No. This was a very specific type of fairy. A very bad Fae with a taste for blood and a thirst for mayhem. I knew what it was as soon as I saw the throats ripped out of those officers. This was a creature that wanted them to know they were dying, that fed on their terror as much as on their blood. They were killed by a sluagh, a

63

type of undead fae creature that is trapped between life and death because the afterlife itself has rejected it, so now it wants to rack up enough corpses to bribe the universe to either give it eternal life, or let it die. They're nasty, dangerous, and they kill just for shits and giggles. And now we're going to track this down before it kills anyone else."

"This is a new one on me," Becks said. "How bad are they?"

"Pretty bad," I admitted. "They're supposed to be worse than redcaps, and you remember the one of those I dealt with last month. I expect this thing to give me all I can handle. That's why I'm taking backup." I nodded at Glory.

"Yeah...backup," Flynn said, and I could tell the morning's revelations still weren't sitting well with her. No surprise, really. It had rocked me, too. But I saw the need for it. Becks wasn't nearly as pragmatic where I was concerned. Guess that's why they say love makes you crazy.

I looked around the table. "Okay, we know what to do. Let's meet back at the war room at six tonight. Faustus, it's your turn to pick up sushi. And don't skimp on the yellowfin this time."

The demon gave me a mocking salute, and he and Watson headed out the front door. I turned to Mort. "Sorry we got your place shot up again."

"This time it wasn't your fault, Harker," Mort said. "Be careful, will ya? I still want my ride in that meat suit of yours, and it will be a lot less fun if you're a corpse when I take the wheel."

That was perhaps the least comforting reason anyone had ever given for wanting me to stay alive, but at that point, I kinda had to take any well wishes I could get.

11

T his sucks," I said, letting my head fall back against the driver's seat of my car. Glory and I had just finished our sixth fruitless search of a self-storage facility looking for the sluagh. The part of town near Mort's had a ton of these places, and it had taken some fast talking to get into the last couple. The first few, I just drove in behind somebody who had a code, but I wasn't as lucky after that and had to pretend to be looking for a rental unit, which meant dealing with perky office people and pretending to give a shit about their first month for a dollar specials and their 24-hour security cameras. It only took me a quick glance down each alleyway with my Sight to see there were no traces of any Fae, but I still had to put up with the bullshit until I could get back to the front gate. By this point, I was pretty sure I never wanted to own enough crap to need a self-storage joint.

"Where else do you think the bastard could be hiding?" Glory asked. "The storage place made sense, because it could be out of sight and try to clean itself off, but...wait a minute...oh, that's not good."

"What?" I asked. She had a look on her face that was halfway between horrified admiration and pure horror. I wasn't sure if she'd had an epiphany about where the beastie might be hiding, or if the lunch from Phat Burrito wasn't agreeing with her. My stomach felt fine, so I was pretty sure it wasn't the burrito, but I had a lot more experience with solid food and processed cheese than Glory did.

"What if the sluagh isn't hiding, but hiding in plain sight?"

"You mean instead of going to ground somewhere until everyone stops looking for it, going somewhere with a shitload of people and milling around aimlessly like a normal person? That's...pretty good, actually." It made sense. Most Fae could mimic humans almost perfectly when they wanted to. The sluagh would be on a weird mix of adrenaline rush and blood frenzy, but it could keep its true form hidden until it was too late for its victims to escape.

"Where would we find a crowd in this part of town?" Glory asked. "It's the middle of the afternoon on a weekday, so I guess the office buildings downtown, but..."

"Those people aren't moving around very much, and it would be hard to hide amongst an office full of people who all know each other," I said. "We need a place with a bunch of strangers, pretty mobile, with a lot of entrances, and preferably a public restroom that's largely out of sight for it to clean off in."

"That sounds like...oh no."

What I assumed was the same thought struck me as Glory spoke. "Yeah, that could be bad." I straightened up, pulled on my seatbelt, and put the car in gear. When I pulled back onto Clanton, I made a left onto South heading back toward Uptown, then turned right onto Tyvola.

"Would it really...?" Glory asked as I wove in and out of traffic. Fortunately, there weren't a ton of cars on the road at this hour, but I definitely didn't want to draw the attention of the police. They would *not* be helpful and might end up getting more of their own killed if they got involved.

"Yeah, it really would," I said. I focused on the road until I turned left into the parking deck at SouthPark Mall, one of Charlotte's top-end shopping destinations. Even at midday on a Tuesday, there were hundreds of cars in the Nordstrom's deck, and hundreds more scattered around the massive structure.

One of the region's gleaming monuments to commerce, SouthPark Mall had over a hundred-fifty stores, ranging from Apple to Tiffany & Co., not to mention restaurants to blow all budgets. It was the place to be seen if you were shopping, and as Glory and I strode through the glass doors of Nordstrom's, there were plenty of people to see. Yuppie women in yoga pants, men in khakis and polos, teens with perfectly tousled hair and studied rebellion literally written all over their shirts were everywhere. Yeah, if I wanted to hide in plain sight, this was the sight to hide in.

Glory and I stood out, although after about twenty steps through the store, I amended that to just me, since my Guardian took a quick detour behind a clothing rack and stepped back out looking like every other overpriced pair of Botox injections in the store. Must be nice being able to change your appearance at a thought.

I stepped into the men's department, placed my hand on a suit hanging near the back of a rack, and whispered, *"Tralatio."* I felt a tingle all over me as the dirt, blood, and sweat from my clothes and body was suddenly lifted off me and deposited onto the suit. Now I was underdressed, but at least I was clean and underdressed, so I was a lot less likely to inspire a security escort, and just garnered some side eye instead.

"You totally ruined that suit," Glory muttered.

"I totally don't give a fuck," I replied.

"That's rude."

"They were charging nine hundred bucks for an off-the-rack suit. I am *not* the one being rude here. See anything?"

"Not even a blood trail. You?"

I peered around using my Sight, but the store was unsurprisingly devoid of anything magical. It was pretty devoid of personality, too, despite the presence of a pompous twit playing a grand piano by the escalators, so I wasn't surprised when there was nothing magical in the vicinity. "Nothing. We should check the rest of the mall."

"What about blood? Shouldn't it leave some kind of trail?"

She was right. Even if it wasn't doing anything magical, the creature should leave at least a faint blood trail until it could get cleaned up. "This is going to take a minute," I said. "I need somewhere to cast."

"Changing room?"

"Too public. Let's find a bathroom."

Of course, the nearest public restroom was for friggin' ever away from the store, out the front, down the main drag of the mall, past a couple of random kiosks of crap like sunglasses, drones, and copper healing jewelry. Finally, we turned down a deserted corridor that led to the mall offices and a set of bathrooms. Glory took the opportunity to browse in some store that I couldn't pronounce the name of or really tell what they sold from the window, while I went into the can to cast my spell.

The place was fortunately deserted, so I went all the way down and set up shop in the handicapped stall on the end. If you ever find yourself in a public restroom needing to do spellwork, I highly recommend taking the extra few steps to gain the wider stall. Your elbows will thank you for it. I stood in the center of the stall, trying diligently to ignore the smells around me, and gave a safety flush before getting to work. I reached into my pocket for the small Kershaw liner lock knife I carried and sliced open my thumb. Then I squeezed three drops of my blood into the toilet, closed my eyes tightly, and plunged my hand into the thankfully clean water. I made it a point not to touch any of the porcelain, not because it would screw up the spell, but because it was gross.

I focused all my senses on the sensation of the water around my hand, letting the blood diffuse through the water and bind to my skin. The open cut on my thumb pulsed in time to my heartbeat, and I felt the ripples emanate from it, resonating with the blood in the water. I pulled my hand out, looking at the thin sheen of crimson coating it. As I watched, the blood vanished from my hand, but I could still feel it pulsing, almost like it was squeezing my fist. I moved my hand nearer to the water, and the sensation got stronger. As I pulled farther away, it weakened. The spell was working. Now I just had to get near somewhere the sluagh had been, and I would be able to sense the blood. I only hoped I wouldn't run into too many people with bloody knees, or paper cuts, or anything else that made them bleed. That could be awkward.

I dried my hand with paper towels, ignoring the stares of the man in the starched shirt and tie washing his hands, and walked out. I'm sure he thought I was the most disgusting thing he'd ever seen, but if I could keep a psychotic fairy from murdering anyone in the middle of the mall, I could handle grossing out a yuppie.

I met back up with Glory outside a store and noticed the three shopping bags she now carried. "I wasn't in there that long," I said.

"Long enough," she replied. "Did you get it cast?"

"Yeah."

"Which hand?"

I held up my left.

"Good to know," she said. Then she took up a position by my right elbow. "Don't even think of touching me with that hand until you scrub it down. I know what you had to do to make that sympathetic magic spell work."

"Oh come on, you can't get sick."

"No, but I can get grossed out, and if anything will do it, it's a public restroom."

I couldn't argue with her there, so I didn't. I just started walking down the middle of the mall, letting my hand drift along and hopefully find a murderous creature.

"Do you feel anything?" Glory asked.

"Glory, it's been ten feet."

"So? Some of these people might be bleeding."

"Do you see any of them bleeding?"

"You do not have to be bleeding visibly, Q," she pointed out.

"No. No one is...wait a second." My hand pulsed and I looked around. "That way." I strode across the mall to stand outside a women's clothing store, the pulsing on my hand growing stronger with every step. I drew up just short of the door as I saw a pair of twenty something girls walk out in a rush, one with her head back and a friend with a tissue clasped to her nose.

"False alarm," I said. "Chick with a nosebleed."

"Well, at least we know it's working," Glory replied.

And it was. The spell worked on a kid with a skinned knee, a bald man with a harried expression and his hand clutched to his gut that I suspected of a bleeding ulcer, a woman with no discernible injuries but who also gave off no magical aura to my Sight, and a teenager with a slightly split lip and a scowl on his face that said louder than a billboard that somebody had backhanded the shit out of him, probably the surly fat man walking beside him griping about the boy's grades. Glory put her hand on my arm to keep me from giving the fat bastard a lip to match his son's.

But that was it. All perfectly mundane. No sluagh. No murderous creature of any kind. Not to say we didn't spot some magic. There was certainly some of that going on. A glamour on the makeup counter girl at Dillard's, a stay-fresh spell on the cookies in the display case in the food court, and a few masking spells from various creatures infernal and divine taking an afternoon stroll through the sea of humanity. But no threats, other than overpricing.

Until we came to the queue outside The Cheesecake Factory. As we neared a clump of people waiting to be seated, my hand gave the strongest pulse yet. "I think we're close," I said to Glory.

I dropped into my Sight, allowing me to see the magical spectrum, and there it was. I could still see the glamour it cast over itself of a balding man with a slight pot belly and a cheap burgundy windbreaker, but underneath that was the gaunt, twisted image of a bloodthirsty monster.

We'd found our sluagh. Now we just had to get it out of the fucking Cheesecake Factory before it turned the crowd into a dessert of a different type.

1 2

How do you want to handle this?" I asked as we walked toward the crowd.

"Let's try to take him down before—well, shit," Glory said as the hostess smiled at the sluagh and ushered him into the restaurant.

"You were about to say we should take him down before he got inside, huh?"

"Yeah, that would have been nice."

"Oh well. Guess we do this the hard way."

"Like there's any other," Glory said, walking up to the hostess stand and bending down to talk to the pretty young Latina working there.

I stepped over to where a dozen people were milling about, held my badge in front of my chest, shielded from the restaurant, and said, "I need everyone to remain perfectly calm. We are going inside to apprehend a suspect. We do not expect him to become aggressive, but I'd like everyone to move away from the door just in case."

"What did the guy do?" said a burly man in an ill-fitting polo shirt. He looked like the type who wore a lot of pro-military garb but had never actually worn a uniform and would love a chance to be a hero without actually putting himself in any real danger.

"Unpaid parking tickets," I replied. "A couple hundred of them. He owes enough in fines to pay my salary for two years. Nothing interesting, nothing dangerous, just a jerk who won't do his civic duty and pay his fees. We'll have him out of here in just a minute, and then we'll have freed up another table so y'all can get in there and eat. Sound good? Good." I tucked my badge away and turned back to the entrance of the restaurant, when a huge commotion at the other set of doors, the ones leading outside, drew my attention.

"Mother. Fucker," I muttered under my breath as I saw a dozen CMPD officers in riot gear streaming into the restaurant.

I had a fleeting thought of getting the cops to stand down before the sluagh saw them, but it was about a mile too late. He was already on top of his table, glamour gone and razor-sharp claws out. A wicked grin stretched his face wider than a human possibly could smile, and double rows of pointed teeth glittered as he licked his lips.

"Come to papa!" the creature bellowed, and the people at the nearest tables, who had been focused on the cops pouring in from the parking lot, now turned to see the monster in their midst.

It had the anticipated effect, which was pure fucking pandemonium. Women screamed, men sprang to their feet and toppled chairs, men screamed, babies started to cry, and people bolted in every direction. The situation went from "challenging" to "mortally fucked" in about two seconds.

Two of the cops were bowled over by fleeing customers, and the rest concentrated on getting their fallen comrades to their feet and getting out of the way. Glory went into crowd control mode outside, snatching people up and flying them to safety before they got trampled by the herd of terrified humanity. That left me to deal with the sluagh, except that there were about a hundred people trying to get through both exits, and I had no good way to get inside.

But no good way doesn't mean no way. My energy was still low from the fight earlier, but it didn't take magic to draw my pistol and fire three quick rounds through one of the tall restaurant windows, up near the ceiling where they hopefully wouldn't ricochet into anyone. The glass shattered, and two massive panes fell to the floor, creating an instant entrance. I vaulted through the opening and started hopping from table to table trying to swim upstream and get to the monster before it started slicing people open.

I wasn't fast enough. With mayhem all around, the nasty little bastard took the chance to add bloodshed to the terror and confusion, reaching down from its perch atop a table and slicing deep furrows down the back of a twenty something man in a Panthers jersey and jeans as he pushed a woman and little girl toward the exit. The guy fell writhing to the floor, and the sluagh spun, looking for another target. Its claws flashed out, and a woman dropped to her knees as the top of her scalp peeled back. I watched in horror as the evil Fae drew back its hand and shattered her skull, scooping out a fistful of brains and devouring them on the spot.

I still had my pistol in my hand, so I paused atop a relatively stable bench and fired three rounds at the creature. Two hit, and the little beastie turned its attention fully to me. It wasn't hurt by the lead rounds, but I damn sure made it sit up and take notice. I knew I couldn't shoot it and do any real damage, because I didn't carry cold iron rounds as a general rule. But if it was coming at me, it wasn't killing civilians, so that's all I could focus on.

It grinned at me, reached down into its chest, and pulled out one of the slugs. It licked the bullet clean of its blood and tossed it negligently over its shoulder, then sprang toward me, hopping from table to table and vaulting fleeing customers like it was some kind of demented game of Frogger. It moved faster than it had any right to, and was nimble as fuck, and I barely had time to find a clear patch of floor to jump down onto before it perched on a booth railing about eight feet away and launched itself right at me.

If I hadn't learned to fight sparring with Count friggin' Dracula, the speed of the creature would have gutted me. As it was, I managed to step forward and crouch, altering the creature's path so it passed over me, and I snagged it by the lapels of its blood-soaked windbreaker and slammed it to the floor. It lashed out with its right hand, slashing a long furrow through my coat and into my left forearm, and I pulled back, calling up a little power to harden my skin against the creature's claws.

"Nice one, dickhead," I said, flinging a baseball-sized flame at the faerie's face. I expected it to duck to one side, but it dove forward instead, going for my knees. I sprang up and to the right, landing awkwardly on a table, which toppled over, taking me to the floor in a thunder of broken dishes and mediocre chicken marsala. I had just enough time to get to my feet before the scrawny bastard was on me again, but this time when I grabbed it, my magic protected me from getting sliced and diced. I picked the sluagh up and flung it across the room to slam into a wall, and it lay there dazed for the few seconds I needed to check on my arm and make sure I wasn't going to bleed out.

I wasn't, but when I looked back at the creature, it was gone. The rattle of automatic weapons fire told me without a doubt where it was, and I spun around to see the thing going straight for the phalanx of SWAT officers.

"Fuck," I muttered. There was no way this ended well. "Glory!" I shouted. "Keep those people down!" If we got out of this without more civilian casualties, it would be a miracle. I wracked my brain for something I had on me that could kill this little fucker. Bullets were out, because lead didn't do shit. My knives were silvered, but unless I could chop its head off before it disemboweled me, they weren't going to be enough. I was too low on power to blast it into oblivion, or even to call up my soulblade.

Then something in the corner of my eye caught my attention. It was crazy, but it just might do the trick. I jumped over the divider separating the booths from the bar area, then hopped up onto the bar and reached up. My hands latched onto the wrought-iron decoration above the bar, and I pulled with all my might.

This really needs to be real wrought iron and not just plastic or some bullshit like that, I thought as I grabbed it, but I knew from the first tug that it was at least really metal, and hopefully really iron. I pulled with everything I had, and after agonizing seconds, a chunk of wrought iron ivy wall art came loose in my hands. It was about three feet long, and unwieldy as all fuck, but it was iron, and it was heavy enough to leave a mark. Which was better than anything else I could come up with.

I looked to where the sluagh was battling the cops, and my gut lurched at the sight. Six of the cops that had come inside were flat on their backs, either sprawled on the floor or draped over tables and chairs, obviously dead. I could see throats ripped out, chests punched through, and one female officer lying three feet away from her severed left arm. Two of the others were trying to hold the doorway against the beast, while the other four were out shepherding people away from the scene. Neither the cops nor the sluagh had noticed the shattered window yet, but it would only take a few seconds, and then there would be no chance of catching the thing without even more bloodshed.

I sprinted across the restaurant, leaping over an overturned table and almost losing my footing in a puddle of spilled gravy. When I was about eight feet from the thing, I shouted, "Hey, asshole!" hoping to grab its attention.

It worked. The monster turned to me, its grin widening when it saw me charging. That grin disappeared when one of the officers that had been holding a riot shield to keep the creature from pushing through the door decided it was hero time. He dropped the shield, which was doing its job and keeping both him and the people behind him alive, and drew his pistol. The pistol did part of its job, in that it pumped a bunch of bullets into the back of the monster, but it failed in the most important part—killing the damned thing.

The sluagh staggered forward, then whirled around with almost unbelievable speed and sliced both the cop's hands off at the wrist. The officer dropped to his knees, blood fountaining from his stumps, and his fellow shield-holder dropped his big chunk of Plexiglas and knelt to try to help his fallen buddy. He wasn't going to be able to help anyone, though, because in the next instant, the sluagh shoved a hand straight through that cop's chest, bulletproof vest and all, and yanked out the man's heart.

All this happened in the few seconds it took me to cross thirty feet of restaurant floor. From the shooting, to the amputation, to the evisceration. It all happened before I could reach the fucking thing to jam a yard of wrought iron through its guts. I did, though. I skewered the bastard on a twisted chunk of forged ivory, and used the makeshift spear as a lever, picking the faerie up and slamming it to the ground. It died, the vicious fuck, but I swear it looked me in the face and grinned as the last light fled from its eyes.

Less than a minute. The whole thing, from the cops charging in like over-armed elephants to the sluagh breathing its last on the floor of the restaurant, took less than a minute. I counted eight dead CMPD officers, a pair of diners gutted like fish, and one woman writhing on the floor who looked to have been trampled. And one dead Fae. One.

Then my eyes caught sight of the faces of two of the cops. My gut clenched as I recognized them. It was Deputy Chief Stephens, the woman who made it very clear that she would like for me to go to prison for a very long time, and Captain Herr, Flynn's boss and one of the legit decent people in the department. Stephens's throat was missing, and she lay on the floor in a massive puddle of blood.

I looked at Herr, one of the very few cops I'd ever really trusted, one of the guys who proved himself a solidly moral human being on multiple occasions, and closed my eyes. All he wanted to do was help people. He didn't know how to live in my world and should never have tried. But he did, because that's where people needed his help. And now he was lying with his guts ripped out on the faux marble floor of a chain restaurant, empty eyes staring at the ceiling.

I let the magic shielding my skin fade and turned to look out at Glory and the surviving officers, wondering if there was anything I could do to help pick up the pieces after this disaster.

And found myself staring down the barrel of two AR-15s held by very angry-looking SWAT officers.

"Get on the ground!" one of them yelled at me, and the other one lowered his weapon to pull out his handcuffs.

Well, shit.

13

———————

C MPD Headquarters has multiple "interview" rooms where the cops talk to suspects, and over the years I'd seen the inside of most of them, usually at the bequest of my now-fiancée Detective Rebecca Gail Flynn. She wasn't always as enamored of me as she is now. In fact, for a while she was convinced that I was the greatest threat to public safety since, well, ever.

But it had been a few years since I'd been an involuntary guest of the constabulary, and after sitting handcuffed to a table for a few hours, I was beginning to remember how much I disliked it. And by "sitting handcuffed to a table for a few hours" I really mean that I jimmied the cuffs after about five minutes and spent the rest of the time sitting in the wobbly chair with my feet up on the table. After about an hour of having my balance screwed up by the uneven chair legs, I swapped chairs with the interrogator seat, which hadn't been rigged to have one leg shorter than the other, and took a nap.

I woke to the sound of the door unlocking and rubbed sleep from my eyes as Chief Putnam stormed in and slammed a thick manila folder on the table. "Get up!" he barked.

I looked at him. "Was that supposed to confuse me, since I was theoretically still shackled to the table, or startle me, because you saw on the camera that I was asleep? Either way, no joy, Chief."

"Get. Your. Ass. Up." He almost spat the words as he leaned over the table. "You're lucky I don't have you—"

I stood up. "Have me what, Chief? Shot? Been there, done that. Locked up? There's not a jail that can hold me. Killed some other way? Better men than you have tried. Now why don't you back the fuck off and we can talk about the shitshow of a day your department has had."

"I'm going to lock you up under the fucking jail, Harker. We're going in front of the judge right now, where you'll be booked on multiple homicide charges and remanded without bail into my custody, where we will unfortunately lose track of you in the mayhem that is law enforcement in a major city. Sometime in the next two weeks, I expect we'll remember you're down there at the very end of our holding cells, without food or drink. But I'm afraid it will be too late by then. You're done, Harker. I'm through playing nice with you and that band of freaks you've got running roughshod through my city. I'm through letting you corrupt one of the best detectives in my department, and I'm sure as hell through—"

"Talking really wants to be the next word out of your mouth, Chief." I didn't raise my voice. I didn't yell, despite the fact that a very loud bald man with a vein pulsing in his forehead and burst blood vessel in his left eye was screaming at me from less than five feet away. I didn't lean forward, I didn't threaten, I didn't even *move*. I just let him look in my eyes. And I let him get a *good* look.

The eyes are windows to the soul, and that's more than just a turn of phrase with a magic-user. I usually keep my truth hidden behind wisecracks and sideways glances, but I let Putnam stare right into me and see what was there. All the fire and fury, all the pain and loss, all the hellfire and brimstone I'd walked through to get to that moment. I let him see it all, and it rocked him back on his heels.

As it should. It's no small thing, really seeing into someone's soul. When the soul you're looking at is the kind of scarred, battered thing that mine is, it's doubly unsettling. To put it mildly, I've seen some shit, and now Putnam was getting an eyeful of it. He sat down heavily in the uneven chair; all his bluster gone in a glance.

I pulled my chair up and sat across from him, leaning forward with my elbows on the table. "I'm sorry about your men. Especially Captain Herr. He was a good cop, and a good man. But you know damn well I am not responsible for his death, your deputy chief's death, or any of the others. There was a monster in that restaurant that they were not prepared for, and they never should have set foot in that place. Those officers didn't stand a chance. It's awful, but that's not on me. Now we can sit here until either someone from Homeland Security comes to spring me, or I get fed up with pretending you can keep me here and just leave, or we can work together and get to the real root of the shit sequoia that was today."

"What is that, exactly?" Putnam's voice was subdued, and there was a lone drop of sweat rolling down his bald pate and trickling along his jawline, but otherwise he held his composure pretty well. It seemed like I probably wasn't going to have to fight my way out of the station, which was great, since I wasn't sure I had enough in the tank to do it without somebody getting hurt.

"DEMON," I replied. "Those assholes have been stirring up shit all over the country for months now, and they were the ones that caused the shootout at Mort's, which caused the sluagh to go apeshit on the people at the mall. If there's no bloodbath in the parking lot, the little Fae monster doesn't get their blood up and decide 'fuck subtlety, let's cause a ruckus.'"

"I thought you worked for them."

"No, I work for the Department of Homeland Security's Paranormal Division. In theory, DEMON handles cryptids and monster-type stuff, and we handle magic and demon-type stuff. In practice, there's new leadership over there and they've decided to destroy any monster, magical being, or person with any kind of supernatural ability."

"Seems like a pretty good idea after today," Putnam said.

"Yeah, I might have to object to that," I said. "When they tried it on me, it involved a Nazi scientist torturing the shit out of me. So forgive me if I don't go along with the idea that I should be killed just because I'm a little different."

"A little different? How fucking old are you, Harker?"

"That's not important. Besides, it's rude to ask."

"You're not a lady. How old are you?"

"As of my last birthday, I'm one hundred and…twenty-four years old." I was a little embarrassed that I had to do the math, but after the first eighty or so, birthdays stop being something you pay much attention to.

"You're not just a little different. You're a super-powered immortal wizard, who took great pains to remind me not two minutes ago that you can't be held in any jail and that it's unlikely I could kill you if I tried. Tell me why I shouldn't be afraid of you. Go ahead, I'll wait." He leaned back, arms folded across his chest and his jaw jutting forward like a pissed-off bulldog. Of course, bulldogs always look kinda pissed off, so I guess that's redundant.

"Because I'm one of the good guys, Chief. I've proved that time and again. I've proven it here, in Atlanta, in San Francisco, France, Germany, Austria, Arizona… Hell, I've taken out bad guys on five continents. I'm missing Australia and Antarctica, by the way, so if you know of anyone that needs handled there, I'd like to fill out the checklist."

Putnam sighed, seeming to deflate a little more. I looked at him closely, really stretching my senses to try and hear his heart rate, breathing, any of the clues Luke can pick up off a person. I got nothing. His demonic mojo was pretty diluted by the time it made it through both my parents and got to me, which sucked in times like this, but I could still go outside for lunch, so I was pretty happy with the tradeoff.

"What am I supposed to tell my people, Harker?" Putnam looked at me, and I didn't see a pissed off cop, or an authoritarian asshole trying to throw me under the jail. I saw a man who had to send other men and women into dangerous situations and sit back at his desk hoping they would all come back safe. I could see it weighed on him, the mark of a decent leader. But I could also see the fury behind the strain. This was not a man accustomed to being told that he couldn't do something, and that coupled with the anger at losing people under his command made for a volatile situation.

"Tell them that you're working on it. Tell them that you need to bring in some help, because there are things that are outside the capacity of a normal police department. Tell them there's federal interference and let them hate me and the people from Homeland. Tell them whatever you need, but let me get out of here and get back to tracking down these assholes from DEMON before they cause another bloodbath on Charlotte's streets and you lose more officers to things they should never be facing in the first place." I put every ounce of persuasion I had into that. It was the best speech I could come up with that didn't involve me blowing something up for emphasis, and for about half a minute I thought it had worked.

Then Putnam shook his head and stood up. "Can't do it. I'm sorry, Harker. You're probably right. This isn't what we're made to deal with. This isn't what my people are trained to do. But it's still my city, and my responsibility, and—"

"And your fucking pride is going to get more people killed," I said, cutting him off. "You want to go out hunting down rogue government operatives, fine. Just stay the fuck out of my way. Because I promise you one thing, Chief. These are the last hours I waste sitting here in your fucking jail while the bad guys are out there hunting the people I care about."

I stood up and turned to the door, but Putnam's next words froze me with my hand on the knob.

"We're not going after DEMON, Harker. You can have them. There were no agents in that restaurant killing my men. That was a monster. Far as I'm concerned, DEMON has the right idea. We're going to hunt down every creepy-crawly critter and magical bastard in this city, and we're going to make this city safe for humans to walk the street or eat mediocre dessert again. We're not hunting DEMON. We're hunting monsters."

He walked around the table and over to me. Putnam stood right in front of me, chest to chest. I had maybe an inch on him, but he was a big man, thicker through the shoulders and arms than I'd ever be. "We're hunting monsters, Harker. And when we find them, we're going to kill every last one of them. And woe be unto any son of a bitch that gets in our way."

Then he left the room, leaving me standing open-mouthed and staring into the open doorway.

14

Two days later, I stood in my apartment in a charcoal pinstripe suit, a pressed white dress shirt, my only pair of decent shoes, a pair of Ecco loafers I'd picked up the day before, and a tie. A real one, with no clip or anything. I even remembered how to tie it myself, after a couple of YouTube videos to refresh my memory. I leaned on the back of one sofa looking out at the skyline. Charlotte's got a nice skyline. Like most places, it looks better at night, because big buildings from a distance aren't really that pretty in the daytime, but they look somehow magical when they sparkle against the black backdrop of a night sky.

"Penny for 'em," Becks said as she stepped into the living room. She was in her full dress uniform, which I hadn't seen her wear since she graduated from the Academy. The dark blue looked good on her, but I'll admit to thinking that literally everything looks good on her. She had a lot more ribbons and doodads on her uniform than at her graduation, but the one that caught my eye was the black piece of elastic around the gold shield on her chest. I had a fleeting thought that it sucked that it was such a normal occurrence to have to wear it that cops just all had those little pieces of elastic at the ready.

"Just thinking about how much these things suck," I replied. As she walked over to stand beside me, I flashed back to my earliest memory of someone dying, and the feelings that stirred in me. The first funeral I went to was much like today's memorial would be—part service and part circus.

Abraham Van Helsing was a very famous man after the publication of Stoker's book about my parents' and Van Helsing's first encounter with Uncle Luke, and his passing was a monumental event at the time. My parents wanted to attend the service quietly, but once the crowd caught sight of my father, the legendary Jonathan Harker, there was nothing quiet about our presence. I was ten and my brother James was eight. Little Orly was home with our housekeeper/nurse-maid/cook Mrs. Levering, because my mother didn't want to have to deal with a fidgety toddler amidst the sea of people.

I remembered making our way to the front of the church and stopping beside his son and daughter-in-law to share our condolences. Marissa, Abraham's granddaughter, was my age, or close to it, and she looked terribly sad. I stepped over to her and said, "I'm sorry your grandfather died. He was a very nice man."

She looked up at me, her eyes red from crying, and hugged me tight. I was even more awkward in 1906 than I am today, so I simply reached behind her and patted her on the back. After a long, increasingly uncomfortable moment for me as she sobbed quietly on my shoulder and I stood there with absolutely no idea what I was supposed to do, she let go and stepped back.

"Thank you," she said. "He liked your family a lot. He talked about your parents all the time."

With that done, we took our place beside the other surviving members of Stoker's novel, most of whom had contributed to my name as well as Uncle Luke's legend, and James and I did our very best to sit still as the priest droned on about Van Helsing's accomplishments and the wonderful things he did in the world. I gave up trying to figure out who he was talking about after a while and let my eyes wander the sanctuary.

It was as I noticed the barest flicker of movement in the far corner of the sanctuary that I jumped a little. I quickly turned to

James, but he was leaning against Mother, his eyes closed. Father was on the other side of her, and I was between James and Arthur Holmwood, Lord Godalming. I looked up at the young noble, who bore a long, twisting scar along the left side of his face as a reminder of his entanglement with my mother, her friend Lucy, and Count Dracula. Holmwood looked down at me, nodded to let me know that he had seen the same thing I had, and pressed a finger to his lips. He also opened his coat to show me that underneath his best waistcoat, he had a large Bowie knife strapped to his chest in a harness that would allow him to draw it easily. I recognized the weapon from the book—it was Quincy Morris's knife. I gave Holmwood a nod to indicate that I would stay quiet, but I knew there was no real need for alarm.

Dracula was simply there to pay his respects to an old adversary who had become a trusted friend and partner. I knew this, as did my parents. We had all been with Luke two nights prior after we stood vigil for Van Helsing's death. He was heartbroken at Abraham's passing, and that was one of the few times I ever saw him consume enough alcohol to have any effect. I could almost feel his eyes on me, and I looked deeper into the shadowy nook that hid him from the rest of the church and nodded to acknowledge his presence.

Finally, the interminable service ended, and we all filed out. Father and I walked hand in hand behind Mother and a very sleepy James, but Father stopped at the door to the church. "I'm sorry, dear. I seem to have forgotten my hat. Please wait for us in the cab. I'll be along shortly."

Father had not forgotten anything. I watched him nudge his hat under the pew in front of us when it was time to stand. Mother gave him a steady look, then nodded. "We will be waiting. Quincy, would you like to come with us?"

"No, Mother. I believe I will walk with Father," I replied. My curiosity has a long history of getting the better of me. It's one of the few constants in my life.

We turned and walked back to the front of the church, where a lean figure in a flowing black overcoat stood leaning on the casket, his head bowed. As we approached, I heard something I had never before heard pass my "uncle's" lips.

"Amen," Luke said, then stood and turned to us. "Jonathan, Quincy, it is good to see you."

"Were you…praying?" Father asked. "I believed you were long past any belief in God."

"I believe in God, my dear boy," Dracula replied. "I just also believe He's a capricious bastard who pays far less attention to His creations than they desire or deserve. But Abraham believed, and the nearer he came to meeting his God, the more fervently he believed."

"I've heard that often happens," Father said, a small smile upon his lips.

"Very true, my boy. As Abraham believed very strongly in his God, I thought it could do no true harm to ask for a bit of kindness on the behalf of the old bastard."

I wasn't sure if he was calling Van Helsing a bastard, or God, but I thought both were equally inappropriate in a church. "You shouldn't talk like that at a funeral, Uncle. It's not polite," I said, with the judgmental certainty that only a child can levy upon a situation.

"You are right, young Quincy," Luke replied. "You are absolutely right. But as both Abraham and his God deemed me a monster, I am relieved of any duty to pretend to be anything else."

I felt my brow furrow as I tried to decipher his words, failing miserably. "Are you still drunk, Uncle?" I asked.

Luke laughed, a big, open sound that I had never heard from him before. He was not a man prone to laughter. Too much death can have a negative impact on the sense of humor, I'm told. But this laugh filled the room and bounced off the ceiling before settling down around us. "No, my dear child, I am not. I am merely feeling something I have not felt in many, many years. The loss of a friend. It makes me sad, and capricious, and impolite. I shall strive to do better henceforth."

I had a sneaking suspicion he was mocking me, but I couldn't put my finger on it. My sense of sarcasm was honed later in life. At ten I was still a fairly guileless child.

"We are having a small gathering at our home later, Luke," Father said. "You are, as always, welcome."

"I do not think all of your guests share that sentiment, Jonathan."

Father nodded. "I believe you are correct. The offer stands, nonetheless. I have faith in our collective ability to hold their baser instincts in check."

"I appreciate it, but no. Today is a day for the living to remember the dead. The dead should stay clear of such affairs. Please give my love to Mina."

"I will," Father said, bending over between two pews to retrieve his hat. "Come along, Quincy."

I turned to follow Father up the aisle to where Mother and James waited for us in a handsome cab, but when we were halfway to the door, I turned to look back at the coffin. I saw Luke, once again turned and staring down at the casket holding his most legendary adversary and his most secret friend, and I could have sworn I saw his shoulders shake with sobs as he wept for the passing of Abraham Van Helsing.

I jerked out of my reverie to the sound of my apartment door opening. Pravesh came in, trailed by Becks.

"Are you ready to go?" Keya asked. She wore a black pantsuit with a jacket cut to hide her sidearm. I planned to leave my pistol at home, figuring anything stupid enough to attack a cop funeral would either be gunned down in seconds, or bullets wouldn't do anything against it. Either way, my nine-millimeter wouldn't be needed. Pravesh held something out to me, a black leather rectangle. I took it and flipped it open to see the gold Homeland Security badge nestled there.

"What's this for?" I asked. "I've got my credentials. Figured that was all I needed."

"It is all you need to do your job, Harker," Pravesh said, pulling her own badge out of an inside jacket pocket, opening the wallet, and tucking the flap into her breast pocket so the badge faced out. There was a black band across her badge as well. "This isn't for your job. This is so you can show your respect."

I nodded, looking down at the badge in my hand. I did respect

Captain Herr, and I respected the badge. I wasn't so sure about the current chief, but today wasn't the day to answer those questions. Today was a day to show the families of fallen officers the esteem we held them in. "Thanks," I said. I turned to Becks. "You got—" I closed my mouth as I saw her hand extended with a black band dangling from her fingers. I strapped it across my badge, tucked the end of my wallet into the pocket of my jacket, and said, "Okay. Let's go."

"Before we do," Pravesh said. "There may be some grumbling at our presence. Yours in particular."

"People who know what went down blame me," I said. "Yeah, I figured. Becks, you should sit up front with the department. We can hang back along the wall. I don't want to cause a scene."

"It may be unavoidable, but we can do as much as possible to mitigate it," Pravesh said. "There will be a host of politicians, and officers from all over the United States. This is a memorial service for one of the largest line-of-duty deaths in history, featuring two ranking members of the department along with the rank and file officers. There will be people from every branch of law enforcement there. We will do our best to be unobtrusive, and hopefully the spectacle will allow us to remain unnoticed."

"Should I stay home?" I asked. "I don't want to make things harder on the families."

"No," Becks said, her voice iron. "Captain Herr liked and respected you, and you felt the same way about him. You should show that publicly. For the department, for him, and for you."

"Okay," I said, nodding. "But the first sign of anyone wanting to start a scene, I'll vanish. But there's something else we need to talk about."

"What's that?" Flynn asked.

"If there are going to be that many cops and notables from all over the U.S., it's going to be a perfect target. Maybe not for DEMON, or monsters, or anything that's in our normal wheelhouse, but mundane threats are still threats."

"That's what we're covering," Faustus said from the doorway. He had on his human face, and Watson and Jo stood in the hall behind him.

"We've got this part, Harker. Us and every Homeland, FBI, and other hired gun Pravesh could round up from any of the alphabet soup agencies," Jo said.

"I have snipers stationed atop every building within a mile of the procession, and the church has been swept for any threats several times with multiple detection methods. Now come on, it's time to go."

"Okay," I said, heading to the door. "Let's go say goodbye to a good man."

Again, I said to Becks.

Again?

I've done this a lot.

Part of the trouble with living forever.

Not just that, I replied. *It's not just funerals. Some of those are kinda cathartic, even celebratory if the person lived a long, full life. No, I've been to too many of these—funerals where the guest of honor is too damn young.*

That's part of the trouble with being a hero, Becks said.

Is that what we are? Sometimes it's really hard to tell.

15

As hundreds of men and women in dark suits or blue uniforms streamed out of the First Baptist Church and began a long procession down to the unveiling of a monument in Marshall Park, Pravesh and I hung back to wait for Becks. She caught sight of us and veered off from where she walked next to Chief Putnam and a tall White man I didn't recognize.

"Hey," she said as she got close to us. "I can't walk with you guys, I—"

I held up a hand. "It's cool. We're not going to the memorial dedication anyway. Don't want to give anyone an excuse to start anything."

Flynn looked confused. "You were just in the church. Why would you think someone would start shit at the monument dedication?"

"It's outside, easier to make a scene and get away with it. Nobody in their right mind is going to start shit in a church in the South, but if some hothead who lost a buddy or two sees me standing near the back of the crowd out there, he might decide to throw a punch. I don't need to be the center of attention today, and certainly not like that."

"Besides, we have another event we must make an appearance at," Pravesh said, earning her a dirty look from me.

"Where are you going?" Becks asked.

"Mort's," I said. "He decided to throw a wake for his customers that were killed in the shootout. It's his way of keeping the monsters from taking advantage of most of the state's upper-level law enforcement being in one place. He asked us to stop by."

"He asked *you* to stop by," Pravesh corrected me.

"Yeah, that."

"Why you? Does he have something up his sleeve?" Flynn asked. She didn't trust Mort. Good call, as a rule.

"He almost certainly has something up his sleeve, but I don't think it's directed at me this time. He wants me to go talk to a few key leaders in the supernatural community to make sure they understand who started this shit, and that it wasn't CMPD. The beasties are just as on edge as the cops, and they're way more accustomed to hunting humans than the police are to hunting monsters."

"When did Mort become all civic-minded?" Becks asked, looking over her shoulder to Putnam and the other cop. The new guy was tall, good-looking, and rugged. He carried himself like a man who could take care of business, with a little of the alpha male swagger that always made me wary of the douche that lurked just beneath the surface. He had a sparse beard, brown hair going gray at the temples, and a chest full of commendation ribbons.

"He didn't," I replied. "Mort just knows that if open war between the cops and the critters breaks out, it's bad for business. Who's the new guy?"

"Major Ivan Strunin," Becks said. "He's down from Raleigh for the service, and he's staying for a few days while we're short-handed. He's a deputy chief there, heads up their SWAT and crisis response units."

"Looks military," I said.

"Iraq," Becks agreed. "Two tours before coming back and going into law enforcement. Supposed to be a good guy, real hands-on type. I've barely dealt with him since he's been here. Had a little on my plate. I need to get back over there. Putnam's smitten with Strunin's service record. If somebody's not there to rein him in, the chief will give away his office." She gave me a hug and a quick kiss on the cheek.

"Try not to blow anything up." With a nod to Pravesh, she turned and moved to catch up with Putnam and the new guy.

I looked at Keya. "That was a little unfair," I said. "I hardly ever blow things up anymore."

"Since when?" she asked, starting toward her DHS-issued Suburban.

"I don't know," I called after her. "Today?"

The parking lot was packed when we pulled up to Mort's, with a big sign on the door that said, "CLOSED FOR PRIVATE EVENT." I parked on the side of the building and headed around to the left.

Pravesh stepped out of the car and called after me. "Harker, the door is the other way."

"We're going in the back way," I said. "I made a deal with Mort that I wouldn't come barreling into the joint, and he promised to meet me in the back room when I arrived and let me know if I was going to have to fight anybody the second I showed my face."

She closed her door and followed me around to the smooth block rear wall of Mart's bar. "There's a back door?" she asked. Not even a seam showed in the tan paint job.

"There is," I replied. "Sometimes." I put both hands on the door and called power. My nerve endings were still a little raw from the exertion a few days prior, but I was almost back to full strength. I felt pretty certain I could handle most anything waiting in the bar, as long as it was local. Anything from another plane might give me a bit of trouble. "*Ostendo,*" I said, pushing energy out slowly across the surface of the wall.

The paint rippled as my power coursed over Mort's wards, and about six feet from me, a rectangular section of wall vanished, replaced by a sturdy metal door with a pair of deadbolts. No knob, and it opened out. This was not meant to be an entrance. That didn't bother me. I'd made a lot of entrances where none were designed, but this time I wasn't planning on blowing anything up. Instead, I knocked.

A few second later, the door opened up and Faustus's head popped out. He had ditched the human suit, and now his obsidian pate gleamed in the summer sun. He gave me a pointy-toothed grin and threw the door wide. "Come on in, Q. The party's just getting going. There's a faerie in the back corner of the main room pretending to be a Roma woman telling fortunes, a siren is up next for karaoke, and two werewolves have already been kicked out for shedding in the punch. I figure we've only got about another hour before things really start to get fun."

We followed the grinning demon into Mort's back room, an extra-dimensional space that pretty much looked like whatever Mort wanted it to look like. Today, that meant it looked like a 1920s speakeasy, complete with poker table, a long wooden bar with a vampire bartender, and half a dozen round tables, each holding an assortment of supernatural creatures.

These were Mort's best customers, the ones he counted on not to stir up shit, and the ones who were most likely to bring him information worth real money or be otherwise useful. The rest of the bar was open to any supernatural creature or magic user who knew about the place and was willing to abide by the rules of Sanctuary. Those rules basically boiled down to "Don't start any shit on the premises and you'll be protected to the fullest extent of Mort's power." I didn't know exactly what kind of power Mort had, but as a hitchhiker demon that had spent some time working for a Lord of Chaos, he had some juice. Enough that I nearly always abided by his rule of Sanctuary, and I'm not usually one for following orders.

Mort himself was standing at the end of the bar farthest from where we came in, his back pressed up against the wall leading to the main room. He was in a new body, but that was nothing new. This time he was a beautiful Black woman with dark skin and a shaved head. She reminded me of Lupita Nyong'o, and I suppressed the urge to walk over to the demon, cross my arms over my chest and say, "Wakanda forever." Mort's eyes caught mine and he gave me

93

a nod, acknowledging my presence but making no move to come greet me.

Instead, I was greeted with a wall of silence as every demon, creature, and person in the room cut off what they were saying and turned to fix me with a flat stare. I've been glared at by a lot of people in my life, but this was the first time that two dozen beings of various origin all shot me a dirty look at the same time.

"Looks like you're popular," Pravesh said.

"I get that a lot," I replied. "What can I say? I'm a lovable guy."

A guy, human from the looks of him, stood up from a table in the middle of the room and walked over to stand directly in front of me. He was tall and broad, and looked like he spent a lot of time in the gym. His hands were beat up and scarred, making me think he punched things for fun and profit, and he had a toothpick jutting out of the corner of his thin lips. He stared at me for a few seconds as if trying to figure out what to say, then a grumble issued from the depths of his throat. "You aren't welcome here. Leave."

"Mort invited me," I said. "Fuck off."

His eyes popped wide and his nostrils flared. This was not a guy who was accustomed to being told no. I didn't mind. I've had many years to learn how to effectively disappoint people on many planes of existence.

"I oughta—"

I kept my voice very low, so as not to share my threat with the bar. "You oughta sit the fuck back down before your mouth starts writing checks your ass can't cash," I said. "You know who I am, you know everything they say about me, and you know that if even half that shit is true, I've killed more men than cholera. Now you've done your part to make me feel unwelcome, you've bowed up to The Reaper so all your friends see how brave you are, so just turn around and strut on back to your table before I decide that Mort's Sanctuary rule was made to be broken. Again."

He stared at me for a long moment, and I held his gaze. This was the key encounter. If he threw a punch, I was going to have to beat every son of a bitch in the building, and probably kill a fair number of them. If he was smart enough to back down, I could offer my condolences to the families of the deceased and be on my merry way before anybody got drunk enough to let Mort have a turn at the karaoke machine. I've heard Mort sing. I'd rather go back to Hell.

We stood there looking into each other's eyes like something out of a movie, and I couldn't tell if we were supposed to shoot each other or make out, when he finally turned and stomped away. "Your funeral, Reaper," he called back over his shoulder.

"Thanks for the warning," I said to his back. I looked around the room. "Anybody else got a problem with me being here?" Silence greeted me. I stood there for a few more seconds, scanning the room, then walked over to sit next to Faustus at the bar. Sitting at the bar gave me both an elevated perch, which was a little easier to jump up and fight from, as well as the option to turn my back to the bartender and look out over the room, which I did.

"Watson and Jo decided not to come along?" Pravesh asked.

"I didn't invite them," Faustus said. "They wouldn't have been very welcome. This is pretty strictly a mundanes-free event. You need to either have magic or *be* magic to get in the door. And I didn't want to hear what kind of a fuss your friend Jack would kick up if he got here and wasn't allowed in. I don't know if you know this, but he's kind of a dick."

"Yeah," I agreed. "I noticed."

Mort came over, leading a slender woman with dark red hair and an athletic build. She wore all black, and her eyes were red from crying. "Quincy Harker, I'd like you to meet Monica Remingham. Her husband was the werewolf that was killed here Tuesday."

I reached out to shake her hand, saying, "I'm sorry for your loss, Mrs. Remingham. I truly wish I could have stopped it."

She looked in my eyes, and there was a fire there that no amount of tears would extinguish. "Thank you, Reaper. That's very kind of you. Now when are you going after those bastards? Because I'm going with you."

16

I showed the vengeful wolf-lady over to a table where we sat down with Faustus and Pravesh. Mort bailed the second he could, making some feeble excuse about not wanting to leave the demons alone in the front room with the peaceful lycanthropes. I figured the were-bunnies could handle themselves but didn't argue.

"Mrs. Remingham," I said, but the woman leaned in and cut me off.

"Don't try to talk me out of this, Mr. Harker. I'm going after the men responsible for my husband's death. He wasn't just my husband; he was my *mate*." She glared at me, and I watched her eyes flash a vibrant yellow. This wasn't some grief-stricken human woman looking for comfort. This was a pissed-off werewolf looking for blood.

"What does your Alpha have to say about your desire for vengeance?" Pravesh asked. Her voice was cool, but her foot was jiggling under the table, a rare show of nerves for the lamia.

"I don't have one yet. David was our Alpha, and the boys are going to get together tonight after the wake to roll around in the dirt and figure out who's leading the pack now." That explained her no-bullshit attitude. As the Alpha female of a pack, she would have been a co-leader with her husband.

"What does that mean for you?" I asked. "I don't know a lot about pack politics, but I know your status would be in jeopardy after the death of the Alpha."

"I don't give a fuck about status. If I have to go rogue, I will. But I am not going to sit on my tail and let the bastards who murdered my husband go free." Her hands briefly thickened, and a fine coating of russet fur began to appear before she wrested control of her body back from the wolf. From the lycanthropes I'd talked to, it as a constant tug-of-war between their human and animal sides, and extreme emotion could force a shift. The last thing I needed was for her to wolf out on me in the middle of the bar, especially in a bar where most of the clientele were looking for any excuse to kick my ass. All it would take was one hint of me threatening a paranormal, and I'd be in a melee.

"I won't ask you to sit this fight out, Mrs. Remingham, but—"

"Monica," she said. "Call me Monica."

"Okay," I replied. "I'm not going to keep you out of it, Monica. I've been in a similar place to where you are now, and I know what that desire for revenge can do to you. I also know what it can do to you if you actually get the revenge you're looking for, but it's not my place to lecture you on thinking about the repercussions of your actions. I'm not that much of a hypocrite."

She gave me a doubting look. "You think you know what it's like to have someone murder the love of your life. Really?"

"I know what it's like to watch it happen right in front of my fucking eyes, and I know what it cost me to kill the son of a bitch that did it. But this is neither the time nor the place for group therapy, so that's as far as I'm going to dive into that. You want to help me go after DEMON, fine. You're on the team."

"Just like that?" Faustus asked. "You're not going to grill her about her motivations, or run a background check, or anything? You're not going to check her credit?"

"I'm not selling her a car, Faustus. I'm letting her come along and help us gut a bunch of assholes with guns. And what could show up on her background check that would be worse than mine? Or Luke's?

Or yours, for that matter, demon. I mean, between you and Luke there are whole shelves worth of stories written about you."

"Bookcases, Harker," the demon replied with a mock bow. "Entire bookcases."

"My point exactly," I replied. I turned my attention back to Monica. "Have you ever fought with a group before? Other than hunting with the pack, I mean."

"No."

"Okay, then when we get into the shit, you'll need to hang back at first and let the more experienced people dive in. Then when everything goes sideways and my plans turn to shit, you can jump into the free-for-all."

"Don't worry," Pravesh said. "It usually doesn't take long for Harker's plans to fall apart."

"Didn't Sun Tzu say something about that?" I asked.

"Nah, pretty sure 'Quincy Harker is a fucking idiot' isn't in *The Art of War*," Faustus said with a smirk.

"I think we've made enough of an appearance that our departure won't be seen as an insult to anyone I don't want to insult," I said. "You can either stay here and meet us at my place later or follow us now."

"I can go now. I can't decide if this is depressing or disgusting." She waved a hand at the bar. "I mean, look at them. Three days ago, most of them had never even spoken to David, and looked at all of us like we pissed on the carpet. Now they're all banding together in solidarity for the supernatural community. It's all bullshit. They didn't know David, they don't like shifters, and they'd be just as happy if this was a purely demon bar. Demons and vampires, that is. Pretentious bastards." She stood up and looked at us. "Well? What are we waiting for?"

Pravesh and I shared a look. This one was going to bear watching. She had a temper to match her fiery hair, stereotypes be damned, and I didn't trust her to keep enough of a rein on her emotions to work with a team. Maybe we'd get lucky and I could send her to chase down a runner or something else to keep her out from underfoot.

"Nothing," I said, standing up. "Let's go."

J o and Watson were sitting in the war room playing chess when we walked in. "Did you know Jo cheats at chess?" Jack asked.

"How do you cheat at chess?" I asked.

"I do not cheat at chess. Jack just sucks," Jo replied. "Who's your friend?"

"This is Monica," Pravesh replied. "Her husband was killed at Mort's the other day. She is a werewolf. She wants revenge."

Monica glared at the slender woman's back as Keya walked over to peer at the board. "Just feel free to share my business with the whole room, why don't you?"

"The whole team," I corrected. "And we will. Everybody here needs to know what you're capable of and why you're here. This is Jo Henry and Jack Watson. Both human. Jo has a magic hammer, and Jack has the superpower of being fucking insufferable. He's also a good shot."

"You've got two humans, a demon, a lizard—"

"Snake," Pravesh corrected.

"Snake, sorry. And a half-vampire. Anyone else in your little Scooby gang?" Monica asked.

"There's also my fiancée the cop and my uncle, Count Dracula," I replied.

Monica froze in mid-stride, then slowly turned to look at me. "Are you fucking kidding me?"

"About which part?" I asked. "The fact that my fiancée is a detective with the Charlotte-Mecklenburg Police Department, or that my uncle is Count Dracula? And neither, by the way."

"Dracula is real?"

"You're a werewolf in a room with a snake-woman and the demon who coined the term 'Faustian bargain' and you're having trouble believing in Dracula?" Jo leaned back in her chair and laughed. "I like this one, Harker. Where the hell did you find her?"

"Mort's," I said, ignoring the daggers Monica was staring at Jo. I didn't think she was likely to break out into violence quite yet. "You guys see anything out of the ordinary in the parade?"

"No sign of DEMON or anyone looking to cause trouble. A few anti-police protesters, a few random people with signs protesting gay rights, and one man with a large sign that just said 'IMPEACH' in all capital letters," Jack said. "I'm not sure I understand you Yanks and your protests. It seems that you will throw one at the drop of a hat."

"It's been known to happen," I said, taking a seat at the head of the long conference table. "Jo, is your mother around?"

"No, she's picking Ginny up from school. Why?"

"I just need to know if it's going to cost me a dollar every time I swear, because talking about DEMON brings out my more colorful language," I said.

"Nah, you're clear for a couple hours. They've got a lesson after school. I don't remember if today is yoga or tae kwon do. Or maybe both."

"Good. Do we have anything new?" I asked, mostly to Pravesh, since she was the one with information sources better than Google or randomly punching people until they told you what you wanted to hear.

"I do not," Keya said. "DEMON has not had an official presence in Charlotte since you destroyed their base of operations. Their presence in Washington is also dramatically reduced, but no one in Homeland Security seems to actually know who the organization reports to, so it is difficult to get any solid information."

"Hold up," Jo said. She'd been leaning back in her chair with her feet on the table, a sure sign that she didn't expect her mother to come in anytime soon, but now she dropped down, fully engaged. "Are you telling me that this secret government agency is so secret that nobody even knows who they work for?"

The slightest hint of red tinged Pravesh's brown cheeks. "That does seem to be the case. They had offices scattered all over town, in the OPM Building, the Hoover Building, even in DHA Headquarters, but they were all small cubicle farms with fewer than ten people. They all thought they worked for research and grant-making organizations funding the study of the existence of cryptids. My director sent teams to interview everyone who worked there. None of them knew that monsters really exist, much less were being hunted and exterminated by their department."

"Monsters? Better watch your tone, lady," Monica muttered.

Pravesh turned to her and hissed, her fangs showing. "My tone is fine, wolf." She looked at me. "We have found no central headquarters, no equipment storage facility, and no real leadership. The finances for the organization are buried in the budgets of over a dozen agencies, from the FBI to the Bureau of Land Management. Whoever is in charge of DEMON, they have some very smart people working at hiding their money."

"But what's the point?" I asked. "DEMON has been operating for years in a role almost identical to what we're doing. Why did they suddenly go all aggro on supernaturals, and why do they exist in the first place? It doesn't make any sense."

"I can answer the second question, Quincy," Pravesh said. "They are a government agency. The United States government thrives on bureaucracy and redundancy. If one agency does something well, then three agencies should be able to combine their efforts to cost five times as much and be half as effective. That certainly explains why they exist to me—government stupidity. I do not, however, under-stand why they have changed course so dramatically in the past several months."

"Are you fucking kidding me, Scales?" Monica asked with a sneer. "DEMON's been the fucking bogeyman ever since I was a pup. Maybe not to you, because you can all pass, but for people like me, who either have traits that can't be easily hidden, or certain times of the month when they don't look even remotely human, those bastards and their Hunters have been what mothers warn their cryptid children about."

"I've met a few Hunters," I said. "They didn't seem all that bad to me."

"That's like you telling a Black guy you don't get nervous when a cop pulls you over, dickweed," she shot back. "Of course they were nice to you. You're the fucking Reaper! They thought you were one of them, not one of us. If they'd known you weren't really human, they would have put one between your eyes before you could blink." She held up a hand. "Yeah, yeah. I'm sure some of them are okay people, but that's just it—they're all *people*. Humans. Humans hunting monsters. It's right there in the name—Hunter. They only exist to put bullets in people like me. You only care now because it's started to splash over into your neat little world, so now you give a shit. If they were only killing weres and trolls and faeries, you wouldn't lift a finger to stop them."

She was right. I was ashamed to admit it, but nothing she said wasn't true. As long as DEMON had stayed out of my way, I was content to let them go about their business with no interference from me. "Well, they're not just killing weres and trolls and faeries anymore," I said. "They've declared war on me and mine, so let's figure out where they are and how we can take the fight to them."

Monica held my gaze with a steady look of her own, then finally nodded. "Okay," she said. "Let's do it."

Then my phone rang, and the day went sideways in a hurry from there.

17

"Harker, we've got a problem." Flynn's voice was hushed, as if she was trying not to be overheard.

I used our mental link, reaching out to her silently. *What's wrong?*

Oh good. I wasn't sure where you were, if you were close enough.

I'm home now. I'll fill you in tonight. What's going on?

I think Strunin's up to something. He's been in a conference room with the chief and the SWAT commander for the last two hours, and now dispatch is calling up a bunch of off-duty officers and telling them to meet at the Transit Center downtown for crowd control at eight tonight.

Why would there be a crowd at the Transit Center? Do they expect a run on the bus lines?

SWAT stages there to use off-duty buses when they need to move a lot of riot cops around downtown. When the protests got out of hand after Keith Lamont Scott was killed, the Transit Center was one of the places we staged to be able to move around the Center City quickly.

You think he's planning to mobilize against...what, exactly? I felt a chill run down my spine. *You don't think he'll try to mount an assault on Mort's, do you? That will just get a lot of cops killed.*

I don't think so. Everything about his bearing says he's not worried about this going sideways. He thinks he's got the situation completely in hand, whatever it is.

Okay. I'll poke around and see if I can come up with anything. Keep me posted.

Will do. Love you.

Love you, too. Stay safe.

I severed the active part of our connection, leaving us linked, but just the tendril of awareness we shared all the time. Looking around the room, I said, "We might have a problem. CMPD is getting their riot cops together for something they think is happening downtown tonight. Becks thinks it's got something to do with the memorial today. We need to find out what's up."

"I will call my office and get our people on it," Pravesh said, pulling out a cell phone and heading out to the balcony.

"I'll call Jason. He's...he was David's Beta. He can get in touch with the pack and find out if they know anything." Monica moved over to one of the sofas in the living area of the den and pulled out her own phone.

"I'll head back over to Mort's," Faustus said. "I can take the temperature of the room, see if anyone wants to retaliate against the police for what DEMON did."

"That would be a touch misplaced, don't you think?" Watson asked.

"Demons and monsters aren't known for their discretion and restraint," Faustus replied. "More like they'll take any excuse they can find to rip out someone's throat. And if there's the thinnest veneer of an excuse, they can get the more peaceful cryptids to go along. The only thing keeping most of the weres and vamps from becoming crazed murder hobos is their leadership, and the feds created a big void in that leadership a couple days ago."

"Where does that leave us?" Watson asked. "I'm afraid I don't have any local contacts with unsavory characters, present company excepted."

"I hate to say it, but Jack's right," Jo agreed. "What do you need us to do?"

"One of you get online and see if you can find anything on local activist social media pages. Jack, poke around at the local extremist groups and see if they've got anything planned. This could be a mundane group of assholes and the cops are completely justified in smacking them down."

"But you don't think so, do you?" Jo asked, her brown eyes worried. She was a lot different from the skinny girl I'd met the night she graduated from college. That night she'd been shit-scared of the new supernatural world that had just jumped out of the bushes and tried to rip her to pieces. Now she was self-assured, strong as hell, and cool in a fight. She also swung that hammer like Babe Ruth swung a bat.

"No," I admitted. "I don't. Becks thinks this new guy Strunin is trying to get Chief Putnam's attention and snag a job big enough to transfer down from Raleigh for."

"And rousting a bunch of monsters the night they buried Captain Herr would be just the kind of feather his cap needs."

"Exactly," I agreed. "Now I'm going down the hall for a bit. I need to do some scrying, see if I can find out anything on my own, and that takes more focus than I can get in here. I'll be back in about an hour."

"We'll call if we need you," Jo said.

"Don't bother," I replied. "My cell won't work inside the casting circle. Scrying interferes with the signal. But I'll just be in Unit Eight. The same key that opens this door works there, too. If you need me, come get me."

I guess she probably said something in agreement, but I was already halfway to the door by the time I finished my sentence, much less when she replied.

———————

My footsteps echoed off the bare walls of the apartment I reserved for casting rituals and scrying. The faint remains of the chalk circle from where I planned to summon Michael a few days before still showed on the floor, so I dampened a paper towel in the kitchen sink and scrubbed it out before I settled in to scry. Keeping one apartment just for this kind of magic was one of the better ideas I'd had since becoming a property owner.

I owned the whole building, and when Luke's house was destroyed a few years back, we just took over the rest of the condos on my floor and I paid my neighbors exorbitant fees to relocate. And by "I paid," I mean I wrote checks drawn on some of Luke's accounts, which he kept filled by selling off random antiquities whenever his balances got too low in the seven figures. Now we had this apartment we kept empty plus separate apartments for me and Becks, Luke, Cassie and Jo, Faustus (and Jack when he was here), Pravesh and Glory, and a couple more we kept furnished and empty in case members of the Council or other allies needed a place to crash.

I drew a fresh circle on the floor in chalk, not bothering with inscribing and placing wards around the perimeter. Once I got myself settled and the circle powered up, I figured I'd be safe enough. It's not like what I was doing would draw the attention of anything nasty. I hoped. Then I took a bowl down off the lone piece of furniture in the place, a small shelf unit filled with casting supplies, filled the bowl, and carried it into the circle, being careful not to spill any water on the chalk. I probably should have filled and placed the bowl first, *then* drawn the circle, but ritual magic was never my strong suit, so it was very on brand to do shit out of sequence.

I placed candles at the cardinal compass points and lit them with a whisper of power, starting at the northern candle and working clockwise. Then I sat cross-legged in the middle of the circle and pulled the bowl into my lap. I pushed just enough power into the circle to energize it, but not enough to make it into a beacon. I didn't need every magic user in the city getting curious. Once the surface of the water stilled, I used a silver ceremonial knife to prick my thumb and let exactly three drops of blood plop into the water.

Pressing my thumb into my jeans to clot it, I focused my attention on the bowl and opened my Sight. My blood mixing with the water gave it a slight glow in the magical spectrum and provided me a focal point to slowly pour power into the bowl, barely more than a trickle until the surface of the water was uniformly coated in glowing pink light as my blood and my magic diffused through the liquid.

That was the easy part—getting the magic into the water. It wasn't the easiest of elements to work with, but it wasn't as hard as fire or air. Earth was the easiest to manipulate, because it moved so much less on its own. But now that I had infused the water with a little essence of Quincy, I breathed deeply and let my consciousness seep into the smooth surface. I used the bowl as a lens, directing my Sight outward much farther than I could See normally. If it were real physics, it would probably have something to do with using the bowl as a parabolic reflector to collect and focus the light to go farther and more direct, like a flashlight. But since it was magic, it was all metaphor. So I metaphorically used the bowl like a parabolic reflector, focusing my soul and power and giving me reach all across the city.

I let my Sight float up through the ceiling of the apartment, then through the roof of the building. I scanned around the city, looking for anomalies or magical hot spots. There were several chunks of downtown that lit up like Christmas trees. Spirit Square fairly vibrated with magical energy. The old First Baptist Church-turned performance venue had all the mojo of holy ground mixed with all the lust and fury and fervor of a theatre and concert hall. That place had more soul than Al Green, but it wasn't anything I hadn't seen before.

The Tryon Center art gallery was the same way, a collector of creative energy that infused that power back into the people who passed through, but there was nothing malevolent there. St. Phillip's Church glowed a bright white in my magical vision, a lighthouse of divine energy and sanctity. Still not what I was looking for. I needed to find something new, maybe something angry, but something that wasn't a place, but centered on a person, or maybe a group of people.

I scanned the Epicenter, hoping against hope that I wouldn't have to go back to that place. Last time I was there, I died and went to Hell. Literally. It took some fast talking and calling in a favor from an Archangel to get me back topside, and I still got the creeps just walking past the big shopping area. It was mostly dark, a few souls with a little bit of power flickering here and there, but nothing powerful enough to be worth the police department's attention. I scanned the rest of downtown in ever-widening circles, coming up empty, empty, and even more empty. My loops around the city had grown almost big enough to reach my building when something caught my "eye" off to the north.

I focused my attention, and knew I'd found the jackpot. There were all kinds of sparkly magical souls flowing into the same spot from all over the city, with a heavy stream of them coming from the direction of Mort's. I sent my Sight over to take a peek, and when I saw what it was, I knew there was going to be trouble. I pulled my mental "eye" back in and opened my real eyes, letting my Sight go as I did. I stood up, managing not to spill water on my pants, and scrubbed out a section of circle with my toe. The magic dissipated, and I walked over to the kitchen, poured the bloody water down the sink, and filled the bowl with cold water to soak. I'd come back to put all my implements away later, if there was a city to come back to.

Becks, I thought, reaching out to her.

Yeah? You got something?

I think so. I'm pretty sure whatever your boy is planning on interrupting is going down at Romare Bearden Park. There's a lot of magical activity over there, and more supernaturals heading there by the minute. Looks like by the time it gets dark, the place will be crawling with magical folks of one type or another.

Just in time for Strunin to come barging in with some bullshit about not having a permit to gather or some crap like that.

Yeah. My best guess is it'll be a memorial for the cryptids and supernaturals killed the other day. A lot of the energy signatures I saw were coming from Mort's.

Great, so they've been drinking all day.

Drunken magic users and pissed-off cops. What could go wrong? I thought.

Harker, you prick, Becks replied. *You just had to ask.*

18

It didn't look like much to the naked eye, just a buttload of middle-aged hippies in flowing skirts and dudes with pot bellies and ponytails. That's what passed for gatherings of witches and magic users in North Carolina, at least that particular Tuesday night. They milled around the park as the sun dipped down, chatting pleasantly amongst themselves, some having picnic dinners that probably all consisted of tofu and gluten-free everything with spring water harvested from the top of the Himalayas by Nepalese virgins and some such shit. It wasn't my scene, but it was pleasant enough.

I sat on a big chunk of rock beside a fountain/wall/sculpture thing that was looking cooler by the minute as the sky got darker and the color-changing LED lights became more visible. There was a nice gentle rainbow effect scrolling from one end of the wall to the other, making a soothing ripple with the reflection of the water in front of it. I had a decent vantage point on the bottom half of the park where most of the witches were gathered, and since I had a flask with me, I was able to overpower the smell of patchouli with the glorious fragrance of whisky instead.

Anything? Becks asked.

Not yet. You see anything coming my way? She was positioned at the top of a parking garage along one of the streets bordering the park, binoculars trained up the street to where the cops would be coming from if they really were planning to roust people.

Clear on my end.

"Jo, you see anything moving?"

"Nothing doing here, Harker," Jo replied from her parking garage facing the transit center. "There are a few buses idling that have their Not In Service lights going, but that's all."

"That'll be what the cops use," I said. "Let me know if they load up or move."

"Got it."

"Glory? Anything on your side?" I asked, speaking into the air. Probably the biggest benefit to having the Regional Director for Homeland Security's Paranormal Division on our side, aside from not going to prison for half the shit I got into, was the badass toys Pravesh brought to the table. All I had to do was say that we needed some of those earbud thingies like they use on TV, and she showed up an hour later with a Pelican case full of little radios and transmitters. I didn't know how well they'd hold up if I had to start flinging around any serious power, since magic can sometimes interfere with unshielded electronics, but for the moment they were great.

"I met a really nice lady named Salem. I think you'd like her. She's got great hair and really amazing hummus," Glory replied.

"That's awesome," I said. "Does she know anything about a planned protest, police involvement, violent magic users, or basically anything I'd give a shit about?"

"There will be five or six speakers paying tribute to the fallen members of their coven and the greater supernatural community, and there will be a ritual to honor the dead and to help them on to their next life. The whole thing was planned by a group called Charlotte for All, and the lead speaker is a woman named Pastor Judy Colborne. Is that more what you were looking for?"

I leaned back against the rock behind me, honestly a little stunned. "Uh…yeah, that's pretty much exactly what I was hoping for. Nice one, Glory."

"Thanks. Now I'm going back to my hummus. According to Salem, there's about ten minutes until full sunset, then half an hour until the speakers start."

"Don't get too full to fly," I said, smiling.

"Don't forget to go fuck yourself," the angel shot back. If she wasn't careful, she was going to end up owing the swear jar more than me.

"What did she mean, 'members of their coven,' Harker?" Jo asked. "I thought you said the only humans killed were cops."

"I did."

"That would mean...okay, I give up. What does that mean?"

"It probably means that one or more of the demons that died wore meat suits that they used to join this coven. It happens more often than you'd think. Witches hate demons as much as anyone. Well, maybe not me, but as much as any normal person. But since the more powerful covens do practice magic, they're always an enticing morsel for a demon to infiltrate. That's how the whole Satanic Panic bullshit got started—a Trickster Demon insinuated itself into a coven and corrupted some of their symbology, then painted it somewhere the cops in a small town in Nebraska or someplace like that would find it, and before you know it *Dungeons & Dragons* is Public Enemy Number One and Tom Hanks is starring in a really shitty TV movie."

"Well, that's *one* version of how things happened," Faustus's voice came over the radios.

"You have a different recollection of events?" I asked. I'd spent a great deal of the 1980s in places that weren't the US, and when I was there, I was in New York or San Francisco, and pretty high, so I was just going off what I'd heard.

"There may have been one main hand behind a few key elements of the Satanic Panic," the demon said, his voice cagey.

"You didn't..." I said.

"I...well, I pretty much did," he admitted. "I was experimenting with various aspects of the publishing industry, and I had a few key clients in the late sixties through the early eighties that I thought would make for some entertaining interactions."

"And these were?" I asked.

"Well, one was Anton LaVey, who 'wrote,' and I use that term *very* loosely, *The Satanic Bible*."

"You've got to be fucking kidding me," I muttered.

"Another was a man named Jack Chick, who created and distributed tracts decrying the influence of Satanists in American society. It was simple enough to seed small towns and even mid-sized cities surrounded by more rural areas with Chick's leaflets decrying the rise of Satanism all over America, then make sure that there were copies of LaVey's book found in the homes of particularly gruesome murderers every few months. Add in humanity's natural paranoia and fear of things they don't understand, and within a few years we had a genuine cultural phenomenon, culminating in young Mr. Hanks' appearance in that truly abysmal movie."

"What did you have to do with that?" I asked, knowing damn well the answer wasn't going to be "nothing."

"I financed the film," the demon said. "I made a *lot* of money off LaVey and Chick both, and I used it to become a silent partner in the...well, I hate to use the word *film* to describe it, but that's all I have. Getting Tom Hanks to play the lead in that movie was the culmination of several years' machinations. I was particularly proud of the reach it had. That movie screwed up children's escapist literature for decades, not to mention what it did to *Dungeons & Dragons* sales."

"Why did you care if Tom Hanks was in the movie?" Becks asked.

"Oh, that's simple," Faustus said. "Hanks plays for the other team. He's one of the very few actually good people in the entertainment industry, and I could see a very bright future laid out in front of him. I needed to do everything in my power to trash his career before it got started, thus an impressively bad television movie followed by a dreadful crossdressing sitcom. All me."

"Yeah, that one didn't work out too well for you, buddy. Tom Hanks still went on the be one of the most famous, and famously nice, actors in the world," I said.

"Yes, well, apparently there was someone working on his behalf from the other side that was at least as good at their part of the job as I was at mine," Faustus replied. "That's how the game goes, Harker. Sometimes we win; sometimes they win. If it were easy, we wouldn't still be fighting after all these years."

"Thanks, Faustie," Glory said. "I thought the tracts were pretty good, but Hanks was just too good to stay buried, no matter who was trying."

"That was you?" the demon asked, delight in his tone. "Well done, Glory! Truly. That was one of the few times in that millennia that I was outmaneuvered. I am seriously impressed. And what you did with *Joe Versus the Volcano*? That was a stroke of genius!"

"What did you do with *Joe Versus the Volcano*?" I asked.

"Not much," Glory said. "I just made it suck a little less by getting an internship with the editor and giving him a nudge here and there to cut the film together differently."

"You saved that movie, and Hanks' career," Faustus said. "I was thoroughly bested, and I am not one who says those words often. I doff my cap to you, my dear."

"Thank you," Glory replied. "You were a worthy opponent. I had to use all the tricks in my toolbox to outfox you."

"If we can pump the brakes of the love bus," Jo cut in, "I've got real buses turning left out of the transit center. Three of them, and they look like they're heading your way."

"Okay," I said. "Everybody get ready. Remember, stay to the edges and don't get in the shit. We're here to try and de-escalate and keep people from getting hurt. We are *not* here to kick ass."

"How much did it hurt to say those words, Harker?" Glory asked.

"Oh, you have no idea," I replied. "I think I sprained my brain just thinking it. Now look sharp, folks. We don't need another bloodbath."

19

I stood up on my rock to get a clear view of the entire gathering, and slowly turned around in a circle. There were pairs of bicycle cops at each corner of the park, staying back from the crowd but close enough to keep an eye on anything going on. I noted one patrol car idling at the corner of Third and South Church Street, but there was no other visible police presence. I opened my Sight and scanned the crowd.

The place was predictably bright with magical auras, since almost everyone in the park had some kind of ability, but it was mostly the pale green, blue, and yellow auras of low-powered human witches and magic users. There were a couple of red-tinted demonic auras, and a few gleaming white specks of divinity scattered here and there throughout the crowd, but it was mostly just what it seemed to be—a collection of humans with a little bit of magic getting together. There were no heavy enchantments on anyone, nothing that looked like battlefield magic, and nothing that could obviously be turned offensive easily.

That's not to say that none of the people there could fight. I had no doubt that they could call up some serious pain if they were given the time and the resources to do so, but most of the magic I've seen done by humans is ritualistic and requires specific components and materials to go with the words. What I do is different, more like the way innately magical beings channel energy. I can perform rituals for complicated things, like the scrying I performed earlier that day, or tracking or binding spells. Summonings and Gates require rituals, too. I wouldn't want to try and freestyle a Gate between Earth and Heaven. Too much opportunity for me to mispronounce something and end up in Valhalla again. Last time that happened, I ended up drinking with Thor and lost six weeks in 1989.

I typically just call up power and bend it to my will, manipulating the energy that flows from the earth through all living things into whatever I need it to be. It's a lot less elegant than a nice, clean ritual spell, but it also goes through fewer candles and takes way less time. When I need to blast something back to Hell, I can't always remember the exact right Latin phrase. My magic is more like jazz—a lot of improv and bending notes to get the right feeling across. I sensed a few others in the park that could do magic that way, but it was not how most of them were accustomed to working.

That meant that they wouldn't be flinging any fireballs if things went pear-shaped, but it also meant that they would be less capable of responding quickly to any shenanigans by the police. "Anybody got eyes on Chief Putnam or anybody in the upper ranks of the police department?" I asked.

The resounding silence didn't bode well for the rest of my night. If the brass weren't anywhere to be found, it meant that either they didn't know what was coming, which was bad, or they knew what was coming and wanted plausible deniability, which was worse.

I spotted a witch I knew slightly and hopped down to go give her a heads up on what was about to go down. She saw me walking her way and scowled. I tried hard to remember if I'd done anything specific to piss her off the last time I'd seen her, couldn't come up with anything, and finally just assumed that she fell into the very broad category of "People Who Don't Like Me."

"Tara," I said with a nod, stopping a few feet away.

She turned from the young woman she was speaking to and

looked up at me. "Harker." She managed to heap a *lot* of disdain into two syllables. Tara was in her mid-thirties, about five-six, medium build, with short dark hair streaked through with blue and purple. Might have been magic, might have just been a recent visit to Hair Klaudt, I couldn't tell.

"Can I speak to you for a moment?" I asked, keeping my tone as casual as I could manage.

"I suppose. You aren't here to cause trouble, are you? Everyone is here to offer up our voices and hearts to the peaceful passing of our friends and community members. You've heard of the concept, right? Peace?" With her arms folded tight over her chest, Tara was giving me a serious disapproving elementary school teacher vibe. I wracked my brain trying to remember what I'd done to piss her off, but the list of people I've offended is long and spectacularly diverse, so I didn't manage to drill down onto her.

"I've heard of peace," I said. "Read about it in a book once. Not usually what people call me about, though. And not what I'm here for. Do you know who's running this show?"

Her brow furrowed as she processed what I was saying. "It's a memorial, Harker. Nobody's 'running' anything. We're all just here to gather and be together in our community's time of loss. You know, some people actually like being around others when things are difficult."

That was it. I'm not a very patient man at my best and getting snarked at when I was there trying to actually help out didn't put me in the same zip code as my best. I stepped in close so the other people around couldn't hear me, and I bent down until our foreheads were almost touching.

"Look, you sanctimonious prig, take whatever issues you have with me and stow them the fuck away for five minutes. There are three busloads of riot cops rolling up Tryon Street right now, and they're all itching to unload a fuckload of tear gas and pepper spray on anyone they think might know anything about the cops that died this week. Now tell me who set up this fucking love-fest so I can get them to clear these people the hell out of here before the shit hits the fan for sure." I could feel power leaking through my eyes and knew they were glowing, probably red. That's what usually happens when I get really pissed, and snotty witches have always been able to push my buttons.

Tara took a step back, her face going pale as she stared at me. She was a witch, but not a very powerful one, and I was willing to bet she'd never been around anyone who could do so much as light a candle with their power unless they cast a circle and mumbled in Latin for ten minutes, so seeing me go all X-Men on her in the middle of the park was a level of power she wasn't accustomed to.

"I-I don't know who set it up. A friend of mine posted the announcement to our coven's Facebook group. It was from something called Wiccans of the Carolinas, or something like that. It gave the time, date, and location, and said there would be speakers, singing, chanting, and a time for healing. We all decided to come out and show our support."

"Did you know any of the people killed this week?" I asked.

"No. They weren't anyone I'd ever met. I—*we* don't spend a lot of time with other covens. I think most groups are like that. I just thought it might be nice to have an opportunity to meet more practitioners. Expand my social network, you know?"

"No, I don't know," I replied. "My network has too many people in it already. But if you don't get your people the fuck out of here, that number could go down. I don't know what the cops have planned, but there's a lot of angry people in uniforms this week, and it won't take much to set them off."

"I'll get our people out and spread the word. Maybe we can keep things from going bad." She turned to the women she'd been talking to when I walked up and waved them over. "Thanks, Harker. Maybe you aren't such an asshole after all."

"I probably am," I replied. "But what did I ever do to you? All I remember is you hating me from the moment we met. Did I sleep with your older sister or something?" I was pretty sure I hadn't, since I'd lived like a monk from the time I moved to Charlotte until I got together with Flynn, so it was meant to be a joke.

Imagine my surprise when Tara said, completely deadpan, "No. You slept with my mother. In 1974 in New York City. She said she met you at Studio 54 and you were the coolest thing she'd ever seen. You hooked up with my mother, Harker, and you never called her again. That's why I've never liked you. Because you're a dick."

I looked her up and down, a sinking feeling in my stomach. "How old are you, Tara?"

She laughed. "Don't flatter yourself. I was born in 1980, to a pair of very loving parents with a father that was present for every important moment in my life. But my mother...she still holds out hope that you're going to swoop in and take her out of her boring suburban life. You showed her something bigger than herself, Harker, then you dropped her right back into reality and walked away without ever looking back. That was a dick move. Helping us tonight makes up for a little of that, but not all. Now go away while I try to get these people out of here. They see me with you, any trust I've got with them goes out the window." She turned and walked away, leaving me to think that even if she wasn't my daughter, I probably wouldn't have minded if she was.

Then the sound of diesel engines reached my ears, and I knew shit was about to get real.

20

Strunin, the new guy Becks had called out to me at the funeral, was the first one off the lead bus the second it stopped. He had a megaphone and was still in his full-dress uniform. As he marched toward the park, a steady stream of riot cops poured out of the three buses and formed up in a double rank of grim-faced police officers, all along the sidewalk on Church Street. They were all kitted up for urban warfare with helmets, all-black tactical uniforms, thick kneepads and elbow pads, face shields and assault rifles. Every other one held a big Plexiglas shield with POLICE written on it in big white letters, like there was any doubt who the jerkoffs in the flak jackets and combat boots were. It looked like a *Call of Duty* cosplay contest, or maybe a meeting of the *Resident Evil* fan club.

What it didn't look like was a peace-keeping mission. These guys were loaded for bear and judging by the ones I got a clear look at, they were itching for a fight. Strunin walked up to the edge of the grassy oval and stopped at the far end, opposite where I was sitting.

He raised the megaphone to his lips and called out, "This is an unlawful gathering. Romare Bearden Park is now closed. Everyone here must disperse immediately. Anyone remaining in the park after this time will be considered to be trespassing."

"Park's open 'til midnight, asshole!" one of the male witches yelled, holding up a middle finger.

Is that right, Becks? I asked.

Yeah, she replied. *Because there are so many events that take place at night, and due to its proximity to the Knights baseball stadium, the city decided it just made more sense to have the official hours of the park from 5 a.m. to midnight, instead of trying to close it down at dusk like the rest of the city parks.*

A rare moment of sanity from a municipal government, I thought. *Whatever shall we see next? Horseless carriages? You find out anything else about this bright idea?*

Nobody here is talking, Becks said. *I think this is a Strunin special. He seems to think if he can get his face on the eleven o'clock news, it'll help him snag Herr's desk, or maybe even Deputy Chief Stephens'. And if he lets the rank and file who are pissed off about the deaths of so many officers this week blow off some steam, it makes him more popular among the department.*

Smart, I thought. *Asshole move, but a smart one.*

That's the book on Strunin, from what I heard talking to a couple friends in Raleigh. He's an asshole, but a really smart one.

Great. A smart, ambitious asshole with a few dozen riot cops at his back. This was going to be a long night.

Strunin put the megaphone back to his lips. "I repeat, this is an unlawful gathering. Anyone remaining in the park will be subject to arrest and prosecution. Please disperse immediately." When no one moved, Strunin waved over his head, and the riot squad began to advance.

I decided I needed to at least try to cut this shit off before it got out of hand, no matter how little hope I held out for being able to do so. I hopped down off my rock, muttered "cover me" to my invisible crew, and pushed my way over to a middle-aged matronly-looking woman with close-cropped salt-and-pepper hair and a flowing white robe. She had a multi-colored stole around her neck embroidered with the symbols of a bunch of the world's major and minor religions. I even recognized most of them.

"Pastor Judy?" I asked.

She looked up at me, and when she got a good look, she jumped a little and took a quick step back. "Yes? Who are you?"

"I'm—"

Tara stepped up and cut me off. "His name is Quincy Harker, Pastor. He's...a fringe member of the community, but he knows a lot of people. He's a pretty powerful practitioner."

"I could sense that," Pastor Judy said, still eyeing me up and down. "What can I do for you, Mr. Harker? You probably noticed that we have a bit of a situation brewing that I need to deal with."

"You don't have a situation," I said. "You have a colossal shitshow. Those cops are looking for a fight, and since you guys look like the easiest asses to kick, you've been elected."

She looked me up and down, and I couldn't decide if I felt like I'd disappointed my grandmother or been called to the principal's office. A little of both, if I'm being honest. "What do you suggest we do about that, Mr. Harker?"

"Get the fuck out of here. Run, don't walk, to your cars and haul ass. Don't engage. Don't try to reason with them, or de-escalate, or talk anyone down. They're not here for that. Most of them are here because they just buried a friend today and you're the most visible sign of the people who killed them, and the guy leading the charge is here because he wants a new job and a big fat raise. None of them are here because they want to hold hands and sing Kumbaya."

"Do you know the history of religious persecution in the United States, Mr. Harker?" Pastor Judy asked.

"You want me to start with the desecration and demolition of the indigenous people and their beliefs, or do you just want to jump to a dozen or so trees in Massachusetts sprouting strange fruit at the tail end of the seventeenth century? Because none of that matters now. What matters tonight, right here and right now, is that there's a couple dozen cops armed to the fucking teeth and spoiling for a fight, and it won't take more than a wrong word from one of the ten or twelve motherfucking *demons* in your crowd to set this whole place on fire. Now are you going to fucking pay attention or are you just going to get people hurt?"

I've been called a lot of things in my life. Some of the least complimentary of them have been mentioned repeatedly. "Tactful negotiator" is never an appellation that anyone has aimed in my direction. Tonight was no fucking different. I could see Pastor Judy shutting down as my voice was growing louder, and I couldn't rein in my fucking temper in time to keep her from dismissing me completely. So what happened next was, in part, my own damn fault.

Pastor Judy looked placid as a swan on a lake, but the steel in her eyes and the vein throbbing at her temple gave a solid hint about the frantic paddling going on underneath her surface. She pushed past me and stalked toward Strunin and his goons, a solid, no-bullshit march that made me think my first impression might have been right. Pastor Judy had almost certainly been a principal at some point.

"This is a public park, Officer. We have every right to be here," she called as she approached Strunin.

To his credit, the glory-hound cop didn't draw down on the short woman who looked like she should be hosting a public access cooking show, but the twitch in his right hand sure made it look like he wanted to. *Becks, you still at the garage?*

No. I'm almost to the park. I wanted to be there to report to Putnam on what went down in case it gets ugly.

Oh, don't worry. It's already ugly. We're just waiting to see if it becomes catastrophic.

"Anybody look like they want to start something?" I asked the team over the radios.

"Clear here," Glory said. "I've got eyes on one demon, but he looks more terrified than scheming."

"That's how I like my demons," I replied. "Faustus?"

"I gathered three of my more hotheaded brethren and removed them from the scene of the protest. We're at Valhalla enjoying fish and chips."

"They have fish and chips in Norse heaven?" I asked.

"Valhalla is a restaurant, you Philistine," the demon replied. "It's across Church from the park. Best fish and chips in the city. Perfectly crispy, and a decent beer selection as well. You should try it sometime. When I'm nowhere nearby, of course," he added.

"Of course," I said. It was a pretty good idea, honestly. He got three demons away from a potential storm of chaos, and he got to have dinner. Little bastard was pretty smart, not that I'd ever tell him that. "Jack, what are you seeing?"

"This lot seems pretty agitated by the appearance of the police," he replied. Jack was down at the benches nearest Church Street, so he was right there by the riot cops. He'd managed to insinuate himself in the middle of a group of pissed-off millennial witches talking shit about the government and police in general, and the police presence at a peaceful memorial in specific. His radio kept cutting in and out, and I couldn't really hear what was going on at his end, so I was counting on him to make some real noise if he needed help. "I don't think they'll strike first, but they don't seem like the type to back down if the constabulary are determined to become aggressive."

That's our Jack. Never use one syllable when five would do.

"Monica, where are you right now?" I asked. After a few seconds with no response, I called again. "Monica? Gimme your location, Fuzzy."

Nothing. *Dammit.* I looked around, but the park was too full of witches and riot cops for me to catch a glimpse of my MIA werewolf. If I was lucky, she was herding any of her pack members to safety. If my luck ran the way it normally did, she was somewhere stripping down and getting into her fur so she could lead that pack into the fight. Served me right for bringing an unknown quantity to a riot.

I shook my head at my own stupidity, then whirled around as I caught a flash of movement out of the corner of my eye. "You scared the shit out of me, Luke," I said to my uncle, who suddenly stood at my elbow.

"Apologies, Quincy. Cassandra felt that I may be of assistance, so she relayed your location to me after I had breakfast."

"You eat at home or takeout tonight?" I asked.

"None of your business," Luke replied. He never liked to talk about his feeding habits, which I couldn't blame him for. But it was one of the few things I could manage to needle him about, so I took every chance I had to poke the bear. Or vampire, as the case may be. "What can I do to help?" he asked.

"Take this, and if things get violent, try to make sure nobody gets killed." I handed him one of the in-ear transceivers and waved a hand at the crowd. "You kinda get what's going on, right?"

"The witches are here to perform a ritual, and the man currently arguing with the fierce small woman is trying to make himself look good to his superiors by 'cracking down' on an 'undesirable element.'"

I raised an eyebrow. "That's pretty astute, actually."

"I called Detective Flynn before I left home."

"Smart."

"I am over half a millennium old, Quincy. Stupid vampires do not live this long. I will observe from the far side of the park," he said, blurring out of sight. He must have eaten well. Luke usually isn't *that* fast.

I turned my attention back to where Strunin and Pastor Judy were talking, their postures intense. Pastor Judy stood like a rock—resolute, feet planted, arms folded. She looked like a woman waves would break over and retreat back into the sea. Strunin looked like a caricature, like something out of an editorial cartoon, looming over the unfazed witch like a blue-clad beast, all loud noises and sharp edges. She was implacable; he was unrelenting. She was stoic; he was raging. She was calm seas; he was hurricane weather.

I took two steps toward the pair of them, only to freeze in place as a water bottle tumbled through the air, moving as if in slow motion, lobbed in a high arc from somewhere in the middle of the crowd of previously peaceful hippies and spellcasters to slam down into Strunin's unsuspecting shoulder, exploding in a shower of water and a shout of surprise and pain. Pastor Judy ducked from the splash as Strunin went to the ground clutching his "wounded" shoulder. He scrambled back to his knees, then his feet, and ran back to the line of riot police, grabbing his radio and barking orders as he did.

The line of police advanced, shields up and faces grim. The witches milled around, looking for the jackass who threw the bottle. Then the tear gas started, and shit went completely sideways.

21

The first thing I heard was a rapid-fire *pap-pap-pap,* then I saw a host of small red and white spheres arc up and smack into the ground. They burst in a spray of burning, stinging gas, and my eyes immediately began to water. My lungs felt like they were on fire, and I was coughing and sweating with tears pouring down my face.

I managed to focus just enough to call power and wrap myself in a shield of magic, filtering out all the gas and irritants. *Becks,* I called through our link. *They just opened up on the crowd with little balls of what feels like pepper spray!*

Shit. Those are pepper balls. They'll sting like a mother but won't cause any lasting harm so long as nobody has any really nasty breathing issues. Are you okay?

I'll be fine. This is bullshit, Becks. I gotta do something. I scanned the crowd, looking for Pastor Judy, but where she had been standing, now all I saw was a swarm of dark blue and black uniforms. Seemed like Pastor Judy was going to be spending her evening as a guest of the city.

I pulled in more energy and let it out in a slow, steady stream, unlike my normal explosive blasts. *"Impetus,"* I said, focusing on spreading the wind as wide as possible to blow the smoke back on the assholes who cut loose on the crowd. It didn't have any effect on them, since they were all in full gas masks, but at least the witches weren't coughing their heads off.

"Hey, they're beating up Judy!" somebody yelled, and because I'm a suspicious prick, I immediately slipped into my Sight. Sure enough, the shout came from the vicinity of one of the red auras I'd noted earlier. Seemed the demons in the crowd were taking advantage of the confusion to sow a little discord. Assholes.

Of course, when the people nearest the crowd of cops saw that they did indeed have Judy and several others face down on the ground, one guy with a cop kneeling heavily on his back and neck, they went apeshit. A couple of young male witches ran forward, and one actually tackled the kneeling cop off of the man he had pinned. That went about as well as you'd expect, since that cop had three of his buddies around him, and seconds later the scruffy blond witch was curled up in a ball trying to protect his head as he got the shit stomped out of him.

"Everybody get clear," I called into the radio. "This is going from fucked to super-fucked, and fast. Glory, help make sure Jack can get to safety. Jo, don't come down here. Becks—"

"I'm a cop, Harker. This is my job. I'm on my way."

"Pravesh, you got any help you can send in?" I asked.

"I'm sorry, Harker. I cannot commit any of our personnel to a purely non-magical conflagration between the police and a group of humans. If you see any specific supernatural threats, I can deploy our people, but as long as everything stays mundane, my hands are tied."

I knew that. It sucked, but I knew it before I asked. Pravesh's mandate with the DHS Paranormal Division was pretty strict—if it was magical or monstrous, she could do whatever she wanted about it. But if it was a human threat, it had to be left to human authorities. "Okay, I'll do what I can."

"Q, don't do anything—"

I cut Glory off. "Glory, I'm in the middle of what's about to turn into a riot between the police and a fuckton of witches, with a sprinkling of demons in the crowd stirring shit. I feel like the doing something stupid train has left the station." I plucked the radio from my ear and jammed it into my pocket. I didn't need to trash Pravesh's expensive shit, but I also didn't want to listen to my friends offering up their "helpful suggestions."

I looked around. The blond witch was now face down with his hands cuffed behind his back, and the police officers restraining him and the other "leaders" of the memorial weren't overtly beating the shit out of anyone. I caught sight of Strunin behind the line of riot cops and started moving in his direction. Maybe if I could talk some sense into him, I wouldn't have to see any more blood on the streets this week.

I didn't get within fifty feet before a cop shouted at me to stop. I held up my DHS badge, and he raised a funny-looking rifle and aimed it at me. I was still shrouded in magic, so as long as it wasn't a high-caliber round, I was probably safe, but I stopped. "What the fuck is that? A paintball gun?"

I watched the corner of the young cop's mouth twitch into a smirk, and he squeezed the trigger. It was absolutely a fucking paintball gun except he was shooting those damn pepper gas balls at me. The little red and white balls slammed into my chest and shoulders, and I instinctively hardened the shield around me. It took a little concentration to keep my face shield porous enough to get me some air, and still filter out the gas, but after a few moments of coughing and cursing, I managed.

Meanwhile, I never stopped marching toward the little fuckwit who was shooting me, and he never let up on the trigger, keeping a steady stream of paintballs coming at me. They bounced harmlessly off me, and I kept shouting "Federal fucking agent!" at the top of my lungs.

As I got close, another pair of cops got shoulder-to-shoulder with Paintball Boy, one with another pepper ball gun, and the other with what looked like a fucking grenade launcher. *That* would be a problem. I was not shielded enough for a goddamn grenade. Paintball Boy Two raised his rifle and started shooting, but he was aiming straight for my face. He didn't hit as often as his buddy, but it was way more annoying to have projectiles bouncing an inch off my eyes. I raised the hand that wasn't holding the badge and started to call up energy, preparing to blow the pepper balls back at them, when the asshat with the grenade launcher opened fire on me.

I heard a hollow-sounding *whump* and felt my chest explode as something slammed into me, knocking me flat on my back. My shields fell, and I immediately started to cough as the powder inside the pepper balls filled my nose and lungs. I rolled over and looked around, trying to see through streaming eyes what the fucker had shot me with, and saw a hockey puck-looking hunk of rubber lying on the grass beside me. I had just enough time to think *that's a fucking rubber bullet?* before five hundred pounds of asshole wrapped in tactical gear plowed into me.

"Stay down, motherfucker!" one cop screamed in my ear as he dug his elbow into the back of my neck.

"Get on your stomach, asshole!" This cop was yelling at me from my waist, where he had hold of my hips and was trying to flip me over.

"Fuck you, I'm a federal agent!" I growled at the one on my neck.

"I don't give a fuck," he yelled. I felt pain explode in the side of my head, and I wasn't sure if he'd punched me or elbowed me, and frankly, I didn't give a shit. I was *done.*

"ENOUGH!" I shouted, and called up a blast of power strong enough to move a Buick. It was more than enough to blast two cops off my back, and I saw one of them bounce off the grass in front of me. I didn't know where the other one went, and I didn't care. I was ready to put an end to this shit, and if it meant that my relationship with CMPD was effectively over, so be it. They were the ones who opened fire on unarmed people with fucking pepper spray and rubber bullets from fucking grenade launchers. I got to my feet just as another cop reached me, and I bent at the waist and flung him over my head onto the turf.

"Strunin!" I shouted, amplifying my voice with magic to make sure I was heard. "Get the fuck over here!"

As I looked for the ringmaster of this shit circus, I saw a line of riot cops all aiming either pepper ball guns, rubber bullet grenade launchers, or in a couple of cases, their service weapons at me. I called up power and wreathed my fists in flame. "You can try, fuckers, but it isn't going to end well." I let a little power leak into my eyes, just enough to make them glow red. The riot cops held their position, but nobody opened fire.

After a few seconds of standoff, Strunin stepped around the line of men aiming their weapons at me. "Who are you and what are you doing?"

"You know exactly who the fuck I am, you son of a bitch. I'm Special Agent Quincy Harker from Homeland Security, and I'm trying to keep you from fucking up any worse than you already have. Put your goons back on the buses and lets you and I go talk this out."

"I don't take orders from you, Mr. Harker. In case you don't know what it means, this badge says—"

I held up my credentials in one hand while keeping the other wrapped in fire. "This badge says you goddamn well do take orders from me, you officious shitwad. This is a gathering of Wiccans and practitioners of magic. Sounds Paranormal to me. And I work for the Department of Homeland Security, Paranormal Division. That means this whole fucking thing is my goddamn jurisdiction. Now tell your men to *stand the fuck down.*" I put away my badge and poured power into both hands, increasing the intensity of the flame until it glowed white hot. There wasn't really any fire, just the illusion of it, but Strunin sure as hell didn't need to know that.

Strunin motioned to the men beside him, and they lowered their weapons. He walked over to stand almost nose to nose with me. "Okay, talk. And it had better be good, or you're going to end up under the jail. I've heard of you, Quincy Harker. It won't take much to get a warrant to lock you up until you're old and gray."

"Better men than you have tried, Ivan, old buddy," I said. "You want to have this conversation out here in front of God and everybody, or you wanna go back to the station where we can have a little privacy?"

He spread his arms wide. "What are you afraid of, Harker? Anything you have to say to me, you can say in front of my men."

That was the straw. The camel's back was strained already, but that was the straw that fucking shattered it. Those two little words. "First off, they aren't *your* men, you carpetbagging asshole. You came down here in your starched uniform with your brass all shined up and stuck your nose so far up Chief Putnam's asshole you were breathing through his fucking belly button. These aren't *your* men, you fucking twat. These are Captain Herr's men, and they fucking buried him today, so show some goddamned respect and at least let them finish shoveling dirt on his coffin before you try to swoop in and grab his desk. And this?"

I gestured at the cops in body armor. "What the fuck is this? Are you *trying* to start a goddamned riot? This is a fucking Wiccan memorial service, not a goddamned anarchists rally. These people just wanted to say a few prayers, burn a little incense, and chant a little to honor their friends that died. There were probably a couple of acoustic guitars floating around, too, so you saved the city from the insidious threat of yet another shitty rendition of 'American Pie.' Congratu-fucking-lations."

I stepped closer, letting the fires in my hands flicker out and fade away, but pouring even more blazing light out of my eyes. "You came in here swinging your dick around and started shit with a bunch of hippies who probably never raised a fist to anyone in their lives. They weren't a fucking threat. You know better than to try to go after the real threat, because you saw the tape of what happened at SouthPark when human cops try to go up against the shit I deal with every day. But you needed to come in and look like a badass to Putnam and make the morons with more tactical gear than brains think you were fucking Rambo, so you rolled in heavy on a bunch of New Age crystal-gazing suburbanites. I guess the only thing we've got to be grateful for is that most of them are White, because if there had been more Black people here, they'd all be fucking dead."

Strunin's face flushed red and he opened his mouth to speak, but I reached forward and let the fire bloom from my hand again. "No. You keep your goddamned mouth shut. You take your fucking *Call of Duty* cosplay brigade, load them back onto their little school buses, and get the fuck out of this park. Go tell Putnam you fucked up and that he should expect to hear from a buttload of lawyers tomorrow because every one of these people are going to sue your nuts off."

"You finished?" Strunin asked. He was almost vibrating he was so pissed off.

"I think so."

"Good. Now get the fuck out of this park before I arrest you and every other person standing here for trespassing. This has been declared an illegal gathering, and we are authorized to use non-lethal force to disperse the crowd." Strunin raised his hand, and a solid dozen pepper ball guns and rubber bullet launchers were instantly aimed at me.

"You really want to do it this way?" I asked, pulling in energy to slam a massive shield in place in an instant.

"I really do."

"Your fucking funeral," I said. Then I took one step forward and laid Major Ivan Strunin out with a right cross to the jaw. His eyes rolled back in his head, and he was unconscious before he ever hit the grass. I saw a streak out of the corner of my eye, and half a second later, Luke was standing next to me behind a pile of discarded weapons and riot gear. I saw confused cops looking at their suddenly empty hands, and before they could reach for the pistols on their hips, a brilliant white light erupted above me, turning the night sky bright as noon.

"GO HOME," Glory shouted from the supernova flare she wrapped herself in. The angel floated twenty feet above the ground, and all I could make out of her form was a pair of massive wings and a blinding light. "GO HOME AND CONTEMPLATE YOUR ACTIONS HERE TONIGHT."

The police looked around at each other, then a couple of them looked at me. I shook my head and yelled, "Get the fuck out before she fucking lights you on fire, assholes!"

That got their attention. Between me knocking out their boss,

Luke stealing their guns at super-vamp speed, and Glory putting on her Avenging Angel show, the fine men and women of the Charlotte-Mecklenburg Police Department decided that discretion was the better part of valor, and hauled ass back onto their buses and away from the park.

As the last bus rolled out of sight, Glory drifted down to stand next to me. "That was almost really bad," she said.

"Yeah, if you hadn't scared the shit out of them, I don't know how it would have turned out," I replied.

"If I have to be honest, and I pretty much do, it was actually kind of fun."

"Well, I'm glad you were here, even if you did enjoy it a little more than you probably should have. You helped keep a bad situation from turning into a truly catastrophic one."

"Don't speak too soon, Quincy," Luke said, looking over to where one of the younger witches had just dropped to her knees and started weeping like her entire soul had shattered.

"Oh shit, what now?" I asked.

"It's Pastor Judy," Glory said, her voice sad. "She's dead."

"Fuck," I replied. "Heart attack from all this bullshit?"

"Much worse," Luke said. "I can smell the blood from here. No, Quincy, the good pastor's throat was cut. She was murdered."

22

It was nearly nine hours later when we walked into our headquarters apartment and hit the switch for the shutters. The *whir* of aluminum fins sliding into place over the floor-to-ceiling windows was barely audible over the hum of the air conditioner, and completely drowned out by the steady stream of profanity I was spewing. I walked across the room and pressed the button to lower the interior shades as Luke followed me inside. It was still dark, but the sky was lightening in the east as sunrise approached, and I needed Luke for this meeting. He didn't have to sleep during the day, but he certainly had to stay out of the sun, thus the light-tight conference room.

"Thank you, Quincy," he said as he took a seat at the conference table.

"Can't have you bursting into flames in the middle of the den, Uncle. I don't want to replace the carpet."

"You always were the most caring of your siblings."

I ignored him, pulling out my phone and sending a group text to the rest of the team, telling them we were home and to meet us ASAP. A few minutes later they started to trickle in, either bleary from lack of sleep or even more bleary from waking up in the pre-dawn hours.

Jo padded in, barefoot and with her hair pulled back with a broad headband. She didn't acknowledge anyone, just went straight for the coffee maker and put in a K-cup. Glory, Jack, and Faustus all strolled in right after her in various states of dress. Glory had on sweats and a black tank top with a twenty-sided die set on a "1" with the words "Crit Happens" written on it in red. Jack was fully dressed, but his hair was sticking up in wild clumps all over his head, his eyes were blood-shot, and the shoe on his prosthetic didn't match the sneaker on his factory-issued foot.

Faustus looked like Faustus. He was dapper in a French Blue dress shirt with white cuffs and collar, black dress pants, and loafers that probably cost as much as my car. I never asked the demon where he got the money for his expensive clothes, or if they were even real, because there are a lot of things I need to know in this world, but how my Hell-spawned friend financed his designer threads was not on the list.

"Where are Pravesh and Flynn?" Watson asked as he sat down heavily. He rubbed his knee, then reached down and adjusted something lower on his leg. "Well, that fucking explains it, doesn't it?" he asked, mostly to himself.

"What explains what?" Jo asked, sitting next to the grumpy Brit.

"Why my fucking hip hurts," Jack replied. "I grabbed the wrong fucking leg. My shoes don't match, and it's throwing me all off-balance."

"You need me to go grab a different leg?" Jo asked.

"No, it's fine. Doesn't hurt when I sit down, and it's not like I've got to walk far when we're done here. Where are they?"

I followed his conversational jump, even if I could tell from the look on her face that Jo didn't. "They'll be here in a minute," I said. "Pravesh had paperwork, and Becks wanted to give Chief Putnam a piece of her mind about what happened tonight."

"Yeah, that was a shitshow," Glory said from a stool by the kitchen. I raised an eyebrow at her. "What? I'm waiting for the stove to heat up. I'm cooking eggs."

"Ooh! Over medium, please," Jo said.

"Two sunny side," Faustus called out.

"I'd love a cheese omelet," Jack added.

"You'll get them scrambled or you'll go hungry," Glory said. "And if you don't like microwaved turkey bacon, don't eat any. Otherwise, shut the fuck up."

Everyone shut the fuck up. Turkey bacon was far superior to no bacon, and nobody wanted to be the one who didn't get bacon. I knew the eggs were going to be scrambled, because that's the only way I knew how to make eggs, and I'm the one who taught Glory to cook. Worked for me—I like scrambled eggs.

Fifteen minutes later, Pravesh and Flynn walked in to the sounds of a bunch of sleepy people clanking silverware around. Becks took one look at us and turned to the kitchen, loading up a plate. Pravesh stopped and said, "Bacon?"

"Turkey," Glory replied.

"Thank you."

"No problem."

I'd forgotten that Pravesh didn't eat pork. Trust Glory to remember. I was glad somebody in our little group was looking out for the rest of us. "Everybody here?" I asked. "Good. If you're not here, now's the time to speak up." My joke fell flat. Nothing new.

Becks stood beside me, not taking her seat. I probed gently along our mental link, but her thoughts were shielded. I could feel the emotional roil she was in, but not what was specifically going through her head. Then she spoke, and it all made perfect sense.

"I've got an announcement," she began. "As of fifteen minutes ago, I have resigned from the Charlotte Mecklenburg Police Department."

A collective murmur of surprise went around the table, then heads started to nod. Becks went on. "What happened last night was unconscionable, and I won't be part of a department that treats its citizens like that. Those witches weren't there protesting anything, they weren't violent, they weren't even *loud*. When Chief Putnam listened to Major Strunin and deployed riot control officers to the scene, I felt there was a high potential for things to get out of hand, and I was unfortunately proven right.

"I went to the chief to talk to him about what happened, and he stood behind his decision and behind Strunin's actions. I asked him to promise me that the department wouldn't use that level of force against unarmed, non-violent citizens again, and he said he would make no promises. The words he used made it clear that he feels like Charlotte is at war with its supernatural citizens, no matter their power level, and no matter their history of violence or non-violence. I can't be a part of that, so I dropped my badge and my gun on his desk, and I left."

I put a hand on her shoulder. "I know how hard that was for you." I did, too. Her father was a CMPD cop, killed by a vampire in the line of duty. I'd been there when he died, and I'd watched every step of Flynn's career, from the academy, to her days in uniform, to promotion to detective, to all the times she tried to arrest me. She was one of the best cops I knew, and this was all she'd ever wanted to do with her life. Now it was over.

Pravesh stood. "While I am sad that we are losing a valuable liaison to the police department, I am pleased that Rebecca has accepted my offer to become the Deputy Director of the Charlotte Region of the Department of Homeland Security, Paranormal Division."

"Okay, you change logos on the credentials and upgrade your flight status, and get to keep your moral compass pointing north at the same time?" Faustus asked. "That's a better deal than my people could have offered, sad to say."

Becks smiled at the demon. "I think I know you too well to sign any deal with you, Faustus."

"A demon can dream, though, right?"

"Now you're a fed instead of a cop," Jo said. "Okay. Does this mean we need another source in the department?"

"I've got a few friends who will keep an ear to the ground for me," Becks replied. "We should still be able to find out most of what we need to know about the goings on inside the CMPD."

"Thanks, Keya," I said to Pravesh. "I'm sure it wasn't easy to make this happen that fast."

"Actually…" Pravesh looked guilty. "I've been trying to woo Detec-

JOHN G. HARTNESS

tive...*Deputy Director* Flynn away from the police department since before you came back from Memphis. Washington was pressuring me to fill the position, and I wanted Rebecca. Until now, she had too much loyalty to the department to consider a change."

"But now that they've proven they don't deserve that loyalty, here I am," Becks said. "I do need one favor, babe," she said to me.

"Anything, you know that."

"I need a gun. I had to turn in my service weapon when I quit the force, and I won't get my new Sig from Homeland for at least a week. My backup piece is my own, but I'd like to have something that carries more than six in the magazine."

"I got you," I said. I unclipped the Glock 17 and the three-magazine ammo pouch from my belt and put them on the table in front of her. "Take this. I've got another setup just like it in our dresser. The mag in the gun is regular bullets; the unpainted spare is the same. The mag with the blue stripe on the bottom is alternating cold iron and silver. The red stripe is white phosphorous rounds. Everything but the fire rounds are hollow point with wax tips filled in with a drop of holy water."

"Good God, Harker," Jo said. "Get specific with your ammunition much?"

I raised an eyebrow at her. "You don't? I've almost died more than once because I had the wrong tools for a job. If I can keep that shit from happening again, I will."

"Makes sense, I guess. I've just never heard you talk gun porn before."

"It's not really my thing, but Becks needs to know what she's carrying around. I don't sit around jerking off to back issues of *Guns & Ammo*, but I know my way around a firing range. But most of the time if I'm going to set something on fire, I'm casting a fireball."

"No more *D&D* for you, pal," Glory said. She turned to Becks. "I'm sorry you had to do this, but it was the right move. Those guys last night, they weren't there for justice, or crowd control. They were there looking for an excuse to hurt people. That's not what they're supposed to be about."

"No, it's not," Flynn said. "And the department has been changing over the past six or seven years. Quicker on the trigger, outfitted more like soldiers than police, more interested in kicking ass than keeping the peace. As long as Captain Herr was around, he kept that kind of shit out of our division, but with him gone…"

She shook her head, and I could feel the regret coming off her in waves. "I don't know. Part of me feels like I should have toughed it out, tried to fix it from within, but I could see the writing on the wall. Strunin is going to get transferred down here into Deputy Chief Stephens's job, and he's going to make changes in Homicide, and that would just make things worse for me. Better to get out now and try to do some good somewhere else."

"Well, that's what we're trying to do here," I said, taking my seat. "Does anybody else have any news? I'll settle for something less earth-shattering than a complete life and career change, but if Faustus has decided to repent and join the Host, I'll just retire here and now."

The demon laughed along with the rest of the table. "Nothing quite that earth-shattering, but I heard from our errant werewolf last night after the riot, and we seem to have a line on our mysterious Ms. Director Shaw."

"Way to bury the lede, Faustus," I said, leaning forward. I wondered about Monica calling him instead of me or Flynn, but it made sense that she would see a demon as more of an ally than a cop or the guy who is literally the star of children's nightmares in the supernatural community. "Monica was out sniffing around looking for DEMON while we were fighting the cops. Good move on her part. All she would have done in the park would have been get hurt or hurt someone else. What did she find out?"

"Well, it seems there is more than one point of Sanctuary in the city, and one in particular caters to a crowd too unsavory for Mort to tolerate."

"That's a high bar for asshole," I said.

"Indeed," Faustus agreed. "It's simply called The Dive, and Monica has picked up some chatter about a new player hiring muscle from there. This muscle is reported to be human, female, and throwing money around like confetti. There's just one problem."

"What's that?"

"Your picture is posted above the bar with a ten-thousand-dollar bounty posted on it. Sanctuary doesn't apply to you, Luke, Glory, me, Jo, or any of our known associates."

"Okay. We use Monica to find out what's going on. She found the place, maybe she can poke around there and find Shaw," I said.

"Monica is leaving town," Faustus said. "This morning. Her pack is heading off into the mountains in the western part of the state to bury their Alpha and determine the new leadership. She doesn't know when she will return, or what her status will be within the pack when she returns. So unfortunately, that source of information has dried up."

"Well, shit," Glory said. "How are we supposed to get in there to find out where Shaw is?"

"We do have one associate that is almost completely unknown to the local supernatural underground. Since he has recently rejoined our ranks, his face has not made it onto The Dive's Bounty Wall," Faustus said, turning to smile at Jack.

Jack Watson, pissy Brit, recent arrival from Merry Old England, and now our way into the most dangerous bar on the East Coast. He looked around the table, took a deep breath, and said, "Oh, bollocks."

23

I fucking hate this," I said to no one in particular. Nobody replied, but I knew they heard me. How could they not, with the four of us crammed into the back of a Sprinter van outfitted with more monitors and listening equipment than most recording studios. We had a monitor feed of the outside of The Dive, a battered white clapboard two-story house with all the non-load-bearing walls and beams ripped out to make as much floor space as possible. That came from a camera on top of the van, which was sitting in the Park N' Ride lot across the street from the bar.

Another monitor was shaky cam footage coming from a pinhole camera built into Jack's glasses. The fisheye lens distorted things a little but gave us a nice broad view of the interior of the club. Which looked like it lived up to every letter of its name. The floors were bare plywood, the ceiling was normal household drywall ceiling with graffiti sprayed and Sharpie'd everywhere, and the walls were covered with bumper stickers and posters from punk and garage metal bands. The place wasn't very full, but it was early yet, barely ten o'clock.

Jack hadn't protested much when we told him he was elected to go in and be our eyes inside the bar. After a couple hours setting up the pickup of the surveillance van and scheduling delivery of all the gear for just after sundown, everyone had turned in to get some sleep. We'd all been up all night, and aside from Luke, for obvious reasons, and Becks, who was too keyed up to sleep after quitting her dream job, the rest of us were exhausted.

That didn't mean *I* got much sleep, because as soon as we were back in our apartment, Becks headed straight for the fridge, pulled out two beers, and came over to the sofa. She passed me a beer and popped the top on hers. I sat down across from her and said, "Okay, tell me the rest."

She gave me a mock innocent stare and said, "What do you mean?"

"Inside your head, remember. I know there's more to it than what you told us in there. What's the rest of the story behind you quitting? Because you're one hundred percent a 'work from within the system' kind of chick, not a 'burn it all down and walk away' type. That's more my style."

She took a long pull off her beer, kicked her shoes off, and put her feet up on the coffee table. She leaned her head back against the couch and stared up at the ceiling for a long moment before she spoke. "Chief Putnam made it abundantly clear that even if he didn't bring Strunin in, and he was almost certainly going to, that I would never be sitting in that, or any other, chair higher than the one behind my detective's desk. He told me point blank that he did not see me progressing any higher up the ranks within the department than detective."

"Is that something you *wanted* to do?" I asked. "Move up in rank, I mean."

She kept staring at the ceiling, so I took the chance to stare at her. My fiancée is ridiculously pretty, with light brown skin, long curly hair, a strong jawline, and cheekbones that could cut you if you weren't careful. But there was a lot of strength in her features, too. She had to be strong, losing her dad at such an early age, becoming a cop, then dealing with me and my world.

My gaze traced the line of her jaw, down the side of her neck, to her hand holding the bottle. Her long fingers had calluses from the firing range, where she went through a couple hundred rounds each and every week, far more than almost anyone else in the department. Her forearms were tightly muscled, long and sleek, like everything about her. Even sitting on the couch with her head thrown back, she looked like barely bridled energy just waiting to unleash.

"I don't know," she finally answered, making me struggle to remember the question. "I know I want, *wanted*, to at least make lieutenant at some point. It would give me a nice bump in pay, and I'd like the chance to run a division. I always figured that was a few years off, but to hear that 'a few years' was more like 'never'…well, that stung."

"Is it a woman thing?" I asked. "I assume it's not a race thing, because Putnam is Black, but I guess that doesn't really make a difference. It can't be a record thing, because you—"

"It's you," she said, and I felt a rush like cold water run down my spine.

"What?"

"Putnam told me that I was never going to get a promotion because of my relationship with you. He said that he, along with the rest of the department leadership, felt like I was serving too many masters, and that as long as I continued to work with you and maintain, as he put it, close contact with people and groups that often run counter to departmental goals, that I wouldn't have any room for advancement. So I told him that it had been a hundred and fifty-something years since any of my people had masters, and he could go fuck himself. Then I dropped my badge and gun on his desk and walked out."

I didn't know what to say. I knew I wasn't popular around the police headquarters, but I thought there was at least a modicum of mutual respect. Seemed I was wrong. A lot wrong. "Fuck. I'm sorry, babe. I didn't know."

"You didn't do anything wrong." She lifted her head up and looked at me, eyes blazing. "That motherfucker couldn't handle the fact that he didn't listen to Captain Herr the better part of a year ago when we both went to him asking for a bigger budget to protect our people from supernaturals. I had a whole damn list that Pravesh helped me build—iron and silver-blended chain mail to go over our vests, incendiary rounds for shotguns, and a supply of holy water in all our teams' vehicles. I spent weeks researching this shit and figuring out the best way to outfit a small, eight-person team within SWAT to specifically practice dealing with runaway supernaturals. I did this right after we got back from Hell, because after the shit we saw on our Archangel hunt, I knew there was no fucking way we could handle some of this stuff on our own, and we weren't..."

She trailed off, but I finished the thought for her. "You weren't getting any help from me. I know. So you took him all this, and he shut you down?"

"Shut me down *hard*. Hell, I even had Pravesh ready to foot half the bill! It still wasn't cheap, but the department has a three *hundred*-million-dollar budget. I was asking for less than a hundred grand. We, *they*, spend more than that every year on tear gas. But he barely even looked at my documentation, just told me to get out of his office with my freak-loving bullshit."

"Jesus wept."

"Yeah. That's the first time Pravesh and I talked about this Deputy Director position. She saw the writing on the wall way before I did."

"She's smarter than the average snake," I quipped. We sat in silence for a while, just drinking and thinking. Well, Becks was thinking. I was watching her. She was still shielding her thoughts from me, which was fine. I didn't need to hear everything that went on in her head, and she sure as shit didn't need to know all the twisted crap that went on in mine. I felt the whirl of emotions just on the other side of her walls, though, and could tell this bothered her more than she let on. "What else is there?" I asked.

"It's stupid."

"I seriously doubt that. You are one of the least likely people I know to be upset at something that's stupid."

She finished her beer and waggled the bottle at me. "Wanna get me another?"

"No problem." I got up and grabbed two more beers from the fridge, popping them open and passing one across the coffee table. "Now spill."

"I feel like I'm letting him down, betraying his memory somehow." She was back to looking at the ceiling, so I watched her swallow fast, several times, as the emotions threatened to overwhelm her.

"Your dad?" I asked.

"No, he'd tell me to get my panties out of a bunch and move the fuck on, that Putnam was a jackass and we both knew it. No, it's… Ben. Captain Herr. He had my back, you know? A lot. When nobody else did. He stuck by me when it looked like you were a murderer—"

"Which time?" I asked, then winced a hair when I realized I was serious, and I'd been suspected of murder enough times that it was a valid question. Oh, well. You live long enough and deal with enough bad people, you're probably going to be responsible for a few corpses along the way. I was responsible for more than a few, for sure.

"When you shot Agent Smith in the head in broad daylight," Becks replied.

"Oh yeah," I said. "That was a rough one." Agent Smith had been a Cambion, the psychotic offspring of a demon and a human, and he had murdered a bunch of people all over the city, including our last Renfield, and blown up Luke's house. I did in fact shoot him in the face, but I am of the considered opinion that shooting mass murderers who are actively trying to kill everyone you love is the very definition of "justified." The American legal system usually agrees with me, but when said mass murderer is also a federal agent, things get complicated.

"Herr stuck with me, no matter what kind of craziness we were involved in, and now he's dead, and I'm just gonna quit? That doesn't feel right."

"No, but it's the best way for you to honor his legacy and keep up the fight," I said. "You won't be able to do shit from within the department. You knew as soon as Strunin showed up sniffing around the empty office, your days of working both sides of the CMPD/DHS street were over. Best case scenario, he'd have stuck you on a desk until you got pissed off and quit. This way, you get to skip the 'stuck behind a desk' part. Now you can keep hunting down bad supernaturals, and hunting the shitty humans who prey on or use supernaturals to commit their own crimes, and keep the city safe from creatures like that fucking sluagh and this nut job Shaw."

"Ugh, Shaw. I'm just glad Pravesh found somebody else to deal with chasing down all her spell components and blowing that plan to shit so we didn't have to deal with that alongside everything else."

"Yeah," I said. "I don't know that bunch from Georgia, but Keya trusts them, so I have to do the same. Now that they're going to keep her from casting her magical cryptic assassination spell, finding her has got to move to the top of our list. It's been a fucked-up week, but now we need to refocus on finding out where she's holed up with her DEMON goons and getting her the fuck out of our city. And maybe get a hint on who's behind her while we're at it."

"That sounds good," Becks said.

"Let's get some sleep and then tonight we can rest all our hopes and plans on Jack Watson's narrow, whiny shoulders."

"Way to inspire confidence, Harker," she said, getting up from the couch. She drained her beer in one looooong swallow and put the empty on the coffee table.

"Well, at least we'll be close by if anything goes to shit."

"If? The way this month's going, that's going to be a 'when' for sure," she said, padding off barefoot toward our bedroom.

I watched her go, thinking how lucky I was to have her in my life. I didn't realize how unlucky I was that she was so damned prescient. Because as predicted, everything did indeed go to shit.

24

"aven't seen you here before," the bartender said to Jack. Her voice came in loud and clear through the mic built into the earpiece of Watson's glasses, making them officially the most expensive fashion accessory any of us had ever worn. Except maybe Luke. He used to have a crown, after all.

"Looking for a change of pace. Bourbon, neat," Jack replied.

"Where do you usually drink?"

"There's a place that used to be okay, but they started letting this asshole back in who got booted a while back, so I decided if they wanted his money, they didn't need mine."

The bartender set a glass on the bar in front of Jack and poured two fingers of Wild Turkey into it. "Yeah, that makes sense. What is it about this guy you don't like?"

"Too close with the cops," Jack replied. "I'm a completely legitimate businessman, but I don't like cops, and I don't like people who hang around cops."

"I get that. A lot of our regulars feel the same way. Especially with the shit the cops are pulling lately." She leaned on her elbows, her bright blue ponytail snaking down over one shoulder. She had on a black tank top that showed off the full sleeves she sported inked up and down both arms. The right was a Dia de los Muertos theme, with sugar skulls and flowers, while the left was a darker, Bosch-inspired tapestry for flames, devils, and tortured souls. She looked at Jack with eyes too green to be natural and asked, "You hear about that?"

"Yeah," Jack growled and tapped the rim of his glass. As the woman poured him another drink, he said, "Jackbooted bullshit is what it is. If they aren't careful, they're gonna turn around one day and realize the city isn't theirs after all."

"They?"

"Mundane assholes and close-minded humans."

The young woman raised an eyebrow, and the camera went to snow for a second. Just as I was standing up to run in after Jack, the image came back, only this time the bartender was staring at Jack with pupilless emerald eyes, and her ears had a distinctive point and no lobe. "Are you saying you're not close-minded, or you aren't mundane?"

"I'm not close-minded," Jack said. "I don't have any magic of my own. My mother did, but it didn't pass down. But I grew up around it, and around supernaturals and folks like you."

"Like me? You think you've met someone like me before?"

"I've dealt with the Fae before. You're Summer Court, if the coloring holds true. Too tan for winter."

The faerie smiled at Jack, and I swear I wasn't sure if the noise I heard was his heartbeat speeding up or his pants getting tight in the crotch. I was really hoping for heartbeat but having spent a lot of years as a man, I didn't have much faith in that.

"Banished from the fields of Summer, sad to say. Seems Titania is more protective of her handmaids than she seems."

"You seduced one of Titania's handmaids?"

"Seduced makes it sound like it was all my idea. Probably more accurate to say I had a…liaison…with one of Titania's handmaids. But since Her Majesty doesn't want to consider the possibility that someone else in her realm might be attractive, I had to leave in a hurry."

"Won't being out of Faerie eventually hurt you?"

"I am allowed to return for one day every decade, under close supervision. Titania wants me to live a very long time, so that I may fully understand what she has taken from me. She doesn't understand that we're going to create our own Faerie, on this side of the mushroom ring, and then all the Fae who are tired of her silly rules and drama can just leave and come here, where they will all be welcome."

"That sounds amazing," Jack said. I thought so, too, but more "amazing" in the "that's total bullshit" sense. I looked to Pravesh, who shook her head. She didn't know anything, either.

"Does that even *sound* like something anyone involved in this shitshow would try to do?" I asked.

"No, but it sounds like what I would tell a bunch of disgruntled expat faeries we were going to do so I could enlist their help and get my hands on their resources," Keya replied.

"You are a devious woman, Director Pravesh."

"I am a snake who works for the federal government, Harker. I think I may be the very embodiment of the word."

She had a point. I turned my attention back to the monitor, where Jack was ogling the bartender's cleavage. We'd decided against earwigs for this op, so I couldn't tell him what a pig he was being, but I was pretty sure he knew.

"Will there be room for any humans in this New Faerie?" Jack asked.

"A limited number of allies will be allowed resident status, and we will allow visitors. If they behave themselves." The smile the bartender gave him said that her definition of "behaving" might not jibe with mine, but from the chuckle Jack gave her, I figured he wouldn't mind. Whatever, if he wanted to sleep with a faerie I didn't care, as long as he didn't get himself killed or come down with some kind of magic crabs that ate the walls of my building or something.

I heard the creak of a barstool as someone heavy sat down next to Jack. He turned to look at the newcomer, and scooted back, both to get a better look, and because the guy was not the type that you really wanted to get too close to. He was big, like bench press Volkswagens big, with long red hair tied back in a ponytail and a thick red beard.

He had arms roughly the size of my legs, and a chest about the size of my first apartment. Jack glanced down and got a look at the hunting knife strapped to his hip and the heavy steel-toed boots the guy wore. He looked partly like he'd just stepped out of *Field & Stream* and half like he ate the guys who hosted survival shows for breakfast.

"Three Budweisers, 'Lena," the new arrival said.

"Three?" the bartender asked. "I see you, and I see Toolbox, but who's the other one for? You know I won't drink that shit."

"I figured listening to this dude's accent, he ain't from around here, so I thought I'd let him know what a good old-fashioned American beer tasted like." He slapped Jack on the shoulder, and I was glad we didn't use earwigs, because it probably would have shot across the room from the impact.

Jack managed to keep his face from smacking into the bar, but he got pretty close. "Thanks, mate, but I've had my fill of American beer. You Yanks can make a fantastic bourbon, but your beer tastes like watered-down horse piss. 'Lena, love, can I get another?" He tapped the rim of his glass. "Pour one for yourself, too."

"Mr. Watson does not understand the concept of frugality with an expense account, does he?" Pravesh grumbled. I looked over, and she looked genuinely grumpy. I was a little surprised, since she'd kept the middle manager side of herself well-hidden until now.

"Be glad he's drinking bourbon. When he comes to my apartment, he goes straight for the Macallan," I replied.

I turned my attention back to the monitor where Jack was facing the mountain of red hair again. "Hey, do I know you?" the big man asked.

"I don't think so, friend," Jack replied. "I'm not from around here."

"Nah," the giant said. "I've seen you before. You got a prosthetic leg?"

Pravesh and I exchanged worried glances. He'd only been in a couple of our encounters over here, but they were pretty memorable, and all involved a lot of gunfire. Anybody that recognized him from one of those was probably on the other side.

"Yeah, I do," Jack said. "Lost it in the sandbox. You over there?

Maybe that's where we met. Or a hospital somewhere if you were injured."

"Nah, I was already enlisted when I got here," he replied. Then his irises went yellow as he let Jack see just a hint of the demon inside his meat suit.

"Shit," I said. "Call everybody," I said to Pravesh. I was already on my feet and pulling open the side door as I threw a long-sleeved shirt on over my shoulder holster. I wished I had my long coat, but it was hot as balls even after the sun went down in the North Carolina summer, and I hadn't left home thinking I would have to deal with people shooting at me. Now it was looking increasingly like I was going to be in a gunfight before I made it home.

"Harker, hold on," Pravesh called. "Let's give him a shot to talk his way out of this before you go charging in. If you rush in now, his cover is completely blown. If he can keep his cool, we might be able to get some useful information on Shaw."

I closed the door and sat back down, then said, "Okay, I'll give him a chance. But have you *ever* seen Jack talk someone *out* of wanting to beat the shit out of him?"

"What's taking so long, Tony?" The voice came from Jack's other side and was accompanied by another rib-rattling back slap. "It's just two damn beers, it ain't rocket surgery." Jack turned to see a massive Black man grinning into his face. The man was pushing seven feet tall, and close to four hundred pounds, and most of it looked like it was muscle. He had a gleaming shaved head and a tightly cropped goatee, with a gold hoop earring giving him a little bit of a pirate vibe.

"I was just asking this fella if we'd ever met before. He looks awful familiar. You seen him?" Red Mountain asked.

Black Mountain looked closer at Jack, then scowled even more deeply as he thought about the question. "Yeah, he does look familiar." He looked Jack up and down. "You got a fake leg?"

"What the fuck, mate?" Jack asked. "Do I have a fucking tattoo?" He leaned over and pulled up his pants leg, exposing the metal rod that came out of his shoe. "Yes, I have a prosthetic leg. Mine is lying some-where under a sand dune in the fucking Afghan desert. Or more likely under several sand dunes, along with the bodies of my mates. Now what the fuck is this? I just wanted to have a drink and maybe meet some like-minded people, since I'm not bloody welcome at Mort's shithole anymore."

"You go to Mort's?" Red Mountain asked.

"Not since he cozied up to the fucking Reaper and the cops. I don't need that shit in my life, mate. People like that are why I left England. Too overbearing. Can't do anything without them jumping right in your shit."

"Can't do anything like what?" Red Mountain asked.

"The fucking Shadow Council ran my mum out of London for so-called 'dark magic' bollocks. Magic isn't dark or light; it's just fucking *magic*. Mum might have done a little work with some folks that don't usually work well with humans, but that's no fucking call to have her booted from the shop she'd run for decades. Bastards." He downed his new drink in one gulp, then tapped the rim of his glass again. "Give us another, love? Looks like you lot are empty. Set them up, too."

"I approve of his efforts to befriend these demons using alcohol, but their metabolism will prevent them from getting intoxicated," Pravesh said.

"I'm more concerned about how complicated this story is getting," I replied. "All it's going to take is one slip and we're going to be picking pieces of Watson up off the parking lot for a week."

"Thanks," Black Mountain said, picking up his new beer. "What are you doing in Charlotte? This ain't exactly a hotbed of magic."

"Or fucking anything else," Red Mountain grumbled.

"A man's gotta work, you know? I'm a lawyer, and I do mostly contracts. There's big banks here, and that means a lot of paper getting pushed around. That means lawyers."

"What's your name, pal?" Red Mountain asked. "I like him, Austin. He's cool."

"Jack," Watson said, holding out his hand to the behemoth. "Jack Walker, Esquire. Pleasure's mine."

They shook hands, then Black Mountain turned to see a third figure join them at the bar. This guy was even bigger than the Mountains, an Everest to their Appalachians, as it were. He was covered in tattoos from his wrists up to the sleeves of his Harley-Davidson t-shirt, with more ink creeping up the side of his neck. He had short brown hair, conservatively cut, but you could tell by his bearing that this guy didn't work in an office anywhere. I picked up on that before I caught a glimpse of the gun riding on his right hip.

"What's going on, boys?" Everest asked, his voice a low rumble like distant thunder.

"Just making a new friend, Harold," Red Mountain said. Jack glanced over at the big man, who had adopted a subservient posture. Head low, shoulders bent, voice soft. He answered the new arrival without meeting his eyes, making it very clear who was the dominant one.

"I like friends," Everest said, pushing off from the bar. Jack spun around and now had a mountain on each shoulder, the bar to his back, and Andre the Giant's scarier kid brother glaring down at him. "What's your name, friend?"

"Jack Walker," Watson said, holding out his hand.

The big man took it, and without letting go of Jack, looked down at the exposed prosthetic. "Funny thing. About three years ago we ran into some busybody assholes who ran with the fucking prick Quincy Harker, and one of them was a Brit with a fake leg. This guy shot me," Everest said, his eyes flashing yellow. He didn't flash them back to normal, though. He started to shift and burst free of his human suit, exposing the demon within.

"Now, before I rip your head off and shit down your throat, why don't you prove to me that you *aren't* the same guy who put a bullet in my chest at the airport that day?"

Jack looked up at the increasingly ugly face that stared down at him. I turned to Pravesh. "I think now it's probably time for me to get in there. Call everybody you can. I expect I'm going to need all the backup I can get my hands on." Then I yanked open the door and sprinted for the bar, hoping there would be some Watson left to save when I got there.

25

The bar was dead quiet when I walked in and slammed the door behind me. I looked around at the warped hardwood floors, punk rock posters and band stickers all over the walls, and tables that looked like they hadn't been wiped down with more than a lick and a promise in a decade, and decided that whatever violent redecorating happened tonight, it would be an improvement.

"'Sup?" I said, looking around the room with a smile. I recognized a few faces, mostly from having punched them at some point in the past, but most of the beings scowling at me were complete unknowns. So either there were a lot of shapeshifters in the bar, or there were a lot of strangers in town who hated my guts. I gave it about even odds, if we're being honest.

Jack was leaning back with his elbows on the bar, staring up into the face of a Rage demon, seven feet of red flesh, horns, claws, and bad attitude. The demon froze with its jaws a few inches from Jack's face, and I wasn't sure if it planned to gnaw his face off or melt it with demon breath. Either one would probably work. It's not that demons have fire breath like dragons or anything—they just have shitty oral hygiene.

"Harker," the demon said as it caught sight of me.

"The one and only," I replied, with a little bow. "Since I've got everyone's attention, I've got a few questions for you fine Pit-spawned fuckwits about a rogue government agency that might want all of us dead, demon and Harker alike."

"Go fuck yourself, Reaper," the bartender said, raising a twelve-gauge pump shotgun over the bar and pointing it in my direction. "Get out of my bar while you can still walk away."

"What? And miss Happy Hour? I heard tonight was two-for-one umbrella drinks, and I do love a good frozen daiquiri." I looked at Jack as if seeing him for the first time. "Oh. Well, I guess if you're going to let assholes like *him* in here, then this might not be the kind of place I want to spend my money in after all."

"Like the lady said, Harker, go fuck yourself," Jack shot back. "Tell you what, I'll even pay for a shot of Fuck Right Off if you'd like. Hell, make it a double, you prick."

I put on my best offended face, which probably wasn't all that good, but since the entire crowd probably wanted to murder me, it didn't have to be. "I'm a prick? *I'm* a prick? You leave me high and dry for a fucking *year* dealing with assholes like these while you prance around in merry old England, and *I'm* a prick? Fuck you, Walker, you poncy git." I walked as I talked, so I was right in front of Jack as I finished. Then I did something I've wanted to do almost since the moment I met the insufferable little shithead. I punched him right in the face.

I landed a right cross to the side of his jaw that spun him around and took out three barstools as he went down in a clatter of wood and brass. The demon and his pals stared in shock at the mess, and I *tsked* at the unconscious Watson lying on the filthy hardwood floor. "Shit," I said. "I really wanted to knock him out of his foot. I'll have to punch harder next time."

I turned back to the Rage demon and looked up at his stunned face. "Sorry, dickhead. You want to kick his ass, you'll have to wait until he wakes up. I'll buy you a drink to help pass the time, though."

I don't think he wanted to pass the time with me. I'm basing this solely on the fact that he opened his mouth in a roar, showing off two rows of teeth with needle-sharp incisors and blasting me in the face with the worst breath I've experienced in a long, *long* time. I'm talking undead Yeti kind of nasty, and that's a high bar. He raised both hands, hoping I guess to bring them down on top of my head and pound me into the ground like a tent stake.

I decided that wouldn't be fun, so I ducked under his left arm and spun around behind the demon, pulling a silver-edged dagger from my belt and jabbing it into the area where his liver would be in a human. I don't know if demons have livers, and don't know where they are if they do. Every time I've killed one, it's been more of a "decapitate or blow to smithereens" kind of killing as opposed to a "carefully dissect for scientific advancement" kind of killing. When you blast a creature into golf ball-sized chunks, it's really hard to tell which organ is which.

The demon let out a yell and spun around fast enough to yank the knife out of my hand. It swiped at my face with one clawed hand while it punched me in the gut with the other. I let myself flop over in the middle to absorb some of the force of the punch, and that saved me from some abrupt plastic surgery. I grabbed its forearm with both hands and slid to the side, twisting its arm as I straightened up. The demon howled as I yanked and pulled until a loud *POP* came from its arm, then it dropped to a knee in pain from its dislocated shoulder. I kicked it in the head, then threw myself to the floor just as an enormous boom split the air.

Thanking my lucky stars, the bartender had to slide the safety off the shotgun, which gave me a tiny *click* of warning before she cut me in half with it. I felt the hail of pellets whizz over my head. I slammed to the floor on my belly, then scrambled to my feet and called up power into a shield centered on my left arm. I turned to the bartender and yelled, "Cut that out!"

"Fuck you!" she yelled back, loosing another blast from the pump shotgun in my direction. The pellets bounced harmlessly off my shield, but the roar of the gun masked the sound of footsteps behind me, and I went down hard as something slammed into my back. My chin smacked into the floor, and I saw stars, then felt another impact as whatever hit me landed on me, driving me further into the wood. I threw an elbow back and felt it smack something solid, so I swung again and again, trying to dislodge whatever was on me. After three solid elbow strikes to the head, the creature let go of me, and I rolled over, shoving a werewolf in hybrid form to the side.

I dragged myself upright and looked around the bar. There were at least a dozen supernaturals arrayed against me, armed with fangs, claws, knives, guns, and glowing magical fists. I gave them my best "crazy bastard" grin and said, "Bring it, bitches."

I spun around and vaulted over the bar, snatched the twelve-gauge from the bartender, and thumped her in the forehead with the butt of the gun. She slumped to the floor, and I caught her collar on the way down to slow her fall. I didn't need her splitting her head open on the floor and adding yet another ton of guilt to my beleaguered conscience. Poor thing could only carry so much. Then I dropped to one knee and aimed the shotgun up, cutting loose a blast right into the middle of a faerie's face as they prepared to leap off the bar onto me with a knife in each hand. The faerie flopped onto their back and rolled to the floor, blood streaming from a shitload of pellet wounds. I figured they'd pop back up in a few seconds, because I seriously doubted the bartender kept cold iron shot loaded. It seemed more like a "calm the fuck down" weapon than a "don't get back up" weapon, and regular bullets were the mystical equivalent of less-than-lethal weapons.

I let loose with two more blasts from the shotgun, just to clear a little space around the front of the bar, then hopped up onto the polished wood surface. I dove forward, leading with the empty gun, and slammed into a man and woman that appeared human, but they certainly didn't fall down like humans. We tumbled to the floor as I crashed into them, but they immediately rolled backward and popped right back up on their feet, ready to kick the shit out of me.

Vampires. They were nowhere near as fast as Luke, but there were two of them, so that made them dangerous. I wasn't going to be able to pull my punches anymore if I wanted to get out of this alive, so I had to hope that there would be enough survivors to maintain Jack's cover story and shifted my ass-kicking into high gear. I pitched the shotgun at one vamp's face, then drew the dagger from my other hip. I transferred it from my left hand to my right, lunged forward, and slammed it hilt-deep into the distracted vampire's chest. He fell back, dead for good, as the silver pierced his heart.

I kept hold of my knife and twisted around to block the slashing claws of the female vampire, who seemed intent on ripping my throat out and drinking from a blood fountain. She raked down my left arm, leaving three bloody furrows all the way from my elbow to my wrist, and grinned at me as my own blood flecked my face. She stopped grinning when I buried a silver blade in her eyeball. Scratch two vamps.

Looking around the bar, I had the Rage demon that started it all lying on the floor screeching about its jacked-up shoulder and trying to yank the knife out of its back, Jack was still out cold, and there were about six faeries, weres, and spell-slingers coming at me from all angles. I assumed the bartender was still laid out behind the bar, but she was the least of my worries. Two guys in motorcycle leathers split apart to flank me, then split apart more literally as they peeled off their human suits to expose the red flesh and gaunt forms of Pit demons. They were skinny little bastards with gangly arms ending in nasty hooked claws, but they weren't very strong or very fast. They were the lowest rung of the demonic ladder, and I didn't bother using magic on them. I just pulled the Glock from the back of my jeans and put two in each of their faces.

Unfortunately, that meant I took my eyes off the faerie in front of me, and they were fast, well-trained, and swinging a combination double-bladed sword/staff like they were a Cuisinart and I was a pile of fries they were about to julienne. I got one arm up in the path of their blade as they swung at my neck, but the sword sliced through my shield like a hot knife through butter. Or like silver enchanted to dispel magic through a mystical barrier, if we're being specific about it. I went down to one knee, my left forearm bleeding around the blade wedged into the meat of it and fired two rounds into the faerie's shin. The mundane bullet wounds would heal almost instantly, but having someone smack your leg with a hammer really hard isn't fun, no matter if it causes permanent damage or not.

The faerie fell to the floor, their sword wrenching free of my arm and clattering to the wood beside them. I blinked away the pain, focused my mind, and shouted, *"Contundito!"* at the top of my lungs. Force streaked from my hands, slamming into the faerie's face and flattening their head. Brains and pointy ears flew across the dingy hardwoods, and the room fell grave-quiet as everyone looked at the carnage I created.

I stood up, cradling my bleeding left arm against my body, and looked down at the faerie's near-headless body. "That's gonna be hard to get out of the cracks," I said, and looked around the room as I holstered my gun. There were five supernaturals still standing, but two of them looked like they didn't have an ounce of fight left in them, and the other three were inching backward to the emergency exit without ever taking their eyes off me.

"You can run, it's okay," I said, and they did just that. There was a little bit of a logjam as a were, a wizard, and a demon in a human suit all tried to cram through one door at the same time, but with a bit of struggle, they managed it.

I peered over the bar, just to make sure the barkeep was still breathing. She was, so I left her there to sleep off her probable concussion. I walked over to the Rage demon and grabbed his wrist with my uninjured right arm. I planted a foot in his ribs and yanked, sliding his shoulder back into place with a *pop* and a scream. Then I bent over and grabbed his chin, turning his face to mine.

"When that prick wakes up, you tell him I'd better never see his face in my city again. If I do, he won't live long enough to regret it. You got that?"

The demon nodded, and I let it go. I turned to walk out the door, not bothering to look and see what the demon was doing. Rule Number One of Badassery—if you look back at the explosion, you aren't really a badass.

Thirty seconds later, I was back in the van with Pravesh, rooting around for a first aid kit. "You can drive home," I said. "I think Jack's bona fides are pretty solid now."

"Probably," she agreed. "You certainly established that he isn't with us. But did you have to leave behind so many bodies? Again?"

"Carnage," I replied. "Just another service we offer."

2 6

An hour later, I was sitting in my living room, with my feet on the coffee table this time, and a Stella Artois in my hand when my cell phone rang. I looked at the display, and it was Curtis, the doorman downstairs. I gave all the security personnel for the building my number, in case they ever needed to call in "the boss" for any reason, but none of them had ever used it. As far as property owners went, I was pretty hands off. I had a management company handle the leases on every floor but the top, and only building staff and my team had the access cards to let the elevators go all the way up. As far as the rest of the tenants knew, I was just some rich dude who bought the entire floor of a building. They didn't need to know that I bought it with money my vampire uncle had hoarded away since the fourteenth century.

"What's up, Curtis?" I asked as I tapped the green button on the screen.

"Mr. Harker, could you come down here, please? There are some men who would like to speak with you." Curtis sounded nervous, so I sat up and grabbed the monster remote off the coffee table. When Dennis went from ghost in the machine to Archangel, we'd had to make some adjustments. I'd gotten a little spoiled having a virtual Casper that could burrow into any computer system in the world in a heartbeat, so having to actually press buttons on remote controls felt pretty tedious. Fortunately, Faustus knew a guy who knew a guy who wired up surveillance cameras in all the public spaces in the building and tied my television into the network, so after a couple of seconds, a view of the lobby from over Curtis's left shoulder popped up on my screen.

"Oh, for fuck's sake, what does *that* asshole want?" I asked, not really realizing that I was speaking out loud.

"This asshole wants you to get your ass down here before I call in a tactical team to drag you out of that apartment by your ball sack, you arrogant prick," Strunin replied, scowling at Curtis, then looking up at the camera and pointing at it. "Now get your ass down here, right now. You're under arrest, Harker. Don't make this harder than it has to be."

I couldn't help it. I knew it wasn't the time, but I couldn't stop my mouth. "That's what she said," I blurted out before I could stop myself. I saw Curtis's shoulders shake in the screen, and Strunin's face turned a shade of purple I'd only ever seen on my barista's hair. "I'll be right down, Strunin. Just give me a minute to disarm. I don't trust you bastards to handle my weapons."

I was already disarmed, at least mostly. I don't just lounge around my apartment with my guns hanging off my belt. I've got decent security, and I figure anything that can get into my home is probably not going to be too concerned about a 9mm round. I dropped my wallet on the table, along with my pocketknife and the pair of silver-edged daggers that I *did* still have around my waist, then gave myself a pat down to make sure I wasn't forgetting anything.

Then I opened a channel to Becks, widening the ever-present connection between us. *I'm heading to the police station. Apparently I'm under arrest. I'll hit you back when I know more.*

Should I be concerned? She didn't "sound" concerned, but there was a hint of worry in her thoughts.

I don't think so, I replied. *I don't think they're interested in the level of property damage it would take to actually put me down, so the worst case is I have to get Pravesh to come flash her badge and bail me out.*

Again.

Yeah, again. Hopefully I can talk some sense into Chief Putnam. I know that won't happen with Strunin. That dude's a prick.

Be careful. I've done some digging into his background, and Strunin is not accustomed to losing. He doesn't take being shown up well at all, and that's exactly what you did at the park. If he gets the slightest chance, he's going to fuck with you.

Well, if he does, he'll learn first-hand how hard I can fuck him right back, I said. *Wait, that...oh, never mind, you know what I meant.*

The mental chuckle Becks gave me was worth stumbling over my thoughts a little. *Keep me posted.*

Will do, I replied. *Love you.*

Love you, too. She shut down the connection on her end, and I headed out to the elevator. I knocked on Luke's door as I passed it.

Cassie answered. "He's sleeping, Quincy."

"I figured. Just let him know I'm on my way to the police station to be arrested. If I'm not back when he wakes up, that's probably where I am. Becks knows what's up, if I need a jailbreak, she'll call in the troops."

"Again, Quincy?" Cassie asked, a wry smile tweaking up one corner of her lips. "I swear, child, you spend more time in the pokey than the bad guys do nowadays."

"Payback for my misspent youth, I guess. I'll probably be home before dark, but if not, that's what's up."

"I'll tell him," she said. "Now give me two twenties."

"What for?" I asked, reaching for my wallet. Then I remembered I didn't have it with me and shrugged.

"You going to see the police, I know you're gonna be using f-bombs like commas. Might as well get the money from you now before you have to spend it all on bail."

I laughed. "My wallet's on the coffee table. You've got a key. Help

163

yourself." Cassie had a master key to every apartment on our floor, since she was working as Luke's Renfield. Just made life easier if she could get into any room and grab weapons or hide evidence as need be.

"You know I will," she replied. "Now go on back to jail, you reprobate."

I waved as I headed to the elevator, wondering what I was being arrested for this time. I had little doubt that I was guilty of *something*, but the number of times what I was guilty of and what I was arrested for lined up was remarkably small.

I sat in a holding cell, staring at the bars. This was a first for me. Not the first time I'd been in a cell. I don't think it was even the first time I'd been in *this* cell. But it was the first time there had been no interrogation, no discussion of charges, not even an accusation. The second I stepped off the elevator, I was tackled, handcuffed, and tossed into the back of a blue-and-white Ford Escape with a light bar on the top and a cage between me and the very nervous officer driving. He either had no idea why I was being treated like the second coming of Hannibal Lecter or he was terrified that I was going to eat his liver with a nice Chianti, because he didn't say a word in response to any of my questions.

We pulled into the parking garage for the police station, and Strunin watched as four officers in tactical gear wrestled me out of the back of the SUV. At least, I assume that was their plan, anyway. What really happened was that I saw them walking up to the door, used a little magic to jimmy the cuffs and the door, and slid out under my own power. I handed the cuffs to the nearest riot cop and started walking toward Strunin.

That didn't go over well, to say the least. I was tackled again, and handcuffed again, this time with a knee to the side of the head for good measure. Then my ankles were shackled together with a longer chain and I was perp-walked onto the elevator leading into the station. They marched me through the squad room, where I got friendly nods from a couple of the detectives and "goddammit, not again" looks from about twice that many others. But instead of taking a right turn into one of the "interview" rooms, they hauled me straight into the holding cells. They took off the leg irons and moved my hands around to the front before re-cuffing me, then slammed the door and left me to my own devices.

I'm not exactly sure the point in them cuffing me again after I had gotten out of them in the car on the way over here, but maybe they just wanted me to tire myself out escaping or something. Being an obliging sort, I spiked the locks with a little magic and tossed the cuffs in the toilet. Then I leaned back on the bunk, hands behind my head, and whistled a few bars of a bluesy tune. I wished for a harmonica, but I don't know how to play one, so it didn't really matter. I lay there for about half an hour, then fell asleep.

I woke up to the sound of the cell door opening, and I swung to put my feet on the floor as three officers in riot gear came into the cell. "Okay, stop," I said, standing up. I was instantly awake, and getting pissed. Whatever game Strunin was playing, it was time for it to end. Right fucking now.

The three men froze. One let his hand drift down to the nightstick on his belt, and I waggled a finger at him. "Don't do anything stupid, son. I don't want to hurt you, but I'm tired of whatever bullshit Strunin and Putnam are playing at, and we're not doing anymore handcuffs, or leg irons, or any of that crap. We're going to at least pretend to all be friends and act like there's some fucking professional courtesy here, and you're going to acknowledge that I'm a federal agent and treat me like a member of law enforcement. Are we clear?"

"Fuck you," the nearest one said, reaching for my arm. I grabbed his wrist and pulled him forward, yanking him in front of me and putting my other hand on the small of his back. I gave him a shove, and he stumbled into the second officer, slamming him into the bars of the tiny cell.

I took one step forward and raised a glowing fist to the third cop.

"Is it worth it?" I asked, giving him my very best Clint Eastwood squint.

"Nope," he said, and stepped aside. "They're in Chief Putnam's office. The County DA is in there with them. You should call a lawyer before you get in there."

"You guys took my phone," I said.

"That might be a problem."

And he was right. It would be, if I had to count on that to communicate. I didn't. *Becks?*

Yeah?

I'm at police headquarters, about to go into a meeting with Strunin, Putnam, and a DA. I think I probably need a lawyer, and maybe Pravesh.

I'll bring her. Don't say anything until we get there.

Got it. See you soon.

I closed down our connection and shut the holding cell door on the two cops who were now untangled from each other and looking really pissy at me. Then I walked down the hall to Chief Putnam's office, not even breaking stride as his secretary stood up and stammered something about meetings and not going in there. I don't know, I wasn't listening.

I walked in and Chief Putnam, Strunin, and a weaselly little guy with a spectacular widow's peak and beady brown eyes were seated all on one side of the long conference table that took up one half of Putnam's office. I mean, this dude had the kind of hair that Lugosi would cream over. It was jet black and tapered down to a point sharp enough to stab somebody with. Thin lips and lug ears completed the unattractive picture, and judging by the off-the-rack suit and the grumpy expression, I assumed this was the DA.

"I heard you guys were looking for me," I said. I pulled out a chair and took the seat directly opposite Putnam. I didn't dignify Strunin or Baby Bela with so much as a glance. "What can I do for you, Chief?"

Putnam leaned forward and leaned his forearms on the table, clasping his hands together in a show of mock concern. "Mr. Harker, you are under arrest for the murder of Judith Fleming, also known as Pastor Judy. We have multiple eyewitnesses placing you at the scene, and a weapon with your fingerprints was found near the body. I hope you didn't have plans for the evening because you'll be spending tonight, and many more nights in the future, as a guest of Mecklenburg County and the State of North Carolina."

Huh. Didn't see that one coming.

27

After half an hour of questions thrown at me by the DA, chief of police, and a very smug Major Strunin, all of which were met with the same one-word response, "lawyer," they processed me and moved me into a different set of cells down the street from police headquarters in the county jail. I got the luxury accommodations, a private room with attached bath, and a lovely orange change of clothes. I was informed by the kind and caring three-hundred-fifty-pound sheriff's deputy that I'd be there until I was arraigned, which might take a few days.

I didn't plan on being there that long. If Pravesh couldn't get me out with her badge, and Faustus couldn't whip up some kind of magical portal or Gate or some other random method of egress, I'd blast my way out through the guards and hope not to break too many of them. Most of them were just doing their job and didn't deserve to have to deal with the kind of hell I could unleash on a room.

That couldn't be said for Fatso McFatass, the deputy who shoved me into my cell. He did his level best to trip me as he shoved me into the cell, no doubt hoping for me to land face-first on the concrete floor with my hands still cuffed behind my back. There were only two problems with that plan: I wasn't cuffed anymore, since I magicked the locks within ten seconds of them going on my wrists, and I knew what was coming so I hopped over his foot. I turned around as I stepped nimbly into the cell and pitched the cuffs to him underhand.

"Here you go, dickhead," I said. "Don't bother coming in after them. You won't like what greets you."

"Is that a threat, inmate?" he growled, stepping forward. He had close to two hundred pounds on me, but he was a couple inches shorter, with short-cropped brown hair going gray at the temples and permanent scowl lines etched into his forehead deep enough to plant corn in. His hands balled into fists at his side, and I could tell this was the point at which I was supposed to either cower in fear or bow up at him so he could beat my ass.

I've long been in the habit of disappointing assholes, so I just leaned against the wall of my cell and smiled at him. "Nah, that's a promise, tubby. Now why don't you get your fat ass out of here and find somebody you can intimidate? I think there's a daycare over in the Government Center. Probably a preschooler there you can scare the shit out of."

He took one more step, reaching for his nightstick, and I called up a ball of fire to float above the upturned palm of my right hand. "This is not the fight you trained for, Butterbean. Now I'm in here for a murder I didn't commit, but that's not to say I don't have a fucking trail of bodies lying in my wake from Cambodia to Kansas. So if you don't want to be the latest on my list of regrets, you'll salvage what little dignity you think you still have and get the fuck out of here."

If he'd been allowed to carry his sidearm into the jail, I probably would have gotten a new bullet hole for that, but I wasn't too worried about one middle-aged deputy who hadn't seen his dick without a mirror in twenty years doing any harm to me with a nightstick. He stood there glaring at me for a few more seconds, his nostrils flaring with every breath, until he finally decided that discretion was the better part of not dying and slammed the cell door. I heard his keys jangling with every angry step as he stalked out of the cells and back to safety.

That might not have been the smartest thing you've ever done, Harker,

Flynn said in my head. I'd opened up the conduit to her as soon as I heard the bullshit I was being accused of, and she'd been able to see everything I saw since.

The list of stupid shit I've done would fill an encyclopedia, I replied. *Any luck getting me out of here?*

Pravesh is working on it, but she can't find a judge that even admits to knowing you're in there, much less willing to do anything about it. Putnam seems to be working with the sheriff to put you under the jail and keep you there.

Yippee, I thought. *The one time I'm actually* working *for the feds, and I end up renditioned to Redneck Gitmo in the middle of my hometown. Tell her to get Jack working on the legal end while she works on the political side of things.*

Way ahead of you, Becks said. *He's already filed a writ of habeas corpus ad something or another to force the city to produce you for prosecution, whatever that means.*

It doesn't mean shit unless he filed another one with the county, I replied. *Part of the crap Charlotte can get away with since the police department is the city, and the sheriff's department is the county, regardless of them using the same jail. If they transferred me to the sheriff's custody, they don't have me to produce me. And it's ad prosequendum, by the way.*

Showoff.

Nah, just old. I learned Latin before it was a dead language, remember? Don't worry about me, I said, feeling the trickle of concern along our mental link. *Worst case, I'll just blast my way out through the walls of the building.*

You can do that?

Probably not, but I can fuck with the locks and just walk out that way, I thought. *Admit it, though. You got a really good visual image of me standing in a circle of rubble looking like a younger Magneto or something.*

It was kinda hot, I'll give you that. Now let me get Jack working on the county angle. Keep your head down and try not to get killed before we can get you out of there.

Will do. Love you.

Love you, too. She closed our connection down to a trickle, just enough for us to feel each other's presence, and I lay down on the metal bunk, wishing again for that harmonica.

It made for a long afternoon and a longer night, made not the least bit better by the spectacularly shitty dinner of lump of gray meat, lump of beige potato-ish things, smear of orange things that might have originated somewhere near a carrot, and a metal cup of water. Everything tasted exactly the same, which is to say like cardboard, and probably had about the same nutritional value. I thought about asking the guard to spit in my breakfast, just to give it a little texture, but I was scared of what he would actually put in there instead.

I spent about six hours all told lying on my bunk staring at the ceiling, trying to figure out the main problems in my immediate life. First, who killed Pastor Judy, and how did they manage to frame me for it? That's ignoring the fact that I was literally standing in front of Strunin when she was killed, something he seemed more than willing to overlook. Given my abilities, and the fact that magic was involved, I couldn't blame him. I can't actually be in two places at once, but he had no way to really know that. If I didn't want the local police thinking I killed someone that I actually *didn't*, I was gonna need to solve that case.

Then there was the Shaw problem. Where was she? *Who* was she, really? What was her beef with me, or was it a beef with anyone and anything that had supernatural abilities? What was her endgame? Was she trying to destroy all supernaturals on the planet? Because that was going to be a tall order. There had been magical creatures since long before there was human civilization, and with the way humans behaved most days, it wouldn't surprise me if they outlasted us. No, it felt like there was someone else pulling her strings, like there was something else going on, and I needed to find her to figure out what it was.

While all that was dominating the foreground of my mind, running along in the back was a question of Glory's divinity, and how we were going to get it back. We literally went to Hell to get her wings back, and I thought once we fixed that problem, that we were good. But apparently not. According to Michael, the Douchebaggiest

Archangel, wings alone didn't make one divine. Which made sense, when I thought about it, since Lucifer got to keep his, and the Morningstar was almost as far from divine as me. If Michael was right, we were going to have to appeal to The Big Guy himself to get Glory resanctified, and He'd been pretty notorious for ignoring prayers for the past few millennia. Unless they came from Sister Lucia, who was busy dying in New York City while I rotted in a jail cell in North Carolina. If I got really lucky, she and I would have one more conversation before she got to take her final rest. But this wasn't the year for lucky, it seemed.

There was a lot to think about, so I could almost be excused for not noticing the deputies until they were right outside my cell, but not quite. I was deep in what I had to consider hostile territory, and there was absolutely no excuse for letting them get close without me knowing it. I got sloppy, and it was only the rattle of keys right outside the door that snapped me out of my reverie and brought me back to the moment.

A moment that saw three burly men and one woman with a snarl chiseled into her face crowded around the door to my cell. One of the men stepped inside and held out a set of cuffs and leg irons with a long chain connecting them. "Put these on," he said.

"Why bother?" I asked. "We all know I'm just going to magic them off the second they become uncomfortable, so why not just spare everyone the energy of getting annoyed and looking surprised, and I just go with you wherever you want me to go?" I was sitting up on the bunk now but hadn't moved to stand. No point in getting too close unless I actually had to kick this guy's ass.

The deputy sighed. "I know." That surprised me. I hadn't encountered the reasonable approach on this trip through the Charlotte City and Mecklenburg County law enforcement systems, so his tired sigh and the sag of his shoulders took me aback for a second. "Look, we drew the short straws to get this assignment, so can you just put the shackles on and not fuck with us? Please?"

I was stunned. "What do you mean, short straws?" I asked, trying to buy myself a few extra seconds to think.

"We're all in the shit with Sheriff Gates," the female deputy said. "We've all screwed up one thing or another over the past few days or weeks, and that's why us four got the job of hauling you out to be released. And no, I'm not supposed to tell you you're being released. He wants us to piss you off so you beat our asses and we get our punishment without him having to actually do the punishing, that way we can't go to our union reps or the county HR about him and file a sexual harassment complaint."

"Or call him out on being a homophobic jackoff," said one deputy, a thickly built Asian man with arms the size of my thighs. If I were one to make homophobic remarks, that would not be the dude I would make them to.

"I'm getting out?" I asked, latching onto that piece of the conversation, since I understood it. The rest of it, including the fact that there might be some cracks in the fabled blue wall, I'd need to process later.

"Yeah, that Indian lady from Homeland Security and the hot detective have been raising hell at the sheriff for the last two hours." This from the deputy holding the chains. I glared at him, but said nothing, but the female deputy slapped him upside the back of his head.

"That's his fiancée, dipshit. Don't talk about her being hot. He'll turn you into a frog or something," she said.

I actually chuckled at that. "I can't really do that. I could burn you alive from the inside out, but I can't turn you into a frog. Give me the chains." I held out a hand.

"Really?" the deputy asked, passing the restraints over to me.

"Really," I replied. "You weren't assholes, so I don't need to treat you like assholes. And you're right, my fiancée is hot." I clicked the cuffs loosely around my ankles and wrists, then stood up. "Let's go, kids. You don't want to see the kind of tongue-lashing Director Pravesh can dish out if she gets really wound up."

I didn't mention that said tongue was forked and had six-inch fangs on either side of it. Let them keep a little mystery in their world. I walked out into the corridor in the middle of a cluster of nervous deputies to go get sprung by my federal agent fiancée and her boss.

S o...that sucked," I said, popping the top on a bottle of beer. It was nice to be home and freshly showered after my sojourn to the city's jailhouse accommodations, but I needed to focus on our plans moving forward. We had to get everyone in one room and get our shit together, or Shaw was going to slip right through our hands while we were distracted by my trumped-up murder charges.

"Your stay in the pokey wasn't enjoyable, Harker? Can't imagine." Jack sat in a chair turned around from the conference table, sipping a glass of my best Scotch. I swear, that dude was an expensive guest.

"The food was pretty awful, but the mattress was great for my back. Oh wait," I corrected, "there wasn't a mattress. So no, I didn't like it. Ten out of ten, would not recommend. Zero stars."

"Now what?" Jo asked. She was on the couch opposite me with Pravesh. Luke stood by the windows looking out at the city. He seemed pensive tonight, like something was bothering him deeply. I didn't want to bring it up with everyone else in the room but resolved to dig deeper when we were more private.

"Now we prove Harker didn't kill Pastor Judy," Flynn replied from her seat next to me.

"You cannot prove a negative, Rebecca," Pravesh said. "And if the police are not willing to accept the eyes of their very own commanding officer, who was speaking to Harker when the murder occurred, it is unlikely that anything outside of a confession from the truly guilty party will suffice."

"Now we need to find the real killer." Faustus leaned forward in his chair and rubbed his palms together. "This is awesome! I've always wanted to be the detective on one of those cop shows. I've seen every episode of *NCIS* three times. I'm ready for this."

"Calm down there, Speed Racer," I said to the demon. "We've got more issues than just my murder investigation. That didn't come out right. Whatever, you know what I mean. We've also got to get Jack in deeper with this Resistance bunch and try to track down Shaw. We're going to have to divide our efforts."

"I will work with Rebecca on the murder investigation. We will have access that none of the rest of you will have, given our status as federal agents." Pravesh looked over at Glory. "Would you like to accompany us? Your ability to take on different forms may prove useful if we have to go unnoticed among people who would recognize us."

"Yeah, I can do that," Glory said. "You good with that, Harker? You won't have me or Becks for backup."

"I think Luke and I can manage. We'll take the search for Shaw, since we're the least squishy of the group, and we have a vested interest in finding that evil bitch."

"As much as I typically dislike using derogatory terms for women, I have to say that Director Shaw certainly qualifies. Although, I have known many dogs who would take umbrage at the comparison," Luke said without turning around. "It will be good to work side by side again, Quincy. It has been a while since it was just the pair of us."

"Won't be just the pair of y'all," Cassie chimed in. "I'll be right back here running things from the command center, and if y'all 'lose' the earwigs I give you, it'll be your asses."

"Don't mess with her, fellas. When she uses that tone, she will one hundred percent whoop an ass," Jo said with a chuckle. "I guess that leaves me running tech for Faustus and Jack while they try to infiltrate this Resistance bunch."

"Capital," Jack said, clapping his hands together. "They have already contacted me about a planning session tonight. It seems that, despite being a touch overenthusiastic, your punch served to supply me with the appropriate street cred."

"That was totally the idea," I said, ignoring the fact that I also really, *really* wanted to punch Jack in the face, so I took the shot when I saw it. He'd never done anything really to hurt me, just left me in the lurch and stuck me with the bar bill more than once, but he just had one of those faces that seemed like it would be improved by the addition of a fist.

"Then we have a plan," Pravesh said. "I suggest we all get some rest, as tomorrow looks to be a busy day."

"Rest?" I looked around the room at the faces of my team, who seemed like the exact opposite of ready to turn in and get some rest. "Pravesh, you've been with us a while now. Haven't you gotten the picture yet that we're usually *starting* our workday when the sun goes down?"

"What do you propose we do?" the DHS Director asked.

"I plan to hunt," Luke replied. "It has been a few nights since I fed, and I expended a significant amount of energy a few evenings back. If you need me...don't." I learned a long time ago not to interrupt Luke when he was hunting, and *definitely* don't bother the man while he's feeding. I'd rather get between a pit bull and a T-bone than try to stop Luke when he's got his fangs out. Just thinking about it brought back bad memories of a Belgian alley, two muggers, and enough arterial spray to make Jack the Ripper nauseous.

"I'm going out, too," Faustus said. "I'm looking for a different kind of action, if you get my drift." Nobody responded to the demon's double entendre, because honestly we were just used to it. Faustus was a player, and players gonna play. "Wanna be my wingman, Watson? That's like your family tradition, right? Sidekick?"

Jack's ears went crimson at Faustus's dig, but he managed to keep his tone light. "No, I think I shall retire early and read. According to my invitation, there is to be a rally of the New Faerie Movement tomorrow night at midnight, and I will likely need all my energy for that. I am afraid you are on your own in your carnal pursuits this evening."

"Your loss, pal," Faustus said, flashing way more teeth than was natural. "My castoffs are usually pretty high quality."

"You're a pig," Jo grumbled at him.

"Demon, Joanna. De-mon. They don't let us be choirboys, and there's a reason for that."

"Yeah," I said. "You pee in the baptismal font and drink all the communion wine."

"One time!" Faustus protested. "One time! And just for that, I'm never allowed back in Vatican City."

"Because the fact that you're a demon has nothing to do with the Church's dislike for you," I said.

"Profiling," Faustus replied. "Speciesist profiling. I'm going to go do my part for interspecies relations. If all goes well, I might do that part two or three times tonight." With that, Faustus stood up, waved a hand in front of himself, and a snazzy gray suit seemed to blur into being along his body. When his appearance settled in, he looked like a mid-thirties Latino with a ridiculous clothes budget, thousand-dollar shoes, and hair that would make Ricky Martin swoon. He dazzled the room with a grin that dimpled his chin and left us with a little wave.

"It's a good thing he's on our side," Jo said. "Because that is a dangerously pretty man when he wants to be."

"More emphasis on the dangerous and less on the pretty," Glory said. "Remember who and what he is. If he's on our side, it's only because our goals align with his for the time being. Faustus is nothing if not self-serving, and we would all be well-served to remember that. Come on, Jo, we're going out. There's a songwriter playing at the Evening Muse that I want to see, and it shouldn't be too crowded."

"Okay, but only if we stop by Cabo Fish Taco for margaritas first," Jo replied, standing up.

"Deal. Let's get changed. Harker, give me your keys." Glory walked up to me and held out her hand.

"Why are you taking my car?"

"Because you're not going anywhere tonight, and NoDa is too far to walk."

"What if I want to go get something for dinner?"

"Your favorite sushi place is literally in the ground floor of this building, and there are ten places to eat within three blocks of here. Now quit being a pain in my ass and give me the keys."

She was right. I was mostly arguing out of principle, because I'd been in jail and was in a pissy mood, so I decided to put on my big boy pants and handed over my keys. If I wanted something more than we could make from whatever was in the kitchen, sushi sounded like a great option.

"Have fun," I said, affecting a "dad" voice. "Be home by eleven and don't pick up any strange boys."

"Finding anyone stranger than this bunch will be a challenge," Glory replied. "Come on, Jo. Let's see what you've got in the way of cute shoes."

Glory dragged Jo out by her wrist, and the last I saw of them was Jo mouthing "save me" as she was pulled out for an angelic fashion show. I just laughed. Glory might have been around for thousands of years, but her drive to play dress up was as strong as if she really was the twenty-something she appeared to be.

"Sushi sounds like a lovely idea," Pravesh said, standing. "Dr. Watson, would you care to join me?"

"Don't mind if I do," Jack said. The pair left, and Becks and I were left alone with Cassie and Luke.

"You want to stay for dinner, Cass?" I asked. "Since Luke's getting takeout tonight, I could probably manage to burn some steaks on the grill upstairs." Access to the roof patio was included for everyone who lived in the building, but the grill was locked up, and I had the only key.

"I'm gonna pass, Quincy. I've got some work to catch up on while Lucas is out tonight, then I'll need to set up our command center for tomorrow night. I've got a couple of receivers for the comm systems, and two or three separate routers so all y'all can message one another fast enough. That stuff ain't as easy as what me and Alex used to do when we was hunting back in the day."

I was consistently amazed at Cassandra Harrison. Not only was she serving as Luke's Renfield, a sizable job on its own, but she also took over a lot of the Shadow Council's tech support work when Dennis got all holy on us. She was sixty-five, but she wrapped her head around the networking at the speed of a woman half her age, and within a week of her taking over as Luke's right hand person and daytime operative, she was integral to every facet of our lives. She was tech support, administrative assistant, bookkeeper, sounding board, and therapist, all while helping Jo raise her daughter, Ginny. She was a remarkable woman, and she was madly in love with my uncle Luke.

Since I don't live in a young adult romance novel, she and Luke never spoke about their feelings for one another. It was the worst-kept secret in the building, but they both had too much respect for her dead husband and for Ilona, Luke's wife and the true love of his life, to ever act on it. Becks and I shared a look as Cassie stood and left the room.

I waited until I heard the door *click*, then I focused my attention on the vampire by the window. "What's up, Luke?" He didn't stay behind by accident. There was something he wanted to say, and he wanted to say it in extremely limited company. I suspect he would have been more comfortable if Becks wasn't in the room, but he knew that there was no keeping anything from her, so she might as well hear it firsthand.

"I believe there is a traitor in our midst," he said, turning to me. There was an anger in his eyes that I hadn't seen in decades, maybe not ever. "Someone set you up, Quincy. Someone is framing you for murder, and I have a sneaking suspicion that they were in this room just now. During your entire recounting of your arrest and incarceration, there were two elevated heart rates among our compatriots. Both Director Pravesh and Dr. Watson seemed agitated by your tale, for no good reason I could ascertain."

"And don't forget Faustus," Becks said. "He is a demon, after all. Betrayal is his stock and trade."

I mulled that over. "Faustus is a reasonable suspect," I said. "He could kill me and send me to Hell to get back in Lucifer's good graces, or he could disgrace me, *then* kill me for an even bigger status boost downstairs. Watson doesn't make any sense. What does he get out of it? He hurts me, he hurts the Council, and that hurts him. He hasn't practiced medicine since he came back from Afghanistan, and his law office is pretty much shut down, from all I can tell. This is his only way to make a living, and I can't imagine there's enough money in selling me out to set him up for life."

"Don't sell yourself short," Becks said. "There are a lot of people who hate you, and some of them are pretty powerful."

"Including at least one highly positioned government official," Luke added.

"At least one," I agreed. "Which brings us to Pravesh. She's the new player in our game, and the one we know the least about. Could be she's tied in with Shaw and this is some joint DEMON-Homeland Screw Harker mission, or maybe she sees taking me down as a steppingstone to go from regional director to the big Kahuna."

"Could be," Becks said. "We should keep an eye on her."

"We must pay close attention to the actions of all of our friends," Luke said. "Someone is working at cross-purposes with us, and until we determine who it is, we cannot fully trust anyone except those in this room."

"Keep your friends close, and your enemies closer, huh, Uncle?" I asked with a wry grin.

"And if you aren't sure which is which, keep those people closest of all," he replied. "Now I shall be off. I hunger, and the night beckons."

With that melodramatic pronouncement, he was gone. Sometimes I wasn't sure which came first, Lugosi's over the top Dracula, or Dracula's over the top Dracula. I turned to my fiancée. "Want some sushi for dinner?"

She stood up and held out her hand. I let her pull me off the couch, and she began to lead me to the bedroom. "Dinner's going to be a little late tonight, Harker."

2 9

B een a long time since we flew solo like this, Luke," I said as we got out of his car the next night. The air was typical North Carolina summer, feeling like someone slapped you in the face with a warm wet towel the second you stepped out of the air conditioning. It took me all of three seconds to feel wrinkled and sweaty, but Luke looked fresh as a daisy, of course. A dead daisy, but one with all its petals intact. He told me once that sweating was one of the things he missed least about being alive. Given the time in which he was alive, I'm guessing dysentery probably ranked pretty high on that list, too. Frankly, he probably didn't even miss real food that much. He was born in a time without Five Guys, a truly dark piece of human history.

"It has been some time, Quincy. That is why I was pleased to join you in this search for clues to the whereabouts of Director Shaw. I do have to wonder, however, at your choice of location to begin your search. Do you really expect to find any information here?" He waved at the front of The Dive, the shitty little monster bar that I'd turned upside down just two nights before.

"It's more about what people don't say, Uncle," I replied. "And about who bolts for the side exit the second they catch sight of me."

"There is an alternate exit?" Luke asked. "I assume that is where you would like me to station myself?"

"There's one that I saw," I said. "I didn't have time to get a good look around, what with the whole riot and murder thing going on. But yeah, if you can be waiting outside the back door for anyone who takes flight, that would be good. There's probably another way out that I didn't see, but if it was my place, the boltiest of bolt holes would be just for me and my staff, and it would take a lot more than the arrival of one dude I don't like to get me to disclose its existence."

"I will be standing by. If no one has come out the door in ten minutes, I will join you inside." Luke blurred out of view, leaving just a breeze and a little bit of waving grass. Sometimes I forget how inhuman he really is. He looks like a James Bond villain, all expensive suits and cultured accent, but when he stands still and you see the total stillness that a creature who doesn't need to breathe can achieve, it's unsettling, no matter how much time you've spent around him. And then he does something like move at full speed, and you realize that in all the time you've known him, you've probably never seen the full extent of his powers.

That kind of revelation was chilling. I'd gone toe to toe with Luke just a few weeks ago, and that was a starved, brutalized, half-dead version of him. And even with that, he almost killed me. Admittedly, I was beaten and half-starved myself, but the strength, speed, and ferocity on display would have been terrifying if he *hadn't* been trying to rip me to pieces. And at the time he was trying to do exactly that, so it was doubly scary.

But that was then, and this was now. This was me walking back into a bar where the owner shot at me and half the customers tried to kill me the last time I set foot in the place. This was me trying to find information about a rogue government agency hunting down supernaturals in a gathering spot for the people they most wanted to exterminate. In short, this was not one of my best ideas. And of course, that didn't stop me.

I walked up the steps, feeling a board wobble a little as I put my weight on it. The place really did live up to its name, all the way down to the shingle hanging off the front edge of the roof over the door. I pushed my way in, ignoring the human sitting on a stool checking IDs. He took one look at my face and booked it out the way I came in. Smart guy. The odds of this visit being quiet and peaceful weren't zero, but you could see it from there.

The bartender scowled and reached below the pitted wood surface as I walked up. I raised my hands. "I swear, I'm just here to talk."

"Nobody here has anything to say to you, Reaper." She came up with a familiar pump shotgun in her hands.

"What's your beef with me?" I asked, sliding onto a wobbly wooden stool at the suddenly empty bar. "I don't know you, and most of the times I've dealt with the Fae have been at least cordial, if not downright friendly."

"I know you, and you killed a friend of mine a few weeks back at the bandshell. They were just trying to get home, and you killed them."

"Just trying to get home? You mean the *assassin*? They tried to murder everyone in the park! They killed a couple of cops and wanted to cut my freakin' head off!"

"I've just met you, and I want to kill you," she replied, those emerald eyes locked onto mine. "I bet that happens to you all the time."

"I'll admit that wasn't the first time it's happened," I said. "But that's over. We can't do anything about your friend's death except to make sure they didn't die in vain. And the best way to do that is to help me find the psycho that's turned the entire federal government into the frickin' Ghostbusters!"

She lowered the shotgun. Not a lot, but enough that it wasn't aimed directly at my face. Sometimes you gotta take the baby steps, and this was one of those times. After a moment's thought, she laid the gun down on the bar and reached over the liquor shelves to ring a small brass bell. The room fell silent at the sound, and all the beings that had been working hard to look like they weren't watching me dropped the pretense and stared right at me.

"Quincy Harker is protected by the rights of Sanctuary tonight, and tonight only. Until sunrise, he may move freely about this establishment unmolested. Any who threatens harm upon him shall face immediate expulsion from the premises and may face further consequences." She focused her attention back to me. "You've got one night. After that, if I see you in here again, I'm not going to listen to your bullshit, I'm just going to shoot you in the face and move on."

I cocked my head to the side and looked at her. She was pretty, with gorgeous tattoos. There must have been magic in getting the ink to stay in her skin, or maybe they were glamours. Either way, the sleeves and blue hair made for a striking visual, enhanced quite a bit by the low-cut tank top she sported. It was a calculated image, one that would make most people forget the fact that looks aside, she was a completely alien creature and placed absolutely no value on human life. I'm not most people, so I knew that if she thought she could have killed me and gotten away with it, I'd be dead. But she didn't, so I was safe. For one night, at least.

Her putting me under the Sanctuary protection didn't mean the rest of the beings in the bar would speak to me, so I switched over to my tried and true method of making friends—buying them booze. There was a pair of burly men at the bar who were either lumberjacks, or lycanthropes, or both, so I asked the bartender to pour me two of whatever they were drinking, and I carried a pair of pint glasses down to the stool nearest them.

"Fuck off, Reaper," the older of the two said as I set the glasses on the bar. He was a thick, round-shouldered man who looked to be in his mid-forties, with a massive Chris Stapleton beard and a ponytail running down between his shoulder blades. He wore a red and black flannel shirt despite the nearly hundred-degree weather, but if the rest of him was as hairy as his arms, it didn't matter because he carried a sweater with him everywhere, even when he was naked.

He reached out with a massive hand and wrapped thick, scarred fingers around the glass, making it look like he was drinking out of a child's tea set. After a long drought that sucked down about half the beer in one gulp, he leaned back on his stool, looked at the ceiling, and made a deep *hurkkkkkk* sound in the back of his throat. Then he leaned forward and spat a massive loogie into the remainder of his beer and slid the glass back over to me.

"I said fuck off." He didn't look at me, but I saw the corner of his mouth twitch as he worked to hold back a grin. I picked up the other beer and walked around to the other guy. He was smaller, with a narrow face and flaming red hair that screamed "were-fox" louder than a megaphone. He reached out to the glass with his narrow fingers, and I held it just a hair out of reach.

"You're not going to have a wank in it, are you? There are things in this world I don't need to watch, and that's coming from a guy who's been to Hell, literally."

He extended a middle finger on one hand to me while reaching for the beer with the other, then sucked down about half of it in a long pull. He didn't hawk up anything into the glass; he just turned it upside down very slowly and poured half a pint of beer out onto my Doc Martens, looking me straight in the eye as he did.

I just let it happen. I've had wet feet before, and those boots had certainly been covered in worse substances. I didn't break eye contact, didn't even put on a glare, just kept my mildest look plastered across my face and asked, "Are you done?"

He reached for the other glass, and I held up a hand. "Nope. No phlegm on the shoes. I've got to have some rules."

"Fine," Foxy said. "Now will you fuck off?"

"No," I replied. "Now I'm gonna ask if you know anything about the crazy chick who runs the crew from DEMON that locked up a bunch of cryptids and supernaturals on the other side of town. I've got a few questions I need to ask her."

"Lemme think about it," he said, looking to the ceiling. About half a second later, he turned his eyes back to me and said, "Nope. Don't know her. Fuck off."

"Okay," I said, turning to go. "But when there are government agents knocking on the front door of your den with tranquilizer guns and scalpels, wanting to chop off pieces of you just to see if they'll really grow back, remember that you could have helped me stop them and didn't." I raised my voice to make sure the last words carried to the rest of the room, then moseyed over to the jukebox.

It was an old-school Wurlitzer, with actual records, that played as many songs as you had quarters, all chosen from the catalog of Johnny Cash, Willie Nelson, AC/DC, Journey, and Creedence Clearwater Revival. I looked for the Wilson Picket classic "Monster Mash," but had no luck. Probably for the best. That one might have pushed the limits of my Sanctuary protections a little too far.

30

The next hour went pretty much the same—somebody would wave me over, I'd buy them a drink, they'd drink some of it and do something insulting with the rest. The best was a fire elemental who wanted a shot of sambuca, swished it around in her mouth, then breathed it out at me in a gout of flame. I had to give her points for originality on that one. But it got me no closer to finding Shaw or learning anything about DEMON and their plans for the cryptic community or me.

I was heading over to a pair of hobgoblins in a dark corner— which, trust me, is where you want your hobgoblins, somewhere with as little light as possible—when a hush fell over the room. I thought I'd finally pushed the monsters in the room to the breaking point and we were going to throw down, but then I followed the gaze of the hobgoblins. Their attention wasn't on me. I might not have even existed for all they gave a shit in that moment. No, they were focused entirely on someone way more interesting, more famous, and more lethal than me.

Luke stood inside the front door, looking over the room like a king surveying his domain. Which he was, in a way. It had been a long time, and I'd largely forgotten the reaction Luke garnered from supernaturals and cryptids who met him for the first time. It's an odd mix of how you'd expect someone to look when they met the Pope, Mick Jagger, and Ted Bundy all at the same time. There's a solid undercurrent of worship and awe, wrapped in a big layer of adulation tinged with a heavy coating of lust, topped off with a sprinkle of wariness and a dash of abject terror. That's what it's like when you're in a monster bar and Count Fucking Dracula walks into the room.

He glided over to the bar, his long coat billowing out behind him like a cape. I tried to keep my chuckle muffled, because he wasn't wearing a long coat when I left him outside. It was June in North Carolina, and even after ten at night, it was well over eighty degrees. He'd obviously run home to get a coat and change clothes when he decided I wasn't getting the job done.

It worked, too. He looked sharp as hell in black dress pants with a pleat you could shave with, a black silk shirt with just enough drape to billow when he walked, a long coat with a tail that didn't quite drag the ground but was pleated with enough extra fabric to make you think about a cape without actually *being* a cape, and a pair of black Berluti shoes with buckles that made you think "old Europe" without having the uncomfortable fit of old European clothing. His dark hair was combed straight back from his forehead instead of his typical loose part, and I would bet a round of drinks for the entire bar that he'd actually powdered himself to look a little paler. Like a man who hadn't seen the sun since the printing press was considered new technology needed help in that department.

The bar was stone silent. You couldn't have just heard a pin drop, you could have heard a feather fall. Every were, vampire, faerie, and monster in the place stared at Luke with eyes (and more than a few mouths) wide open. He took a solid ten seconds after he reached the bar to survey his kingdom, making sure he'd sufficiently wowed the rabble, then leaned in and spoke to the bartender.

"I would like a drink, my dear," he said, his voice as much a purr as speech. "Your finest bourbon, if possible. And might I say that your hair is *exquisite*. It truly sets off the green of your eyes. Did you craft the glamour yourself?"

The bartender, the same self-assured woman who threatened, then tried, to kill me on my first visit, actually stammered. "Y-y-yes, I did."

"Well done, my dear. That is one of the best I have seen since arriving here in the New World." And just like that, Luke made more headway with the bartender in two minutes than I had in both visits to the place. Admittedly, she wasn't predisposed to try to shoot him, but still, every once in a while I just had to stand back and watch the guy work. It was never about him being able to hypnotize people with his gaze. I mean, he *can* if he has to, but he's just so goddamned charismatic I've never seen him need to use it. He can just look at people with his big dark eyes and his movie-star good looks, lay on a little bit of the Old World charm and let his European accent shine through, and before you know it, people are handing him whatever he wants: information, car keys, wallets, undergarments. You name it, Luke can talk someone out of it. I sometimes wondered if he was more terrifying when he was angry or when he was truly working a room.

Then I'd see him angry and remember. Definitely scarier angry.

He took the glass of Pappy Van Winkle the bartender poured him, turned to the room, and raise his drink to the bar. "Thank you for the kind welcome. I know my nephew is not the easiest person to like," here he tipped his head at me, and I raised my hand, guilty, "but it would mean a great deal to me personally if you would give him any assistance you can in his search for this…Shaw woman. She is not just a threat to humans, or to Quincy. She is a threat to all of us, as has been evidenced by her repeated attempts to capture and incapacitate, or even kill, me."

That got a response. A ripple of righteous anger went through the room, oddly similar to the one that happened whenever I walked in. These beings didn't take kindly *at all* to someone threatening Vampire Jesus. I mean, I didn't like it either, but I didn't act like somebody wiped their ass with the Shroud of Turin over it. But if it helped us find Shaw before she hurt anyone else, Luke could play the Messiah of Monsterdom all he wanted. I looked around the room at a bunch of suddenly kind and welcoming eyes and saw a pale hand from the opposite corner of the bar wave in my direction.

I walked over to a table where a wizened little vampire sat, deep in shadow, a voluminous hoodie pulled down low over their face. I couldn't pick a gender, if they even had one locked in, because their features were so obscured. All I saw was the tip of a long, narrow nose, a pointed chin, and a right hand lying on the table with loose skin puddling over emaciated fingers. I couldn't tell if this was a vampire that hadn't fed in way too long, or if someone turned a starving person and left them to suffer forever in this depleted form.

I pulled out a chair and sat opposite them. "Hi."

"Hello," came a reedy voice. "You are looking for the government agents? The ones who experiment on us?" They leaned forward, and I got a better look at their face. He was male, and gaunt to the point of skeletal. Not, as I thought might be the case initially, the kind of skinny that a human gets and would maintain if turned when almost at the point of starvation, but the kind of wispy, paper-thin emaciation that a vampire gets when it hasn't fed in far too long. His skin looked like old parchment left in the sun for a year, bleached and brittle, and the strands of hair that crept out of his hoodie were lank and lifeless.

"Yes," I replied. "The agents of DEMON. Real assholes. Did you escape one of their facilities? Do you need something? Blood? I bet the bartender has a few pints tucked away. I'd be happy to pay for them." I could barely look at his sunken cheeks, his yellowed eyes, the nostrils caving in like someone with a thousand-dollar-a-day coke habit.

He gave me a shaky smile. "That would be nice, Reaper. I prefer to be positive, if you get the joke." I held up three fingers to the bartender, pointed at the vampire, and called out, "B-pos, please, warmed if you can."

"You got it," she replied without a threat or a snarky word. Apparently I needed to have Luke make all my introductions in the supernatural world. A minute later, she came over with a gigantic mug with a straw sticking out the top and set it in front of the vampire.

"Thanks for getting him to eat," she whispered in my ear. "I was afraid he was going to sit back in this corner and shrivel to dust."

"You know I can hear you, my dear," the desiccated vampire said, his voice a hiss like sand across a hardwood floor.

"I know," the bartender said, shooting him a smile. "I just don't care." She walked back over to the bar where she fell right back into Luke's eyes, completely spellbound.

I watched the vampire suck down blood for a minute straight, color and strength flowing back into his face and hands with every precise little slurp. It took him almost a full minute, but eventually he came up for air and smiled at me. "Much better."

He did look better. Almost alive, and much more human. Now that he wasn't dying of hunger, he pushed back his hoodie to show me a thin face, but no longer emaciated. He had high cheekbones and fine features, with a narrow nose that made him look a little vulpine. I'd say he looked a little Fae if I didn't know he was a vampire. "Thank you," he said, extending a fine-boned hand.

I shook it. "You're welcome. I've been a prisoner of these assholes, too. I know how bad they can be."

"No doubt their treatment of you was even worse, given your… unique…nature."

I almost replied with "you have no idea," but I remembered that he literally didn't have any idea how unique my makeup is, so I just nodded. Most of the supernatural world thinks, as I did for the longest time, that I'm some weird hybrid between vampire and human, created because Luke bit my mother, Mina Murray, and his "wives" bit my father, Jonathan Harker (more than once, among other things, but that was *not* a topic to ever bring up with dear old Dad). The common knowledge is that having vampires snack on both my parents without turning them still changed their DNA somehow, and that trait was passed down to their oldest child.

The truth is…more complicated than that, and involved a little of that, but more of a transfer of a tiny sliver of the demonic essence that turned Luke into the original vampire way back in the day. Somehow through his interaction with my parents, then me, and the nibbling he and his wives did on my parents, Luke passed on a hint of the demon to me, leaving me something not vampire, but a long way from human. We tended to keep my demonic heritage a little close to the vest. Wouldn't do to just have that information widely known, especially since I run around with a guardian angel. Who knows what kind of uncomfortable questions *that* would raise.

But most of vampirekind thinks I'm basically the Lite Beer version of them, without the allergy to sunlight or the dietary restrictions, and with lesser enhancements to my strength, speed, and senses. I let them keep that illusion, especially if I think it might be useful. This was certainly no time to disabuse anyone of that notion, since it seemed that my new friend had information.

"Now, what did you want to tell me?" I asked, leaning forward to make sure I caught every word of whatever he had to tell me. I needn't have worried. I wouldn't have missed the bombshell he dropped on me if he whispered it in the middle of a Pantera concert.

"You cleansed their facility on the north end of the city a few weeks ago, correct?"

"Yeah, we went through that place with a fine-toothed comb. Got a few leads, but they all ran cold. I've got no clue where they bailed to after that."

"So you know nothing about their other location just south of town?"

"Their *what?*"

"That is as I thought," he said, leaning back and steepling his fingers. "The laboratory you searched was their main headquarters in the region, but it is not where I was held. They have another facility, one that was operating as recently as three days ago, when I escaped."

Well, *this* just got interesting.

31

The DEMON facility looked like a tornado had ripped through it, a tornado with a taste for CPUs, file cabinets, and anything that could be used to store testing data. It was another nondescript, single-story building, the kind you'll find scattered through industrial parks all over the country. There was a small office and reception area up front, with an abandoned desk and cables where a computer used to sit. The chair was decent, particularly for a government facility, but there were no personal touches around the reception desk. No family photos, no cute cartoons from a page-a-day calendar, not even a plant, or dirt where a plant might have been. It was as sterile an environment as I'd ever seen outside a clean room or a Level 5 infectious disease facility. Don't ask how I know what that looks like. The answer doesn't involve the *World War Z* movie and will probably result in you losing hold of your lunch.

There was a multi-line phone, a notepad for messages with carbons that I slid into a jacket pocket, and a buzzer to unlock the door. I didn't need that, since I just broke out the floor-to-ceiling plate glass window by the door and walked in. The alarm was either disconnected or silent, because nothing indicated it had been tripped.

I wouldn't have put it past DEMON to not even alarm the place, counting on their goons to be able to defend against any intruders.

To the right was a pair of doors leading into a set of bathrooms, and to the left was a large office with a window looking out into the reception area. The office was completely ransacked, with shelves cleared off in haste, cables sprouting up from a wire hole in the desktop like a strange multi-connected fern, and drawers that had been pulled out and thrown into a haphazard pile in the corner. Luke tapped along one wall while I scouted the rest of the room, then beckoned me over as he pulled a hideous painting of ducks in flight down off the wall.

"That's truly ugly," I said.

"We're not here to critique their nonexistent taste in art, Quincy. We're here to find the safe." He tapped on the wall behind the painting and smiled as the hollow sound turned solid. "See if there's a switch somewhere on the desk," Luke said.

"Oh, there is," I said, holding up both hands. "*Impetu!*" I shouted, channeling pure kinetic energy through myself into the wall. A four-foot circle of drywall and insulation exploded outward from us, scattering dust and sheetrock through the warehouse on the other side of the wall. What remained suspended by wooden framing was a safe, about eighteen inches on a side. Luke gave me an exasperated look as the hidden door slid off the front of the safe and fell to the thin gray carpet.

"Found it," I said, stepping up to the safe. "You want me to open it, too?"

He put a hand in the center of my chest and pushed me back. I stumbled a little. He put some *oomph* into it, I guess to prove a point. Then he pressed one ear to the safe just beside the wheel and began to spin it slowly. Three times to the left, twice to the right, and one final time to the left, and the safe opened with a *thunk* and a squeak of seldom-used hinges.

Luke turned to me and smiled. "My hearing is still pretty good, for an old guy."

"Showoff."

He kept grinning as he looked inside the safe, when his smile faded to nothing. It was empty, just like the rest of the building. Not even a scrap of paper remained.

"Nothing up here," I said. "Let's check the back. But be careful. Last place like this I went into there was a werebear, a couple other lycanthropes, and a psychotic faerie princess who threatened to marry me."

"Threatened?" Luke asked.

"She was scary, dude. Like scarier than the faerie princess I *did* marry, and that's a high bar."

"And how does Detective Flynn feel about your earlier marriage?" Luke asked with a teasing smile.

"There are some things we don't talk about very often. That one's on the list."

"Is the fact that you're nearly a century older than her also on the list?"

"That one's at the tippy-*top* of the list," I replied. "I do *not* spend much of my time reminding my fiancée that we're a lot closer to Bella and Edward than I'm comfortable discussing."

"You would need much more hair product to be Edward, Nephew." Luke walked out of the office and through a door into the warehouse, leaving me staring open-mouthed at his back. Did Count Dracula just make a *Twilight* joke? That shit was weird, even for me. I followed him into the warehouse, my mind still firmly in the "boggled" category.

It didn't get any less surreal when we stepped into what would normally be used as a warehouse. You know the type—rows of pallet racks with materials waiting for shipment, kind of like a home improvement store, but usually without prices everywhere and usually a lot smaller. This place was nothing like that. Nothing at all.

The first thing I observed when we walked in was that the whole area seemed to have been built out, and not just some slapdash walls thrown up, this stuff was done for the long haul. There was a drop ceiling, fluorescent lights, crappy motivational posters on the wall, cheap indoor/outdoor carpet, the whole eight and a half yards. We stood at the end of a long hallway, making me think far too much about the lab across town where we'd found row upon row of cages used to torture cryptids and supernaturals in the name of "science."

To our immediate right was a heavy steel door set into a reinforced frame. There was a small sign on the wall by the door that said "Armory," and the door was slightly ajar. I pushed it open, and it was empty, but obviously a military-grade weapons storage. There were racks for rifles, pegs for pistols, space on the floor with dust outlines in the shape of munitions crates, and massive rolling toolboxes with drawers labeled "9mm," "7.62," "5.56," and ".50" with various sets of letters after them, probably indicating silver, iron, or some other type of ammunition. Each of the half dozen toolboxes had a pad on top with a cleaning station set up, including rags, gun oil, and brushes.

I opened a few drawers and a couple of loose rounds rolled forward. A quick sniff of the tip of the bullets told me that my guesses were right—these were not typical lead rounds. The first one I smelled was loaded with white phosphorus, and I recognized the colloidal silver in the wax tip of the next. "These are vamp-killers," I said, holding it up to Luke's gaze.

"No, Quincy," he said, tossing a bullet in my direction. "Those are more flexible. *This* is a vampire-slaying bullet." I gave it a close look and let out a low whistle. The bullet was a type I'd seen before, a wooden-tipped frangible round, dipped in holy water. It was designed to impact a vampire's flesh and split into half a dozen shards of blessed wood, which would carve nasty furrows into the body and kill or incapacitate the vampire.

"That's nasty," I said. "Be better if it were made of silver, though."

"True. Wood through the heart is effective, but so is silver, and it is much easier to penetrate flesh with silver than oak," Luke said. "And of course, the fact that the wood is blessed is irrelevant. The best thing Stoker ever did for me was to promulgate the myth that religious symbols are anathema to our kind."

"I guess we'll take any advantage we can get, and mistakes by our enemies certainly count," I said. "These guys were certainly well-armed. Something tells me there's more backing them than just the DEMON budget."

"I agree. DEMON is a national organization. If they had multiple facilities this well-equipped all across the country, there is no way they could hide that kind of funding in a government budget. They must have a private funding source," Luke agreed. "But who?"

"This is going to sound paranoid," I started, then stopped. Luke made a "go ahead" motion with his hand. "What about Nazis? I mean, that was Heinrich *Himmler* that we dealt with a couple weeks ago. And you know those assholes have gotten bolder the last few years. It might not be as ridiculous as we'd like it to be."

Luke closed his eyes, and I could almost see the thoughts running through his head. "It does have a certain logic to it," he said after a moment. "Not all of the gold and money they stole from their victims was recovered, and we knew there were more of the bastards in South America than we were able to hunt down."

"I was thinking it might be worse than original Nazis spreading their filth to a new generation. It feels like there's a whole new crop of assholes wrapping themselves in the flag of the Reich and goosestepping merrily along these days. All it would take is some billionaire with a YouTube channel and half an ounce of charisma, and those bastards could be right back in power somewhere."

"We killed them once," Luke said. "If need be, we can kill them again."

"No shit," I agreed. "It's a bad day when the humans are the monsters and the monsters are the heroes."

Luke chuckled. "My dear Quincy, around here we call that Tuesday."

I followed him from the armory, shaking my head again. Two jokes in one night? Who was this strange vampire and what had he done with the cold, unyielding block of marble that helped raise me? I wondered for a moment what caused this softening of Luke, then it hit me—Cassie. He started to change not long after she took over as his Renfield.

Any sense of amusement or levity faded the second we stepped into the long room across the hall. The smell of death hit me in the face like a hammer, and I could see out of the corner of my eye that

Luke got it even worse. This was a jail within a long room, with a dozen six by ten cages lined up against the wall. The silver wire mesh facing us was mangled and blown inward in places, and the floor and back wall of every cage was splattered with blood. It looked like someone just walked down the row of cages firing a shotgun into each cell until whatever, *whoever* was in there, was dead. Because you could tell by the height of the blood spatter that the beings murdered in these cages were humanoid.

"Can you...tell what they were?" I asked. My senses are sharp, but there was so much blood it overwhelmed me. I couldn't sort all the smells, and even at my best, I'm no bloodhound. But Luke could name every chemical scent at a Macy's perfume counter if he wanted to.

"I...could..." he said, his voice low and shaky. I looked at him and took an involuntary step back. His face was completely still, devoid of all emotion. It was as if he was a statue carved to look like himself, but I knew that look. This was Luke on the precipice of rage, the kind of rage that he might not be able to pull himself back from if he allowed himself to tip over the edge.

"Luke," I said, reaching out to put a hand on his arm. He snapped his attention to me, locked his eyes on mine, and I just stood there. I didn't freeze, I didn't gasp, and I definitely didn't pull back from him. I knew where he was. I'd been where he was. And more than once, Luke had been the one to pull me back. Now it was my turn.

"Luke," I said again, stronger, looking deep into his eyes. I wasn't saying anything. Wasn't trying to *tell* him anything. Not that it was going to be okay, because that was a lie. Not that we would get the bastards, because the truth was, we might not. And certainly not that we'd never let it happen again, because history had proven us liars on that promise far too many times. No, I just stood there, letting him see himself in my eyes, letting him see who he was to me, letting him remember the pieces of his humanity that he clung to with every ounce of his will.

I stood there, for I don't know how long, until he drew in a shuddering breath, relaxed his shoulders a millimeter, and said, "Thank you, Quincy."

"Anytime," I said, in a tone that said without using the words that I meant that literally. Anything that man ever needed from me, he'd get, without questions. When I went down into my own personal abyss, he was there waiting to pull me out. The very fucking least I could do was return the favor.

He didn't say another word, just looked around the room and said, "There's nothing left here. Let's move on." Then he was out the door in a blur and a whisper, and I was left standing in a charnel-scented nightmare room.

3 2

The rest of the building was nearly as useless, and almost as disturbing. There was a room that could best be described as a barracks, with a long row of bunk beds lining one wall and empty footlockers at the end of each bunk. Well, mostly empty footlockers. The next to last one in the row was still closed, with a combination lock hanging from the hasp. I gripped the lock in my right hand and twisted, feeling the screws pop out of the cheap wood of the trunk. Pro tip—nothing is more secure than the surface it's mounted to. You can install the thickest, heaviest door in the world, but if the wall three feet to the left of it is just drywall and aluminum studs, that door won't keep anyone out. Same for a lock. There's no point spending a ton of money on an expensive lock if you're just going to put it on a cheap hasp in quarter-inch plywood.

I flipped the lid open and looked inside. Apparently whoever owned this footlocker didn't have time to come back and clear out their stuff because it was full of pants, shirts, shoes, socks, and boxers. Either there was a uniform of all black tactical gear, or our DEMON agent was a particularly uninspired dresser, because there was not a splash of color or a single pattern anywhere. Just dry-wick technical fabric super-light long-sleeve shirts, black pants with bunches of pockets, black socks, black combat boots, and a black tactical vest. Even the boxer briefs were black. It was like looking through the wardrobe of a modern-day ninja. Or a hardcore G.I. Joe cosplayer, maybe.

I pawed through the clothes, hoping to find a journal, a laptop, a smartphone, or even a matchbook with a phone number written inside. Nothing. Every pocket was empty, and the only thing in the trunk was a really dull wardrobe. I put my hand on the edge of the footlocker to push myself up, when my fingers brushed the top of one boot. Raising an eyebrow, I crouched back down and picked up the boots. I learned a long time ago not to randomly put my hands into boots or gloves without making sure they were empty first, so I flipped them over and gave them a good shake. I felt something rattle around inside the right boot, then a small bundle wrapped in a red bandanna *thunked* to the floor.

I was surprised, not just because I'd finally found something in this fruitless and depressing search, but also because that bandanna was the first indicator I'd had that these assholes even knew what color *was*. I dropped in my Sight to check out the lump in the supernatural spectrum, and it lit up like Times Square. There was definitely magic here, and it was no joke.

"I got something," I called out, and before I could blink away my Sight, there was a rush of wind and Luke was at my shoulder.

"What is it?" he asked.

"Dunno," I replied. "My X-Ray vision isn't working. The bandana must be lead-lined," I deadpanned.

"I assume that is another of your asinine popular culture references," Luke replied, reminding me that I needed to get him to read more comics. Or watch a movie now and then. Or any of half a dozen TV shows featuring Superman.

"Yeah," I said, taking the fabric by one corner and pulling it up. The bundle weighed about a pound and was maybe eight inches in diameter, including the layers of fabric. The fabric unwound from around the object inside, a metal disk on a long silver chain. As it clattered to the lid of the now-closed trunk, I saw that the disk was also made of silver, with a half-sphere set in the middle of something that looked like metal but was maybe stone. I picked the medallion up for a closer look and heard Luke draw in a hiss of breath beside me.

"Don't sweat, Uncle," I said. "It doesn't feel like there are any active spells on it. There's some kind of passive enchantment, but nothing defensive that will turn me into a toad for touching it or anything like that." It was stone, hematite to be exact, which explained why it looked like metal even from just a couple feet away. The medallion was made of brilliant silver, with elaborate scrollwork around the stone, then a ring of writing, then another ring of elaborate decoration around the outer rim.

"Do you read Faerie, Luke?" I asked, holding up the amulet.

He took a slight step back, not touching the jewelry dangling from my fingers. "No. I have never had need nor desire to learn."

I brought the thing back down and took another close look. Some of the letters looked familiar, but it was all gibberish to me. "Well, here goes nothing," I said, and dropped the amulet around my neck.

"Quincy!" Luke shouted, reaching a hand out for me, but even with his vampire speed, he was too slow to stop me. The silver chain fell around my neck and the medallion thumped to my chest, and... nothing happened.

"Huh," I said. "That's disappointing." I looked around the room, wondering if I was supposed to have better vision, or hearing, or maybe be able to fly. I didn't feel like I could fly, and I didn't feel like spending a couple hours playing Arthur Dent in a warehouse throwing myself at a concrete floor trying to miss.

"What's disappointing?" Luke asked, his voice a little awed.

"It doesn't work," I replied. The tone of his voice was completely lost on me, I was so caught up in my disappointment that the only piece of evidence we'd found turned out to just be costume jewelry.

"I don't think it will work on you," Luke said. "At least not while you're wearing it. But pass it to me." He held out a hand, and I took the amulet off over my head and handed it to him.

Luke slipped the necklace over his head, and I let out a low whistle as his face shifted right before my eyes. His hair went from dark brown, almost black, to a light chestnut color with highlights. High-lights! Luke hadn't had highlights since, well, since he could walk in the light. His features softened, blurring together just a little and losing the most angular sharp edges of his cheekbones and nose. But the two biggest changes were his lips, which plumped up like he'd had a collagen injection, and his eyes, which went from their natural dark brown to a brilliant blue that looked for all the world like the very center of a sapphire. But that was nothing compared to his ears.

Luke's ears were nothing to write home about normally. They were ears. They held up his sunglasses, didn't stick out an obscene amount, and had no lobes to speak of. But now, he had *ears*. These were majestic things, swooping out from the side of his head to long, narrow points that stretched nearly six inches into the air. The whole look combined to make him look much softer, gentler, and, not that I would ever say it to him, *pretty*.

"Holy shit, Luke," I said. "You're a faerie! And you're really cute." Okay, I probably would say it to him.

"I am an attractive man, Quincy. I am surprised it has taken you this long to realize that."

"Yeah, but you're cute now. That's not a word that I think has ever been used to describe you before."

"I am fairly certain that if it was, I quickly eviscerated the person who did so," Luke replied. It was kinda hard to take him seriously as the apex predator when he looked so much like Legolas's older brother.

"So the amulet makes the wearer look like a faerie," I mused.

"More than that," Luke said. "It has other effects as well. I can read the inscription now."

I looked at him. He said nothing. I kept looking at him, and he kept saying nothing. Finally, I sighed. "Are you going to read it to me?"

"If you like."

"Please." Sometimes my uncle is a douche.

"It is a portable glamour that conveys the appearance to all senses that the wearer is one of the Fae. They have all the outward appear-ances, but they also have some of the more detrimental effects, including a sensitivity to cold iron. According to this, it is not fatal, but will disrupt the glamour if the wearer comes into direct contact."

I looked around the room. There were at least twenty bunks, and as many footlockers. All of them except this one were completely empty. "Do you think everyone here has one of those amulets?"

"I can only tell you that most of the beds have been recently occupied. At least fifteen different people slept here within the past two days."

I dropped my Sight back down, scanning the trunks for any residual signs of magic. About seven of them had a faint glow, as if something enchanted had been in them, but was now gone. It was a similar glow to the one surrounding the necklace, and to a lesser degree, Luke. "Looks like they've got eight to ten of those things. That could make things difficult, if we can't tell the faeries from the DEMON agents."

"You can see the magic around me, right?" Luke asked.

"Yeah, but I can't keep my Sight active all the time. It'll wear me out, and it screws with my vision in the mundane world. We certainly don't want me trying to shoot with this trippy-ass filter in front of my eyes."

"Then perhaps you can use it sparingly."

"I'll have to," I said. I sat down on the lid of one of the trunks. "That doesn't address our bigger problem."

"You may have to be more specific, Quincy," Luke said. He closed the footlocker at the end of the bunk next to me and sat down facing me. "There are many things that could be considered our 'bigger problem.' I'll need you to narrow the field a bit."

"This place is empty."

"Your skills of observation are growing nothing but keener with age."

"We just found out about its existence about three hours ago, but when we got here, everyone was gone. How the hell did they know we were coming? Did they close up shop a couple days ago, after the vampire escaped, or did someone tell them we were coming?"

"Or was that vampire released to lure us into a trap?" That's what I count on Luke for—his ability to find the goddamn bright side in any situation.

"If this is a trap, it sucks," I said. "We've been here an hour and we're not dead yet."

"This may surprise you, Quincy, but some people look upon patience as a virtue."

"Those people don't own microwave ovens," I replied with a grin. "But I get it. There could be multiple layers of fucked going on. But one thing is for sure—whoever was here is gone, and they left in a hurry."

"That does seem to indicate some warning of our impending arrival," Luke agreed. "Who knew we were coming here?"

"Not many people," I said. "The two of us, Becks, Cassie. I assume if Cassie knew, then Jo probably knew, or at least knows where we are now. Glory, of course."

"All above reproach. If we cannot trust your lady love, my Renfield, Joanna, and your Guardian Angel, then I believe the correct phrase is 'we've got bigger problems.'"

"You ain't wrong," I said. "The vampire who told us how to get here." I held up a finger. "Jack, Pravesh, the bartender, and if Jack knew, then Faustus either knew or could have found out easily enough." As I named them off, I held up one finger per person. "Assuming nobody in the bar overheard us—"

"They didn't," Luke said, with such certainty that I didn't ask.

"Then there were five people who knew we were on our way here. Jack's a dick, but he's a legacy member of the Council. He's at least as above reproach as Jo. I have to trust Pravesh, because she's saved my ass too many times. Besides, she's my boss, and I really don't want to kill another Homeland Security middle manager. It'll start to be a whole thing. That leaves Faustus, the vampire, or the bartender. I think the bartender is the most likely suspect out of that bunch."

"Why is that?" Luke asked.

"We don't even know if Faustus knew we were heading here, not for sure, so we don't know if he belongs on our suspect list. That vampire looked almost starved into nothingness. I can't believe anyone who'd been tortured to that degree would work with his captors for any reason. That leaves the bartender, who hates me already."

"The number of people who hate you is almost as high as the number of people who think I don't exist. But I don't think you can eliminate Director Pravesh just because you don't want her to be the mole. She deserves careful observation."

I felt a flash of irritation. This fixation Luke had with Pravesh being a traitor was starting to bug me. It was new, and I didn't understand where it came from. But I shoved all that back down, because it would do no good to get in a fight over it. "Okay, then why don't you follow Pravesh and investigate her a little, and I'll tail the bartender home when she leaves The Dive tonight and maybe have a little chat with her when she doesn't have a shotgun pointed at my face."

Luke looked as though he wanted to protest, but I could almost see him going through the exact same internal process I'd just gone through regarding him, and after a few seconds of arguing with himself, he nodded and said, "I will observe Director Pravesh. If she is working against us, I will ensure that she is no longer a threat."

The casual way he said it, without any heat or emotion at all, like he was discussing painting the bathroom, was a little disconcerting. Every once in a while it was good to remind myself that the guy I called Uncle Luke was Vlad Tepes, known as The Impaler, then later as Count Dracula, and he's got a body count that rivals most natural disasters. He's one of the people I love most in the world, but sometimes Luke is one scary motherfucker.

33

Luke and I split up as we left the abandoned lab/office/barracks/whatever the hell it was, with me in my pickup and him deciding just to run, since, as he put it, he didn't have to obey any red lights on foot, and I drive like an old woman. I didn't dignify that with a response. Mostly because he was right. I had a new-to-me Chevy Colorado I'd picked up since returning from Memphis, bright red with black trim, and I actually enjoyed driving for the first time in decades. Most American cars are either boxy, soulless things, or sleek jellybean-shaped soulless things, or soulless SUVs which were like big jellybeans shoved into a box. But while in Tennessee I'd driven an old beater of a pickup and really gotten to enjoy the feel of driving a truck.

There's something about sitting a little higher than the rest of traffic, the stiffer suspension, and the just more massive feel of driving a truck that appealed to me. Even in a compact like the Colorado, it still felt bigger, more solid. And the gas mileage wasn't bad and it had built-in navigation and a hookup for my phone, along with satellite radio. I mean, I'm not a complete Philistine.

I'd just turned the truck toward The Dive when Becks' face popped up on the truck's center dash console. I pressed a button on the steering wheel to activate the Bluetooth and answered the phone. "Yeah, babe. What's up?"

"Where are you?" she asked.

"Down near the state line, just heading up to The Dive. Why?"

"I'm texting you an address off Steel Creek Road. Meet me here as soon as you can."

I felt a spike of worry shoot through my system. "Are you okay?"

"I'm fine. I'm down here at the sniper training grounds and I've got something to show you. How long will it take you to get here?"

"Probably ten minutes. Fifteen if traffic at Westinghouse is stupid."

"Traffic at Westinghouse is always stupid. See you in twenty." She clicked off and I smiled. She was probably right. Estimating arrival and travel times was not my strong suit. I always blamed it on being born when people still traveled by horse-drawn carriage. Flynn blamed it on me not giving a shit if people had to stand around waiting for me. To-may-to, to-mah-to.

Twenty-two minutes later, I walked up to the nondescript concrete block building and grabbed the knob. It didn't turn, and I looked around, finally seeing a small buzzer set into the frame. I pushed it, looked up to see if I could spot the camera that was no doubt trained on me, and heard a magnetic lock disengage. I opened the door and walked in.

The lobby was just as nondescript as the exterior, with two armless plastic and metal chairs sitting against one wall and a wooden door set into the wall facing the exterior. There were no posters, no coffee tables with magazines, nothing. This was not a place designed for loitering.

I stood around for a minute or two, then sent out a tendril of thought. *Becks?*

On my way up to meet you. Sorry. I'm way in the back.

What is this place? It looks like a Cold War bunker.

It kinda is. It's one of the CMPD SWAT training facilities. The sniper range is out back.

What are you doing here? You quit, remember?

"Yeah, I remember," she said, opening the door. "But I still have a couple friends on the force, and one of them is back here in Cyber Crimes."

"Cyber Crimes?" I asked, following Flynn as she waved me through the wooden door, which closed with a much more solid *thunk* than I expected from what looked like a flimsy hollow-core door.

"You know, internet predators, identity theft, hacking...all the stuff most cops think of as BS crimes that are beneath their notice." There was a hint of venom to her voice, and when I looked to her face, I saw the tightness in her jaw, the scowl on her face.

"Something you're leaving out, Becks?"

She sighed. "It's bullshit, of course. My friend here has been working Cyber for ten years. She's good. Damned good. One of the best they've ever had. She can sniff out an online creeper and get him to give up his home address without ever knowing she's a cop. But she'll never make rank because what she does isn't sexy, isn't flashy, and her arrests end up shipped off to the FBI half the time because the bad guys have done a lot worse shit across state lines than they've done here. So instead of having a nice office down-town, she's stuck in a bunker twenty miles from anything with nothing but cost-of-living raises and two kids to raise. I'm just pissed about it."

I thought about it for a minute. "Why don't we talk to Luke about hiring her? To work for the Council?"

Becks stopped and whirled around so fast I almost ran smack into her. "What?"

I shrugged. "We've been down a nerd since Dennis got all sancti-fied, and if she's as good as you make her out to be, we could probably really use her."

"You're not fucking with me, are you, Harker?"

I was honestly confused. "Why would I fuck with you about this? You say she's really good, we've got a need at that position, and Luke's richer than Croesus, so why *shouldn't* we hire her? Besides, our office is way nicer than this."

Flynn got a thoughtful look on her face, then gave a little nod. "I'll bring it up. You just follow me and look at what she's found. I don't understand it, but there's no way it's not significant. It's just too damn weird not to be."

"Well, now I can't wait to see what it is. Lead on, Macduff!"

She turned, laughing. "You know that's not the line, right?"

"I know, but 'Lay on, Flynn!' Just doesn't have the same ring to it."

I followed her down a bland hallway lit with glaring fluorescent lights. It's always good to know that the local police have plenty of money for riot gear but not enough to make their offices where the less sexy members of law enforcement have to spend all their days be the kind of place anyone would want to spend most of a day. The walls were bare, with intermittent faux wood plaques with names engraved in them in white letters. We passed FRAUD, TELEPHONE FRAUD, INTERNET SEX CRIMES, INTERNET WEAPONS, and CYBER HARASSMENT before arriving at TECHNICAL SUPPORT/INFRASTRUCTURE.

"All these investigative divisions, and we're dealing with the person who fixes the computers?" I asked.

"Who do you want on your side, Harker? The person who breaks all the shit, or the person who fixes all the shit?"

I had to give her that. Since I'm usually the one breaking all the shit, having someone around who could fix it was pretty appealing. "Okay, let's meet the Nerd Queen." I followed Becks into the room and froze in the doorway at the panorama in front of me.

When I said, "Nerd Queen," I thought I was joking. Turned out, I was about one thousand percent right. Sitting at a wall of computer monitors was a woman with streaked auburn, orange, red, and purple hair cascading over her shoulders, but there was so much sensory overload going on in the room itself I almost missed seeing her.

The overhead lights were out, but there was plenty of illumination in the room. LED strips ran along the top of each wall, slowly shifting colors in a cascading rainbow that scrolled around the room. One wall was dominated by equipment racks with blinking lights in red, blue, green, and amber scattered across the front of a dozen pieces of equipment that looked both complicated and expensive. Each rack had a smoked glass door on it with a serious cylinder lock. I was kinda glad. It looked like the type of gear that if I bumped into the wrong thing, I could nuke Oklahoma. I mean, it wouldn't be the biggest loss, but I've got nothing specific against Oklahoma, so I'd rather not nuke it.

The other walls were a crazy-quilt of shelves of Funko Pop figurines, the little ones with the big heads, from all kinds of comic books and sci-fi shows and movies. I saw a bunch of Avengers, a few figures I recognized from *Star Wars*, the entire cast of *Breaking Bad* immortalized in melon-headed plastic, a blue phone booth that I think was a *Doctor Who* thing, and a bunch of others that looked vaguely familiar. One figure sat alone, on its very own special shelf with a spotlight shining down on it, and as I looked more closely, I realized that it was Jeff Goldblum from the movie *Jurassic Park*, reclining on one elbow with his shirt hanging open.

Every chunk of wall that wasn't covered by toys on shelves was plastered with posters. Comic book movie posters, science fiction movie posters, horror movie posters—you name it, there was a poster for it. And tacked to the corner of most of the posters were a pair of tickets, presumably from when someone went to that movie. But pride of place, right over the desk, above even Jeff Goldblum's disturbing plastic figure, was claimed by an explosive print of yellow and blue, streaks of color all emanating from a central point and blasting out to the edges, slowly resolving into more and more of those blue phone booths as the whole thing turned into a nerd-tastic homage to Van Gogh, only with Tardises. Signatures littered the surface of the poster, a dozen or more in all. I had no idea who the signatures belonged to, but apparently they were pretty important people, at least to the poster's owner.

"Hi! I'm Joey." I looked down and saw the woman had turned and was holding up her hand. She was tall, even seated, with a huge smile that made me feel instantly welcome. I took her hand, then looked down to take in more of her. She was pretty, with kind eyes and a nice figure, but it was the smile that made the room warm. She wore jeans and a loose-fitting shirt with a scoop neck and a floral print. "I would get up, but..." She let the words trail off as she gestured to a mobility scooter tucked against one wall and a cane leaning against her desk. "It's not the easiest thing to do, and there's no real point if I'm just going to shake your hand and sit right back down, is there?"

"None at all," I said. I was completely disarmed by this woman. I felt like I'd known her forever after just a few seconds, and I felt myself wanting to trust her completely. I wondered briefly if she had some kind of magical ability to put people at ease, then thought that no matter how unlikely it seemed, I might have actually just met one of the world's last few surviving nice people. "Becks says you've got something to show me?"

She smiled again, this time looking over at Flynn. "Becks, huh? Is this the guy attached to that ring you don't wear nearly often enough?" she asked.

Becks nodded. "Quincy, meet Joey Starnes. Joey is one of my oldest friends in the department. We went through the Academy together. Joey, this is Quincy Harker, my fiancé."

"Pleasure's mine, Quincy. Can I call you that?"

"That's fine, or Harker, or Q. Whatever, really. I've been called a lot of things in my time." I was babbling. I never babble. This woman just made me feel so…at ease, I was a little discomfited by it. It was almost creepy. I wasn't used to it.

"Q," she said. "I like that. Okay, Q, here's the short version. Something really fucked up was going on at that rally."

"No shit, Sherlock," I said. "I was there. Somebody murdered a member of the clergy and managed to make it look like it was me."

"Not that," Joey said with a wave of her hand. "We knew *that*. No, this is tech fucked up, not humans are assholes fucked up. This is the kind of fucked up I've never seen before, and that's a short list, believe me."

Great. Not bad enough I'm being framed for murder. I'm being framed for murder by somebody who's not just good at it, they're good enough to make the experts in weird shit think it's weird. Sometimes my life is just a pain in the ass.

3 4

S how me," I said, looking around for another chair.

"There isn't another chair," Joey said. "If I have another chair, people want to sit down. If people sit down, they stay longer. If people stay longer, I have to deal with them. I don't like most people, ergo no chair."

"Makes perfect sense to me. Most days I wish I could surround myself with big-headed dolls and not speak to anyone," I said. I leaned over her shoulder as she turned back to the monitor.

"Yeah, that's not gonna work," she said. "You stand up and go over to the wall. I'll find what I want to show you and put it up on the big screen." She pointed to the only clear space on the wall above her desk, and I realized that it was actually a monitor set into the wall. It was hard to tell, because there were still movie posters all over it—they were just digital and changed every few seconds.

I did as I was told, giving Flynn a "don't you dare laugh" look as I did.

She held both hands out in a faux-innocent "Who, me?" gesture. "Did I mention that in addition to being brilliant, Joey's a little…quirky?"

"Quirky?" Joey asked, shooting Becks a snarky grin. "Your seventy-year-old maiden aunt who doesn't wear underwear and pees in the back yard is quirky. I'm batshit crazy and I've got the meds to prove it. But I'm really good at this stuff, so just stand there and look pretty, both of you."

I folded my arms and watched as the big screen came to life. It was sectioned off into four quadrants, each showing the events at Romare Bearden Park from a different angle. One seemed to be a security camera mounted high above the park, one looked like a professional quality video camera, and two looked like handhelds, maybe cell phones or maybe just jumpy news cameras. It's almost impossible to tell the difference now between a really good cell phone video and a mediocre professional camera shot.

"Okay," Joey said as the images moved in slow-motion through the events at the end of the rally. "The wide shot is from our eye in the sky, which is a CMPD camera mounted on one of the mobile plat-forms we roll out to events where we think we're going to need eyes on a big area. You've probably seen them in mall parking lots on Black Friday, or at outdoor concerts."

I nodded. I knew what she was talking about, a trailer-mounted box that could raise to fifteen or twenty feet in the air, with lights on all sides to help increase visibility in a big area. I always assumed there was some type of surveillance equipment inside. Now my suspicions were confirmed.

"The ground-level steady camera shot is from one of the local news stations. There's a producer over there who owes me money from a poker game, so I erased some of his debt in exchange for getting their raw footage." The more she talked, the more I liked this woman. My wild-ass idea was seeming better by the moment—we should definitely try to hire her away from the police. Shouldn't be hard, since as soon as any of the department higher-ups found out she spoke to us, much less *helped* us, she'd be filing for unemployment.

"The other two feeds are cobbled together from cell phone videos streamed the night of the event. The local alternative newspaper had a stream going the whole time, as did a few of the protestors, and we were able to merge that with some of the less complete footage to make a mostly coherent timeline of events. These are all synched together, as you can see by this frame." She pressed a button and all four images froze. Using her mouse, Joey indicated the same person in the same pose in all four images, shown from different angles. It was a woman in a flowing blue skirt with white flowers, a yellow top, and a broad-brimmed white hat. Her outfit made her easy to pick out from the rest of the crowd, most of whom were wearing black t-shirts with some type of slogan on them.

"Okay, you can see the woman, and watch her movements in the videos to see as she moves through the crowd, people chanting, yelling, waving signs, getting more agitated, and then…this happens." She froze the video again and used her cursor to indicate a person-sized blur on each of the four screens. You couldn't really see it well on the wide shot, but you could clearly see me up in Strunin's face at the bottom of that screen, while the blur slid in from the right, off camera.

"What is that?" I asked, leaning slightly forward to try and see better. I wanted to make sure I didn't crowd Joey's personal space, because apparently that was a big no-no, but whatever was on the screen was blurry, and I couldn't make it out from across the room.

"That's the weird," the tech guru with the multi-hued hair replied. "Look. It's on every view of the scene, at the same place, and it moves. It's not a blotch on a lens, because it wouldn't be on every screen. It's not something tech-based, because these files came from all kinds of sources—phones, professional video cameras, and our surveillance footage. And it didn't get corrupted when it was sent to me, because I took the data off the memory card from our camera myself. No matter whether I got it from the card directly, or got it through email, or downloaded it from a cloud server, the same blotch appears at the same time stamp in the same place on every video. I have no idea what it is. It makes no sense. But I know it's important, and that's what drives me nuts."

"What makes this specifically important?" I asked.

"Watch," she said, pressing her spacebar. The videos rolled, and in four different views we watched as the blur wove through the crowd until it stopped right next to where Pastor Judy had her hands up in the air and her mouth open in prayer or protest, I couldn't tell which. I knew in the pit of my stomach what I was about to see, but that didn't make it any less difficult to watch. While Becks and I stared at the screen, and Joey watched through barely spread fingers, the blur moved up alongside Paster Judy, then the distortion effect broadened to cover them both, and a few seconds later, the blur moved away.

Pastor Judy's image cleared up, and it was almost in slow motion how she reached up, grabbed her throat, then collapsed to the ground. The people nearest her turned around in confusion for a few seconds, then the stampede of running, and presumably screaming, started.

"Fuck," I said. "That was harsh."

"So whoever was hidden in that distortion just walked right up to the reverend, slit her throat, and dropped her to the ground in front of several hundred people. How the hell could anyone have that kind of balls?" Flynn asked.

"Because they were wearing my face," I said.

Becks and Joey both stared at me. "What?" Flynn asked.

"Strunin said they had a bunch of eyewitnesses that saw me kill Judy, so even though I was standing in front of him when she died, he brought me in. Luke's little Barry Allen impersonation a few minutes before gave the police reason to think that I have super-speed."

"You kinda do," Becks reminded me.

"Not like *that*," I said. But she was right. I am faster than a normal human. I could have easily left where I stood with Strunin, run over to where Pastor Judy was speaking, slit her throat, and been back to the cop within thirty or forty-five seconds. But not so fast that he wouldn't have seen me move. And last time I checked, I could be recorded on digital cameras just fine. Frankly, so could Luke, which caused more than one uncomfortable moment for him since most people stopped developing photos with silver.

"Okay, let's try this," I said. I pushed off from the wall and looked at Joey. "You've got a smartphone, right?"

The way she looked at me you would have thought I said she had an ugly baby. Apparently questioning her tech ownership was a major insult. "I'm just going to say yes and not bother educating you on exactly how many and what type of portable communications devices I own."

"Thank heaven for small favors," I said. "Take it out and point it at me, then start shooting video."

She looked confused but did as I asked. I stood still for a moment, then waved, then turned around twice, waved again, and said, "Okay, that's enough. You can stop recording."

She pressed a button on the screen and said, "Now what?"

"Play it back."

She tapped the screen again and raised an eyebrow in my direction. "Am I on there?"

"Yes…" She had that drawn-out syllable like she was concerned she was talking to a crazy person.

"And it looks just like a video of any normal person. No blur, nothing like that?"

"No, it's you, standing there, waving, turning around in circles like a doofus…you know, what you just did."

I let the "like a doofus" part go for the time being. "Okay, we're going to try something different. Start a new video recording."

She tapped the screen again and aimed the phone at me. I stood still, then waved, then I reached into my jacket pocket and pulled out the amulet. Becks looked at me, confused, as I put the necklace over my head and let the heavy chunk of hematite drop down onto my chest.

"Holy shit!" Joey exclaimed. "You just went all blurry! Just like the video!" She turned the phone around to me, but that put her face on the screen.

I pushed the button to flip to the front-facing camera, and where my head should be taking up most of the frame was just an indistinct gray blur. I pressed the button to end the recording, then played it back, holding the phone so that Becks and I could both see. Sure enough, one second it showed me standing there with a necklace over my head, then as soon as the amulet touched my chest, the image diffused outward from the stone until in less than a second my entire image was completely obscured.

"Harker," Becks asked slowly, "why did you get really pretty all of a sudden? And what's with the ears? And that's even before I ask you what *the fuck* happened to the video!"

"This amulet makes the wearer look like they're a faerie. And there's a reason they're called the fair folk. Faeries are *really* pretty. It's easier to just manipulate someone's real appearance to fit an illusion, so the magic takes my features and faeries them up. And as to the video, magic and tech don't always get along very well, so I guess this is one of those cases. It seems like this particular disguise spell doesn't like digital video, but instead of collapsing and dispelling the illusion altogether, it hides everything about the person's image."

"Where did you get the amulet you're wearing?" Flynn asked.

"At the DEMON facility Luke and I just investigated, which was about half a mile from Carowinds, in a sense of kinda creepy irony. The whole place was cleared out, but this was tucked away in the toe of a boot inside a footlocker. Whoever killed Pastor Judy must have been wearing a similar disguise amulet but enchanted to look like me to anyone who saw them."

"Whoever killed Judy was working with DEMON," Becks said.

"And had access to something that would allow them to imprint my essence into the spell. To craft a general illusion, like make someone taller, or thinner, or change their features a little to make them look like a faerie, you just need something from any person with those characteristics to tie the spell to an image. But if you're making an illusion of a specific person, you need something with that person's essence—their sweat, hair, blood, or...other bodily fluids," I said.

"Ummm...ew," Joey said. "When you start talking bodily fluids, it's definitely time for you to be somewhere not my office. It was nice to meet you, I don't shake hands, ever, so thanks for stopping by and I hope I don't get fired for this."

"If you do, call Detective—I mean Deputy Director Flynn. We'll make sure you aren't left twisting in the wind for helping us," I said. I opened the door and stepped out into the hallway, blinking against the glare of the fluorescents after being in the dark room.

Becks followed me out, then passed me in the hall and led the way out of the building. "What does all this mean, Harker? And take that damn thing off. You look like a really dirty Legolas."

"Is that a bad thing?" I asked. When she didn't answer, I took the necklace off and put it in my pocket. "As for what it means, I'm not sure of everything it tells us, but I know one thing for sure—the same people who want to make DEMON agents look like the Fae want to get me in jail for murder. So Either Strunin is in bed with DEMON, or they're both working for somebody else who hates me."

"Any idea who that might be," Becks asked as we reached the front door.

"Unfortunately, my love," I said. "That list is long and varied."

35

T his feels like a really bad idea," Becks said over the comms.

"That's probably just because it's a terrible idea," I replied.

"Oh, look on the bright side, Harker. What's the worst that could happen?" Jack asked, his voice coming through a little staticky, but still understandable.

"Well, let's see," I said, looking around. "I'm walking up to a rally led by a woman who has said more than once that she wants to shoot me, surrounded by more people who want to kill me, and we suspect that somewhere hidden in this crowd are federal agents, maybe disguised to look like faeries, maybe disguised to look like *me*. So thanks for the jinx, asshole. Going silent now." I stopped talking as I got close enough to the field to see down into the stadium.

I stood atop the home team bleachers at the Garinger High School football stadium, looking down on a field jam-packed with people. There must have been a couple thousand beings milling around down there. The stadium lights weren't on, but a portable light rig was set up in front of a small stage with a podium and a mic on it. There were a couple of stacks of speakers pointed out from the stage, and I could see a sound board out in the middle of the crowd where a DJ was playing some random classic rock and Top 40 music.

All in all, it could have been any gathering of people anywhere in the world. It could have been a pep rally, a campaign event, or a protest. Hell, if the stage was a little higher and a little longer, it could have been an outdoor fashion show. Weird place for it, but I'm not the one to judge. If you didn't look incredibly closely, you'd never see the pointed ears peeking out from under hats and hair, or the skin that seemed to have glitter permanently embedded in it. You might think that guy over there in the old-fashioned clothes was just really pale, and the group of men doing standing backflips and other tricks were just exceptionally hirsute. If you didn't know what you were looking for, you'd have no idea that the football field was full of monsters, there to rally the troops to the cause. The cause, in this case, being kicking a lot of human ass and taking a chunk of the city of Charlotte for themselves, enchanting it, and creating a little slice of Faerie on Earth.

It was an impossible dream, but nobody had told our punk rock protagonist because the first thing the bartender from The Dive did when she walked up to the mic was lean down and shout, "Who wants to make some MAGIC!" She shoved a fist up into the air, and a stream of sparks in rainbow hues blasted off into the night sky. Her magical fireworks weren't quite Gandalf-level, but when a couple hundred other spellslingers followed suit and shot their wads into the air, the east side of Charlotte suddenly looked like the god of raves had pissed fireworks and rainbow glitter all over Garinger High School.

"Well, that was subtle," Jack whispered. He was winding his way through the crowd on the far-right side while I dove straight into the middle and started pushing my way toward the stage. I'd modified the spell on the amulet a little, so now I looked like a really dirty and really *mean* Legolas, and the glamour was holding, because anytime somebody turned around to bitch at me for squeezing past them, they just looked at the ground and made room instead.

Jack was in a more conventional, and less comfortable, disguise, since the key to his masque was the pair of yellow contact lenses he was wearing. Those coupled with the sunglasses he wore made it almost impossible for him to see where he was going, and it didn't take him bumping into very many people for us all to be glad he brought along a cane tonight. I didn't ask him if this was the one with the sword in the shaft, or the one with the whisky flask. I hoped I knew which one, but I'd be pretty disappointed if he didn't figure out some way to have the sword cane *and* a flask secreted somewhere on his person. He did have a reputation to uphold, after all.

The mood of the crowd was upbeat, almost happy, but there was a different feeling bubbling just under the surface. It was like the whole place was trying really hard not to be pissed off, but nobody was quite managing the feat. I nodded to a few folks but kept my distance. I couldn't use my Sight for fear that someone else would notice me and look at me in the magical spectrum, which would make my amulet glow like a strobe light. That didn't seem like it would be good for me, so I just kept my eyes and ears open and tried to pick out any disguised DEMON agents by their mannerisms. Nobody looked terribly out of place, except maybe me, as I skulked around the edges of the crowd trying to see if anyone looked out of place, which is what made me look out of place in the first place.

The DJ cut off the music and a squeal of feedback killed all conversation. I turned along with the rest of the crowd to look at the stage, where the bartender from The Dive stood fiddling with the microphone.

"Sorry," she said. "Not really my thing. But, um, anyway… Thanks for coming out to raise community awareness for our work building New Faerie!" She threw her arms up over her head, and the crowd erupted in a cheer.

"My name is Jelena, and I was banished from the Summer Court fifty years ago. I am allowed one day there a year, both to remind me of my 'transgressions,' which consisted of me looking prettier than Titania once—"

This was met with a chorus of boos and a host of people shouting about what a bitch Titania is. I'd never met the Summer Queen and wanted to keep it that way as long as possible. Especially if she was as terrible as the crowd seemed to feel.

Jelena raised her hands for quiet. "Yeah, she's pretty awful. But now, after so many years of being here in this iron-clad shithole, we've *finally* got some hope. We've found someone who is going to let us stop worrying about getting back to Faerie because she's found a way to bring Faerie to us and turn part of this plane into our own Court!"

More wild applause, and I looked around, trying to see who she was introducing. There was a human-shaped being off to the right-hand side of the stage with a long cloak and a hood pulled up over their face. It could have been a woman from the height, or just a small man. Or a faerie, or an elf for all I knew. I was pretty sure it wasn't a hobbit. Far as I've ever known, hobbits are shorter. And fictional. But I'm an immortal half-vampire wizard with a demon riding shotgun in his soul, so I don't put too much stock in what people claim is and isn't real.

Jelena leaned back into the mic, and the crowd quieted down a little. "I first met this woman when I was pretty low. I'd just come back from my annual trip to Faerie, where I was reminded of everything I'd lost, and everything I'd never have again. My bar was doing okay business, but nothing great, thanks to a bunch of assholes all over town screwing with the infernal types."

More boos, and I was reminded why I wore the amulet. There were a lot of people in that crowd who had reason to dislike me. They had even more reason to fear me, but it's been my unfortunate experience that large groups of people, monsters, or supernatural beings somehow manage to lose any semblance of reason they may have once had. There were enough folks here that would love to see me dead to outweigh any healthy terror I might strike in their hearts.

"But then this lady came into my bar, and she told me about a place. A place where our magic could thrive. A place where we'd never have to hide our ears, or our eyes, or our fur again. A place where we could be ourselves, with nobody there to hide from, and nobody to tell us what to do. A place of our own!" She threw a fist up into the air, and the crowd roared its approval.

"Ladies and gentle beings, men and monsters, it is my pleasure— no, my *honor* to introduce to you the woman who is going to help us create a utopia on Earth, a little slice of Faerie right here in Charlotte, and nobody, not even Titania herself, is going to get in our way. This is the woman who has been such an inspiration to me, and the woman who is going to lead all of us cryptids and supernaturals out of the dark and into our rightful place at the front of society and the top of the food chain. Please welcome Adrienne MacDonald Shaw!"

The woman by the stage straightened her head, and with a shrug of her shoulders let the cape fall to the ground behind her. She walked up the three steps to the stage and looked out across the captivated audience. You could have heard a pin drop, even on the grass, that's how quiet it was as the hundreds of beings stood there waiting for this psychotic Moses to tell them how she was going to lead them to the Promised Land. I just stood there, taking my first good look at the woman who'd caused me so much pain, mentally and physically, since I came back from Memphis.

Director Shaw, as far as I could tell the *real* Director Shaw, was a tall woman, pushing six feet in flats, with long black hair hanging arrow-straight to the middle of her back. She was crazy pretty, with high cheekbones, full lips, and big almond-shaped eyes flanking an aquiline nose. She would have looked equally at home walking a runway or sitting on a throne in ancient Egypt. She moved with the kind of grace I usually associated with the Fae, but something in the way she held her head, the way she set her jaw, and the way she was in constant, if minute, motion gave her a decided aura of predator.

The crowd didn't care. They either couldn't see that she was the most dangerous thing within a mile of that podium, or didn't give a shit, because the second she waved to the crowd the first time, they went absolutely apeshit. Their applause and shouting got louder and louder until I felt like my ears were bleeding. I managed to keep from clapping my hands to the side of my head, not knowing if the illusion would hold past me putting my hands *through* the pointed tips of my ears, and when she raised both hands, the crowd fell silent again.

"Thank you," she said, adjusting the mic with the grace of someone that's done it hundreds of times before. "Thank you all for coming and thank you for joining the cause. With your help, we will shake off the yoke of human oppression!"

The crowd cheered again.

"With your help, we will destroy those who hunt us and destroy us!"

More cheering.

"With your help, we will create a Faerie here on Earth that will leave Titania and her pitiful minions gnashing their teeth with jealousy!"

Still more cheering.

"With your help, we will step out of the shadows and into our true roles as the rightful lords and masters of all humanity!"

The loudest cheering yet, and I was starting to get really nervous about the things she was saying.

"With your help, we will grind human society to dust beneath our boot heels and usher in a Peace of the Fae that will last a thousand years!"

Well, goddammit. Eighty fucking years later and half a world away, but it's another charismatic nutty talking about another goddamn thousand-year Reich. I reached out to Becks through our mental link, staying silent so nobody would hear me say anything aloud.

Hey babe?

Yeah, Harker?

I fucking hate Nazis.

Me too.

No, I really hate Nazis.

I know.

This shit is personal now.

It wasn't before?

A little. But now there are people trying to kill me and *there are Nazis. You know what that means, right?*

You're going to do something stupid?

Yeah, pretty much. I closed down the connection and stepped a little apart from the beings nearest me. Putting a little power into my voice to make sure everyone in the stadium could hear me, I called out, "I remember the last person who stood behind a podium talking about a group of people ruling for a thousand years because they were genetically superior. That didn't work out so good for them. Why don't you take your little Magical Hitler Nostalgia Tour back to wherever you came from and let us get on with living our lives?"

Shaw locked eyes with me, and my blood ran cold as a slow smile stretched across her face. "I wondered how long it would take you to muster up the courage to speak. Why don't you take off that amulet and show everyone who's really standing here acting like you give a damn about the supernaturals in this city? Go ahead, *Reaper*, show us your real face."

Fucking hell, I thought. *I have* got *to do something about that nickname.*

36

I looked around, trying to play it off like she was pointing at someone else as my mind raced for a way out that didn't involve a lot of bloodshed. I glared at the man standing next to me and reached out to grab his lapels, hoping to threaten him into distraction, but I felt a jolt as a spell slammed into me and knocked me off-balance. I wasn't hurt, but I could feel the amulet getting warm on my chest, so I reached down into my shirt and pulled it off, throwing it to hiss on the ground. The grass beneath it immediately began to smoke, and everyone around me made surprised and angry noises as my disguise evaporated.

I looked at the faerie standing next to me, a male a few inches shorter than me, with a slight build and long, flowing blond hair. "We don't have to fight, pal. I'm not looking for—"

My words cut off as a fist slammed into my gut, and I doubled over, forgetting for a few seconds the strength of the Fae. I slid to my right, avoiding the rabbit punch coming for the back of my skull, and straightened up to throw a right hook across the faerie's jaw. He spun around and dropped to the turf, giving me a brief respite. I reached under my jacket and pulled out a long knife, sweeping it in a low arc around me as I spun to create some separation. There were a *lot* of faeries and other supernaturals all around me, and I could see Shaw leaving the stage.

"Jack, she's running. Don't lose sight of her," I said over the comms.

"What about you?"

"I got this," I said. "Just stay on that psycho!"

"I'm on my way to you, Harker. Make some light so I can find you!" Flynn didn't sound like she was scared for me, more like she was happy to finally have an excuse to punch something. I didn't blame her. She'd had a really shitty week and not nearly enough opportunity to cut loose with the type of violence that would relieve the tension.

I raised a hand and cut loose with a pulse of brilliant blue energy, summoning up a globe of power to hover overhead, bathing the area around me in an intense cool light and giving Becks something to target on. I wasn't sure if she was running, driving, or if she had Pravesh send in a chopper, and I didn't have time to care, because as soon as I set off my flare, a red-furred form streaked through the crowd and barreled into my chest, knocking me flat. I rolled back as I hit, pushing off with my feet and flinging the were-fox into the air behind me. I was free of the were but had to do some twisting and rolling to avoid multiple kicks and stomps from the crowd of angry magical creatures, all of whom wanted to puree my face with their feet.

I struggled to my feet, throwing elbows and fists with abandon, but trying hard not to stab anyone, just maybe slice them up a little. Yeah, that's my idea of restraint—maiming. I'd just dropped a massive guy that I assumed was a lycanthrope of some sort by driving the point of my elbow right between his eyes, when I heard a crash and shriek of tearing metal, then the roar of an engine. A blaring horn cut through the sounds of the chaos around me, and a few seconds later, the crowd hemming me in dove out of the way as Rebecca Gail Flynn, in perhaps the most badass thing I'd ever seen her do, drove a Homeland Security Suburban through the fence and onto the Garinger High School football field, knocking cryptids and faeries aside as she drove hellbent for leather in my direction.

I ducked a wild swing from a half-shifted werewolf, then slammed a fist into his gut and hoisted him up over my head lengthwise. I turned sideways and chucked him at the grill of the oncoming SUV like a furry spear, grinning at the massive *CLANGGGG* his head made when Flynn drove into the oncoming meat missile at full speed. I knew that despite the massive impact, the were would be fine the next time he shifted, so I didn't waste any time feeling bad. I just ran at the oncoming truck and leapt into the air as Becks jammed on the brakes. I came down on the roof of the Suburban and spun around, cold iron knife in one hand and a glowing orb of magical energy pulsing in the other.

"Back the fuck off!" I shouted, pointing at the stage with my knife. "This woman is no friend of yours! She's the one in charge of all the testing labs that have been torturing supernaturals all over the country! She's the head of DEMON, the group of assholes that started the riot at Mort's! Her bunch of government dickheads made that amulet I was wearing, so one of her people could murder a woman at the rally the other night and make it look like I did it!"

"What, like you're not a killer, Reaper?" A familiar voice came over the PA, and I turned to see Jelena standing there with that same goddamned shotgun pointed at me again.

"Pull that trigger and find out if I am, lady," I growled. "I'm getting real tired of you pointing that scattergun in my direction. If you want to fucking dance, call the tune. I'm right fucking here."

Way to de-escalate, honey, Flynn said in my head.

I'm pissed.

Never would have noticed from your calm demeanor.

Jelena stared at me across the distance for a long string of heartbeats, then lowered the barrel maybe a millimeter. "Talk, Harker. What do you mean, she's behind the labs? And DEMON?"

"I mean she *fucking runs* DEMON! She's the goddamned director of the agency. She's made it her entire fucking mission to wipe out every cryptid and supernatural in the world, and she's gotten a pretty good start." I was shouting, both because of the adrenaline still pumping through me, and to be heard by everyone. I didn't have a PA system, but I pushed a little magic into the words to get them out to everyone.

"Why should we believe you?" Jelena asked from across the field. "You've spent a hundred years hunting us down, murdering us all over the world, and harassing our people. Why should we believe you have our best interests at heart now?"

She had a point. I wasn't exactly a favorite of the supernatural world before Shaw started trying to make me look like I killed people in cold blood, and nothing I could say would wash the blood from my hands. But if it would prevent another bloodbath, it was worth a shot.

"I don't know," I said. "I don't know what I can say to make you believe me. I don't have some bullshit yarn about rainbows and unicorns and mountains of candy and a new paradise where nobody will be mean to you or murder you just because of who or what you are. Shit, you couldn't get that if you were human. You'd still deal with assholes that are pissed off just because you exist. But I promise you, this woman does *not* have your best interests at heart. She has killed more supernaturals in the last two years than I have in the last hundred."

"Liar!" shouted a faerie standing on the ground behind the Suburban. He climbed up onto the roof of the SUV with me and charged, swinging a stick that looked like it had a protest sign attached to it, judging by the scraps of white construction paper still flapping in the breeze. I blocked his first clumsy strike and took one step forward, planting my hand in the middle of his chest and shoving him straight back off the top of the truck. He flew back a couple feet and landed on half a dozen other faeries and weres who caught him like he was stage diving at a punk show.

I didn't even feel the wind as the next guy leapt up clean and landed dead center on the Suburban, crumpling the roof under his mass. I heard him, though, and turned around to see the same half-shifted werewolf I'd chucked into the grill of the SUV standing there slashing at me with his claws. I parried one strike with the knife, but the other hand opened up four deep slashes through my shirt and the flesh of my chest. I drew back, hissing in pain, and lost my balance when a hand reached up and grabbed me by the ankle. I toppled over the edge, looking up as the werewolf licked my blood off his fingers. A petty slice of me hoped it tasted like shit.

Then my back hit the turf and I didn't have time to think about anything else as it was back to dodging and writhing as I tried not to get stomped to paste. I managed it, mostly, until a heavy boot caught me right behind my left ear and starred my vision. I covered my head with my arms, but that left my ribs and back exposed to more kicks, then I felt a pair of strong hands reach down and grab my arms, hauling me to my feet. I almost bounced up, then landed upright, staring into the grinning face of a seven-foot-tall Pit Demon. Its yellow eyes gleamed in the stadium lights, and its putrid breath peeled the five o'clock shadow from my face.

"Ready to meet my maker, Harker?" the demon asked, licking its lips as it drew back a razor-tipped hand.

"Hard pass, fuckwit," I said with a snarl, calling up my soulblade as the demon's arm came forward. I didn't even have to move the blade, just held it upright and let the demon strike. Its fingers were splayed wide, and the sword slid through the middle two like a hot knife through butter, splitting its hand and forearm into two long, flapping sections. I yanked the blade downward as the demon managed to arrest its stroke, pulling the flaming blade free and flicking black demon blood around me in a wide arc.

The creature looked at its newly bifurcated forearm, flapping in the air like a bloody wind chime, and let out a screech that sounded like Freddy Krueger running his gloved fingers down the world's largest chalkboard. I shut it up with a quick cut through its neck that sent its head to *thump* onto the grass at my feet.

I picked up the demon head and held it and my glowing sword aloft, amplifying my voice once more. "Contrary to the dead asshole before you, I did not come here to fight. But if you want a fight, step the fuck up and find out exactly why I'm the motherfucker you tell scary stories about around the campfire. Find out why I'm the bastard your mothers warned you about. You want to step to me? Come up on me and meet the goddamn Reaper, motherfuckers!"

Yeah, babe, I felt Flynn in the back of my head. *You are the absolute soul of diplomacy, aren't you?*

They haven't attacked me yet, have they? I asked.

For the briefest of moments I thought that I'd calmed things down. I had a tiny glimmer of hope that I managed to finally intimidate someone out of beating the ever-loving fuck out of me. Then about fifty of the faeries in the crowd simultaneously yanked the amulets from around their necks, shattering the glamour and revealing themselves to be DEMON agents, all in full body armor and carrying assault rifles.

"Kill them all!" came a voice that I instantly recognized as belonging to Director Shaw, and the DEMON troops opened fire.

37

G et down!" I shouted, mostly to Becks, but also to the beings around me as the DEMON agents opened fire. It was a massacre. Some of the agents were just firing indiscriminately into the crowd, spraying lead around like they were playing a video game, but more than a few of them were cool, calm, and collected, choosing their targets and taking headshot after headshot. These were the ones I was most worried about—the ones that weren't all gung-ho to shed as much blood as possible.

I'd seen men with those eyes before. Hell, I'd *had* those eyes before, and that was a darkness that only the deepest layers of Hell could match. These were the men who lay awake at night, their rifle on the pillow next to them, dreaming of the day when they were given the order, or the permission, to cut loose and kill as many living things as possible in a short amount of time. These weren't people working a job to protect the world from dangerous creatures, these were men who just needed a job that would give them an excuse, any excuse, to point a gun at someone's head and pull the trigger. The only thing that made their eyes bright was watching the light go out in another being's.

One in particular stood out to me, a broad-shouldered, good-looking man with a square jaw and bulging biceps. He had a tiny little smirk at one corner of his mouth, and it twitched with every pull of the trigger. I could almost feel the hatred rolling off him in waves, a deep-seated loathing for all living things. He held the rifle to his shoulder, and he'd pull the trigger, turn to a new target, shoot again. Fire, pivot, fire, pivot, like he was a robot with one simple program— kill as many people as he could in as efficient a manner as possible.

I'd closed to within twenty feet from him before I realized I was moving, and even then only because I saw him pivot in my direction and give that twitchy little smirk. I called power and wrapped my left arm in a shield, raising it just in time to feel a bullet smack into it like a hammer blow. I didn't stop as he fired again and again, never shifting his aim, never trying to shoot me in the legs, just shooting round after round into the forcefield I carried in front of me. I got close and leapt, closing the last ten feet in a mighty pounce that slammed my shield into his face and drove him to the ground. His rifle fell but caught on the strap slung over his head and one shoulder. I landed on top of him and punched him in the face with my right hand, keeping the shield between us on my left.

Good thing, too, since I felt more hammer blows coming as he drew a pistol and fired half a dozen times into the shield before he abruptly went limp. His eyes rolled back and I stood up, looking down at the blood covering my chest and stomach. I felt myself all over, then looked down. The bullets he'd fired into my shield ricocheted, and there was nowhere to go but into him. He basically murdered himself in a demented piece of psychotic justice.

I looked around. Everywhere I turned there were more agents, but the monsters and faeries had shaken off their initial shock and started to fight back. I watched as a werebear crushed an agent's skull, helmet and all, shaking off the bullets like they were spitballs. A pair of Reaver demons stood over the bloody corpse of another agent, arguing over who got to eat what organs. Three faeries encircled a young agent who kept spinning around in circles, his rifle forgotten, reaching out to the faeries with a vacant smile on his face. Every time he stretched out an arm, one of the Fae slashed his arm with a wicked knife, adding more and more blood to the pool he was standing in.

The cryptids were holding their own, but in a moment, that all changed. I was punching a DEMON agent into oblivion when the rumble of diesel engines roared through the night sky. I turned to see what was coming now, and four armored SWAT vehicles barrelled over the same fence Flynn had partially destroyed. The troop carriers bristled with armored riot cops dressed almost identically to the DEMON agents, except for the POLICE name plates velcroed to the front of their flak jackets. The vehicles split, with two peeling off to the right, and two to the left, and stopped at the four corners of the field. The officers disembarked, and a door opened in the back of each carrier, disgorging more cops out onto the football field. Each one carried a wicked little submachine gun, MP-5s if I remembered right, along with their forty-caliber sidearm. A sniper with a rifle stuck his head and shoulders through a port in the roof of each carrier and flipped a bipod down as they took aim at the crowd.

"Goddammit, no!" I heard Becks shouting through my comm, and as I turned back to the Suburban, I saw her fighting her way out of the SUV. "They're going to fucking get killed!" She was pulling on her own flak jacket as she shoved the passenger door open, and she hit the ground running toward the nearest SWAT transport, fishing a badge out of her shirt and making sure it hung visible in front of the big "DHS" emblazoned across her chest in white letters.

I watched in horror as my fiancée sprinted across the field, ducking under swinging fists and shoving beings of all sort out of the way as she hauled ass toward the armored vehicle puking assault troops onto the grass. I looked up onto the roof and saw the sniper bring the barrel of his rifle around to her, and I flung a bolt of energy across the field, striking him right in the face. His head rocked back and forth, and he fell down inside the vehicle. I threw enough fists and elbows to get back on top of the Suburban and knocked out the other three snipers as Becks made her way to a SWAT cop with more stripes on his shoulder than the rest of them.

"Stop." I heard her through our mental link. It was different from

when we talked to each other, more like I was standing on the other side of a wall listening to a conversation. *"Cut this shit out, Sergeant. This is a federal operation, and these people are federal fugitives. Stand your men down, and back the fuck up!"*

I couldn't hear the cop's response, but from where I stood atop a rocking SUV, it looked like he was about to call his men in when something came across his radio that made him freeze.

Harker, get over here! Strunin's on site and he's telling the police to partner up with the DEMON agents and wipe out everyone who isn't wearing a badge!

Fuck. Stop him. They're police. They're not in this to kill anybody, right?

The pause was deafening. *Baby, I love you, but sometimes you are a dumb son of a bitch. Most of these guys are good people, who really do want to help. But there are some out here who want revenge for Captain Herr and the others who died last week. There are some who hate anybody who doesn't look like them, and that goes double for somebody who really* isn't *human. And there are few that are just fucking psychopaths. That adds up to enough "bad apples" to make even the best cop go along with the crowd, either out of fear or just out of wanting to fit in. You can't count on anybody in this crowd to do the right thing. It's a mob, and mobs aren't known for their restraint.*

I thought about it for a second, thought back to some of the things I saw in Europe in the thirties and forties, things I saw in America in the fifties, when everyone was convinced that the Communists were hiding around every corner. I saw it in Cambodia in the seventies, when the Khmer Rouge had an entire nation cowering in fear. Now I was seeing it in my own backyard. The same shit, different zip code. More little men pushing fear and xenophobia and crowds of frightened people going along with anyone who made them feel safe. No matter how many times I saw it, it never failed to surprise me.

Get out of there, I said. *Strunin will recognize you. You can't be there.*

I felt her want to argue, then agree. *Okay. I'm headed back to you. Be there—what the FUCK?!?*

I saw her spin around and knock the officer's hand off her arm, and saw him lean in, reaching for her shoulder. That's all I needed to see, and I was off the roof of the Suburban, vaulting over a vampire who was clambering up to try and get himself a piece of the Reaper. I cleared fifteen feet before I hit the ground, and when I came down, I was at a dead run. I could feel Flynn's anger and fear in my head as the cop grabbed her and spun her around, trying to restrain her with a pair of flex cuffs.

I reached the officer just as he raised a fist to punch Becks in the back of the head and subdue her. That punch never landed. I slammed into the cop's side and stopped cold, transferring all my energy into his body. He flew off his feet and slammed into the side of the armored carrier, bouncing off to land on his knees on the turf.

"Don't touch my girl, shithead," I said, my voice low and cold. I called up power to sheathe my fists in glowing spheres of force and took one step toward the downed officer. He tried to stand, but I laid a magically enhanced fist across his temple, and he faceplanted in the grass.

I turned back to Becks. "You okay?"

"A little shaken, but not hurt. But we gotta deal with these guys right now." She pointed at the SWAT officers milling around. Some of them had their weapons half-raised, but they were looking around like they wanted someone to tell them what to do.

"Stand down," I said to the cop nearest me. He didn't move, so I reached out and snatched the MP-5 from his hand and broke the strap. "I said stand the fuck down," I shouted in his face. "And if you touch that sidearm, I'll shove it so far up your ass you'll brush your teeth with the magazine."

He stepped back, stunned, and I flipped the MP-5 to full auto, then pointed it up into the air and emptied the magazine. The sound of an automatic weapon rattling away has a way of getting people's attention, I've noticed. When all the cops from that armored transport were looking at me, I said, "The guys with DEMON on their chest are terrorists and murderers. They're not the good guys."

I paused for a second. "Frankly, nobody here are the fucking good guys, but those are the worst guys. So go arrest them." The SWAT cops looked at me for a long second, confused. "Go! Arrest them. Or whatever you do."

"I don't think that's how this plays out, Mr. Harker," came a voice from behind me. I knew that voice, so it didn't surprise me when I turned around and saw Major Ivan Strunin standing there. It did surprise me to see him pointing a gun at Becks' head, so I tossed the MP-5 to the turf and raised my hands.

"Okay, Strunin. You've got us. I surrender. Take us in."

"Not tonight, Harker," Strunin said with a grin. "Tonight, we put down this little insurrection. Tonight, we utilize the weapons at hand and our friends from the federal government and we make Charlotte safe for humanity again! Tonight, we kill all the monsters, and I'm starting with you." He swept the pistol away from Flynn's temple and around to point right at my face.

I opened my mouth to try to talk some sense into this psychopath, but the second I drew in a breath, Strunin pulled the trigger.

3 8

I called power to wrap a shield around my face, but before I could even finish the thought, a blade of fire streaked out of the heavens and sliced the bullet in half. One chunk still carved a furrow along the side of my temple and spun me to the ground, blood pooling at my feet, but I was alive.

"Thanks, Glory," I said.

"Kinda the gig, Harker," she replied. "But I will admit, you take a lot more guarding than any of my other charges."

"That's why they pay you the big bucks."

"I gotta learn to negotiate my salary better."

I wiped away a little blood that ran into my left eye and stood up to see a terrified Strunin standing in front of a pissed off angel. Glory looked like a teenage boy's wet dream of angelic vengeance, in a tattered black AC/DC t-shirt and ripped jeans, with her huge white wings spread eight feet across and a flaming sword in her hand. Strunin looked like a B-movie dictator whose plans just went to shit, his white hair sticking up in all directions and his mouth working to get words out, to no avail.

His eyes were locked on the angel with the flaming sword, as anyone's would be, so he never saw the punch from Becks coming. She laid a shot across his temple that spun the man around like a top, and when his eyes could focus again, he turned to her, only to receive a kick in the balls before he could say or do anything. He dropped to his knees, and Flynn stepped forward. She grabbed him by the ears, lifted her right knee, and slammed it into his nose with a sickening *crunch*. Tossing the bleeding Strunin to lay unconscious on his side, she turned to Glory. "Good timing."

"Well, if you're gonna bring the cavalry, you may as well hold off until they're useful." She grinned at us both and gestured to the rest of the field, where Luke, Jo, Faustus, and Pravesh were all kicking ass and taking names. One smaller figure caught my eye, swinging a bo staff like it was going out of style. Everywhere the slender gray-haired woman turned, another creature or cop dropped to the ground.

"Is that...?" I asked.

"Cassie," Glory confirmed. "Luke tried to convince her to stay behind, but she told him to go fuck himself. Looks like I'm not the only one you're a terrible influence on, Q."

"She's...a badass," Becks said, the awe evident in her voice. And she was right. The older woman moved across the battlefield like a whirl-wind of ass-whooping, sidestepping attackers, tripping them, and cracking them in the head with her staff. Every step was sure, every spin was fluid. It was like she was suddenly forty years younger, and when I caught a glimpse of the grin on her face, I could tell she was thrilled to be there, happy to be alive and fighting alongside her friends and her family.

I turned to Glory. "I got this part. Get as many people to safety as you can."

"Got it," Glory said, launching herself into the air and streaking across the battlefield.

I watched her fly away, then reached out to Flynn as a wave of dizziness threatened to send me to the ground. "Shit," I said.

"Harker? What is it?"

"That piece of bullet must have smacked me harder than I

thought," I said. "I think I might be a little concussed. I'll get a sip of Luke juice when we're done, and I'll be fine. Let's finish this shit. With Strunin down, you think you can get the cops out of here?"

"Maybe. I used to be tight with one of the SWAT team leaders. Let me see if I can find him." She turned around, picking up Strunin's MP-5 and clubbing a police officer to the ground with it. Then she straddled his chest and pressed her service weapon to the guy's jaw. "Where's McAllister?"

The officer just stared at her for a second, so she slapped him across the face, her open palm ringing like the gunshots that echoed all around us. "Hey! Simple question, dipshit. Where's Tommy McAllister?"

The cop pointed over at a far corner of the field, and Becks nodded. "Thanks. Now roll over so I can cuff you." She eased up on the guy, who immediately reached for his pistol. I took one step forward and kicked him in the side of the head.

Flynn glared up at me. "You didn't have to do that. I had him under control."

"Misery loves company," I replied. "Now somebody else has a concussion, and my pain is lessened by being shared." I gave her my best pious group therapy smile and reached down to help her to her feet. "Take the tank over to where your buddy should be. I'll keep things corralled around here."

"Keep them corralled?" she asked. "They aren't corralled *now*, Harker." She gestured to the field, and I looked around. She was right. It wasn't a fight anymore. With the police department joining forces with DEMON, it had turned into a bloodbath. In the less than a minute since I ran over to Flynn's side, things had gotten bad for the cryptids. Men in black tac gear were forming up in lines and marching shoulder to shoulder, firing into the crowd of fairies, weres, and other beings. The supernaturals weren't even trying to fight back at this point; they were just trying to get away.

They weren't a mob anymore, or even a group of angry people protesting. They were terrified and trying to run, but they had nowhere to go. The cops and agents had formed a "V" with the point on the field, and they were herding the supernaturals back against the tall fence around the field and the back wall of the field house. A few were able to jump high enough or manifest wings to fly, and they got away, but the rest were trapped in a kill box, and that's exactly what happened to them. The troops advanced, and with every step, more bodies hit the ground. Flynn and I watched, frozen in horror, as what started off as a moment of hope for all these people turned into a massacre.

"Jesus Christ," Flynn murmured next to me. "I *know* some of those cops. How can they do that?"

"They can do it because we aren't fucking stopping them. Get that tank rolling, Becks. We've got maybe thirty seconds before there's nobody left to save." I could see faeries dropping, but as the line of shooters passed them, they got up and limped off the field, dragging other wounded with them. So the cops and agents weren't using cold iron rounds, at least not all of them.

A werewolf in his hybrid form ran forward and spread his arms, trying to block the bullets from hitting the ones behind him. He went down but didn't shift back to human, so he was still alive. They were using normal ammo, so we had a chance. We could save some of them.

"Shadows! On me!" I shouted at the top of my lungs. I dashed a forearm across my face, swiping away the last of the blood running down my cheek, and started for the line of black-clad murderers. For one night only, it looked like I was gonna be reaping for the other side.

Faustus fell into stride with me as I sprinted across the field, and I could see Glory and Luke converging on the attackers well ahead of us. I looked over at the demon, and all his normal swagger was gone. Instead of a cocky grin, he wore a grim look of fury. He glanced at me and nodded.

"I promise not to kill everyone," he said.

"If the uniform says DEMON, drop them," I replied. "They might as well be Nazis, the way they've been going, and you know what to do with Nazis."

"Punch them all. Until they stop moving." Faustus flashed me a hungry grin and veered off to the right to engage an agent with a shotgun. I saw a set of wicked claws appear at the end of Faustus's hands, a fountain of blood, and heard a stifled scream. *That* was a part of his demon form he'd kept tucked away before, and I was kinda glad he had. I was also pretty happy he had those claws right now, though.

We crashed into the line of cops and agents at a dead run, bowling some over and leaving some lying in spreading pools of blood. I kept my guns and blades holstered and focused on the police officers. I didn't want them dead if we could help it. Most of them were doing their job, scared out of their wits by things they didn't understand, and in a lot of their cases didn't know existed until less than a week ago. These men and women didn't deserve to die, so I did a lot of punching, a lot of disarming, broke a lot of arms, and dislocated a lot of shoulders and kneecaps. They were all going to hurt a lot in the morning, and some of them might never work SWAT again, but I didn't kill any of them.

That didn't stop them from trying to kill me, a fact that my bruised forearm and battered body could attest to. The reinforcements on my coat held, but it still felt like a hammer every time the spell-buffed leather stopped a round. And the shield on my forearm stretched to keep my face and head covered, but it couldn't absorb all the kinetic energy of the bullets, so my arm took a beating. As we got into the thick of the fight with the attackers, the surviving supernaturals turned and joined in, but they were indiscriminate in their attacks, to say the least, so I found myself punching cops, smashing agents, and battling the occasional cryptid to boot. We managed to turn the carefully constructed assault line into a chaotic melee of guns, blades, claws, and fists, but we were stuck in the middle of it, too.

I lost track of the others as I plunged further and further into the fray. I got intermittent flashes from Becks as she drove the armored carrier across the field toward the SWAT commander she knew, so she could try and talk him down and get at least one set of enemies off the field, and I saw streaks of white light as Glory swooped in and airlifted wounded supernaturals and cops alike to safety. But most of the time it was punch, parry, duck, kick, energy blast someone, try not to get shot, swear about getting shot, and try to stay alive.

My vision narrowed to just what was in front of me, as I tried to listen for attacks coming from the sides and behind. My whole world was fighting, and bleeding, and making others bleed, and pain, and screams. A mad howl of rage split the air, and I couldn't tell where it was coming from, then I realized it was coming from me. I lost myself in the battle fever like I haven't in a long time. This wasn't the red-tinted haze of unconscious murder that I'd felt when Anna died, when I thought Becks was dead. This was glorious, exhilarating and thrilling, with my blood pounding in my ears and my death waiting around every corner. It was the most intoxicating thing in the world, and the most addictive. And the most terrifying.

Then it was over. There was nothing in front of me to hit. I shattered the orbital socket of a DEMON agent and dropped him to the turf, and there was no one standing within ten feet of me. I looked around, hungry for more battle, but there was nothing left. Just a couple dozen police officers on their knees with their hands in the air, or on their bellies with hands cuffed behind their backs, and a lot of downed federal agents and paranormal beings.

And blood. There were gallons and gallons of blood. It puddled the field in low spots, soaked everyone's clothing, covered everyone's face in a masque Poe would be proud of, and the coppery-tangy scent of it hung in the air like smoke days after a forest fire, thick and cloying. We'd made it through, though some of us only just.

All my people were still standing. Luke looked as if he just stepped out of a Victorian issue of *GQ*, without a drop of blood on his immaculately pressed shirt and pants or a hair out of place. Faustus had a horrific grin on his face as he surveyed the carnage around him. The skinny demon looked like a Tasmanian devil set loose in an abattoir, and the light in his eyes was pure manic bloodlust. Jack leaned on his cane and looked like he could barely stand, but he was still upright, and his British upper lip was still stiff.

Jo bounced back and forth on the balls of her feet, hammer in hand, like a prizefighter looking for someone to punch. She was all coiled energy and bottled lightning, blood-stained but ready to go another three rounds. Cassie used her staff to help her slide down to sit on the grass, then leaned back on her elbows, trying in vain to pluck gobbets of blood out of her hair. Glory knelt beside her, hands on the old woman's shoulders, a gentle warm light telling the tale of some angelic healing taking place.

"Anybody hurt?" I called out. Everyone shook their heads or mumbled some kind of dissent. "Becks, you okay?"

Yeah, I'm good. I found McAllister, and he told his guys to stand down. That's what cut them off like a light switch. He's on his way over with me. I've got Strunin trussed up in the back of the personnel carrier like a Christmas goose, ready to bury under the nearest jail once we get all the useful information out of him. Pravesh is with me, too. She took a graze across her leg, which bled a lot but wasn't as bad as it looks. She says once she shifts it'll be healed.

Good deal. I lost track of her in the fray. Shit, I lost track of everything in the fray.

I know. I was in there. That...was a little scary, babe.

For both of us, I replied. *If we can go another hundred years without having that, it'd be great.* But even as I thought it, I knew it was a lie. It *was* terrifying, giving myself in so totally to the bloodlust and fury, but it was also freeing, and glorious on a lot of levels. I knew that beast was never going back in the cage.

"What about Shaw?" I asked. "Did that psycho get away again? I'm getting real tired of hunting her."

"Don't worry, Harker," Shaw said over *our* comms. "Your hunt is over." I looked up and saw her standing atop one of the abandoned SWAT transports with a wide grin on her face and a fallen sniper's rifle in her hand. "After I kill your friend here, I've got something special planned for you, and it's going to need my full majesty for the job."

I watched as Shaw's skin stretched, then began to split as she grew. She dragged a fingernail down the center of her forehead to the bridge of her nose, opening up the flesh of her face like a zipper, and a demonic face with curly black hair and skin of crimson appeared. She sloughed off her human suit and grinned at me, showing me the lush lips and pointed fangs of a succubus.

"Ahhh. That's better." She licked her lips and scanned the field where no one but my allies were left standing. She hoisted the rifle to her shoulder and grinned as I started running her way. "Let's finish this," she said, and pulled the trigger.

39

Becks, stay down! Keep all the humans behind cover! I shouted the instructions in my mind as I ran full-out for Shaw. I had no idea who she fired at first, just that Becks was still in my head, so she was okay for the moment. I covered the eighty yards to Shaw in a matter of seconds, but she still managed to get off three more shots.

Then I was on her. I vaulted into the air and caught her around the midsection with a tackle that took us both off the far side of the vehicle and crashing to the dirt. I rolled to the right as we slammed into the turf, spinning around to spring to my feet.

Shaw was already standing as I got up, grinning at me with the Remington 700 rifle in her hands. "Let's get personal, Harker," she said, then tossed the gun aside. "You don't mind getting physical with me, do you?"

Her grin was salacious, like everything about her. She was even taller in this form, six and a half feet tall or so, with deep crimson skin, black hair, and pointed incisors that made me wonder if the demon that lived in Luke was some type of succubus or incubus, since their teeth were similar. She was built like a centerfold, with impossible curves and lines of lean muscle carved into her arms and legs.

Those long legs tapered down humanoid calves into equine ankles and hooves black as midnight that left smoking prints as they scorched the ground beneath her.

A long barbed tail snaked up over one shoulder, moving like it had a mind of its own, and her arms ended in human hands, but with wicked hooked claws instead of fingernails. Her eyes blazed yellow in the stadium lights, and even from a few feet away, I could smell the scent she was giving off. She smelled like sex and warm pancakes, like a spicy mix of everything you've ever wanted and known you shouldn't have offered up to you on a silver platter. I saw her smile widen as her scent affected me, and her forked tongue flicked out to dance across overblown lips that were so lush as to be a parody of sexy.

"Ya know," I said, fighting to catch my breath. "I always heard succubi smelled like whatever you love most in the world, but you just smell like a tired stripper eating breakfast at Denny's after last call."

Her smile dropped away and the seductress vanished, replaced by pure demonic rage. She launched herself at me, claws outstretched for my throat and face, but I met her with a blast of energy that slammed her back into the troop carrier. She hit the vehicle with a massive CLANG! and slumped to the ground.

Only for a second, though, because before I could even take a step forward, she slithered forward on her belly and lashed out at me with her tail, driving the spike into the ground where my foot had been half a second before. I danced backward as she slinked forward, spiking the turf as fast as I could lift my feet. After a few steps of this dance, I let myself bobble a little, showing myself a little off balance, and hesitated for an instant before I yanked my foot out of the way. She fell for it and overcommitted, driving her tail deeper into the earth so it became stuck momentarily.

I pounced on her mistake, literally, hopping forward and stepping on the tip of her tail, keeping it buried in the dirt and pinning Shaw in place. I raised a hand to the sky, calling power to layeth the smacketh down on her demon ass once and for all, but ended up flinging a bolt of energy straight up into the sky as Shaw spun around and in a move straight out of 1984, swept my leg and dropped me flat on my back.

I scrambled to my feet as Shaw did the same, using both hands to jerk her tail out of the ground and shooting me a dirty look. "That was rude," she said, her voice a sliding hiss. "There are a lot of things we could do that involved my tail, but none of them involve feet. A lady has to have her standards."

"How would you know?" I asked, calling more power. "You're no closer to being a lady than I am." I flung a blast of energy at her face, then followed up with a lower one aimed to the left, trying to gauge which side she'd dodge to. I stared as she just held up a hand and caught the power in her palm, then licked it up like it was chocolate syrup.

"Silly Harker. You think I'm *just* a succubus? I'm no closer to that than I am a lady. My Master has given me many blessings, some of them designed just for you. The ability to absorb and thrive on your energy is just one of them. The others I had wanted to show you in a more private setting, over hours and hours, but I suppose you won't live that long now."

There are very few things I love more than a good villain monologue. They don't just give me a chance to catch my breath, they almost always happen when something has unexpectedly gone pear-shaped for me, so I get a second to regroup mentally, too. It's half the reason I talk so much shit when I fight: I want to piss the nasties off enough to need to prove their mental superiority. The other half is because I'm a world-class smack talker and it's a sin to leave a talent like that on the shelf.

So while Shaw was fellating her fingertips and telling me how she was going to fuck me to death or something equally improbable and unpleasant (I don't ever *listen* to the damn monologues; I just use them to come up with a Plan B), I flung another three blasts of energy at her, then drew my silver-edged knives and sprang at her. If I couldn't blast her to bits, I'd slice her to ribbons. As long as she ended up filleted on the grass, I didn't really give a fuck about the how.

She sidestepped my first cut, giving me four parallel slices along my forearm in response. Okay, she's fast. Real fast. I spun around, driving a backhand stabbing blow at her kidney, but she dove out of the way into a front handspring, then spun and leapt back at me, claws reaching for my face. I got out of the way of her claws, but not her tail. The barb dug into my right shoulder, and I felt both the burning sting of the puncture and a sense of icy numbness radiating out from the wound.

Succubi have poisoned tail spikes. Good to know. Better if I knew it thirty seconds earlier, because then I'd have paid more attention to her goddamned tail. But I knew where it was now—buried in my fucking shoulder. I jerked free of it, feeling the skin tear as dozens of tiny barbs ripped my flesh on the way out, and spun around, managing to drop my knife and catch hold of her tail in my left hand before she drew it back.

With the last strength in my rapidly numbing right hand, I swept my knife up and cut off the last foot of tail, spike and all, before my fingers quit working altogether and the blade tumbled to the ground.

Shaw let out a horrific scream as black blood pulsed forth from the stump, and she rushed me, both hands slashing, trying to rip me open from nose to nuts. I couldn't get away; she was too fast, and I was down to one arm. So, I did the only thing I seem capable of doing when faced with a threat that can almost certainly kill me—I stepped right the fuck into it.

With one long stride, I stepped inside her slashing strokes, blocking her arms with my own and bringing my left hand up as we clashed together in an awkward hug. She wrapped both arms around me and buried her claws into my back, digging deep furrows all the way from my spine to my sides. I had one working hand, and it was between us, wedged between my ribcage and Shaw's chest. The barb from her tail went in just under her left breast and I used all my fast-dwindling power to drive it up, behind the ribcage, digging through her chest cavity, piercing her lung and finally, with a final thrust, slamming her own goddamned tail spike into her heart.

Her eyes went wide, and she let out a breath with a hiss of a laugh. "I'll just go home, Harker. You didn't kill me, just sent me back to the depths to plan my return. And I will return. My Master has so many more plans for you. So many."

She pulled her claws out of my back and pushed herself back off me, slumping to the grass. "My Master is greater than I! He will destroy you, Quincy Harker, and he will take the demon in your soul for his own, and he will rule for a thousand thousand years! All he has promised will come to pass! *ALL* his promises shall be fulfilled, and his most faithful shall be rewarded. I will be back, Quincy Harker, and I will dance on your grave!"

"Dance on this, bitch," Glory said from ten feet in the air above us, then she swooped down and drove her flaming sword through Shaw's right eye. The succubus's body burst into flames, flared to a blazing white, then flashed out. Seconds later, there was nothing left of Director Adrienne MacDonald Shaw but dust and a lot of blood on the ground.

No small amount of it was mine, and without anything left to fight, I dropped to my knees, flinging the demon's tail spike away. "Fuck me," I muttered. "That sucked."

I lifted my head and looked at Glory. "Thanks for the assist, but could you have stepped in just a scooch earlier?"

Glory didn't say anything, just lifted her hand and pointed back to where we'd all been standing when Shaw opened fire. There was a circle of my friends standing there, and they were all looking down at something on the ground. I could make out a pair of dark dress shoes, and then it clicked. I saw Flynn, and Jack, and Faustus standing there. Glory was with me. I felt Flynn through our link. Cassie was leaning on Jo, weeping as Jo looked down.

That only left…

"No."

40

ecks?

If she responded, I didn't hear her. I didn't hear anything but a hollow roaring in my ears. It matched the growing pit in my stomach, and I tried to push myself up to run, but all I managed to do was sprawl face-first on the grass. I shoved myself back up to my knees, and got one foot under me, then I felt a pair of small but incredibly strong hands slip under my arms and lift me. Glory picked me up and carried me through the air, her wings beating mightily as we cut through the air.

It took maybe five seconds but felt like an hour. I saw every blade of grass, noted every drop of blood on the field, registered every corpse we flew over, then I was down, on my feet for one step, then collapsing to my knees by Luke, my tears mixing with my blood as both poured down onto my uncle's motionless body.

"Luke?" I reached out and shook him. There were three holes in his chest, surprisingly small round holes with not near enough blood to have taken down the King of the Vampires, but he didn't move. I reached for a knife with my right hand, but I still couldn't make it grip the hilt. Feeling was coming back, but not fast enough. My head swam with emotion and pain and blood loss, and I wobbled on my knees. I felt Becks drop to the ground beside me, felt her arms go around me to hold me up, to hold me together.

"Luke?" I repeated, shaking him again.

"They're silver," Becks said. "CMPD SWAT issues silver magazines to their snipers for any situation where they might need them. Shaw shot him with silver bullets."

"He's not dead," I said. I knew I was wrong, but I wouldn't believe it. Not until he turned to dust in front of me, or dissolved into goo, or whatever the oldest vampire in the world would do when he died. As long as he still looked like Luke, he was alive. "Dig them out."

"What?" *Are you nuts?*

"Dig the bullets out," I said. "I can't move my fucking hand. You've got to dig the bullets out." *Please, Becks. I swear he's not gone. If you do this, he can heal. He's in there. I can feel him.*

"Quincy's right," Cassie said. "I can feel him, too. He ain't gone, but he will be soon if we don't get that silver out of him."

"Are you sure?" Flynn asked.

"Yeah," I said. "I'm sure."

"What about Jack?" she asked, looking up to the Brit. "Aren't you a doctor?"

"Not anymore, love," he said, wiggling his cane. "Since the explosion I don't have a steady enough hand to cut on anyone I want to get up off the table."

"It's got to be you, babe," I said. *You're the one I trust. You're the one he'd trust.*

"Okay," she said. "Give me a little room." I scooted back on the grass, then stood as Glory ducked under my left arm and held me up. It was a lot easier to do once she tucked her wings away. Jo and Cassie stood on the other side with Jack, looking down as Flynn pulled out her pocketknife, flicked it open, and closed her eyes for a moment.

Here goes literally everything.

You got this, babe. There's no one I'd rather have doing this.

There's legitimately everyone *I'd rather have doing this*, she sent back to me, but I felt her smile a little at the encouragement.

Then she buried the tip of her knife in the hole for the first bullet and started to dig. It seemed like it took hours, but after a minute or two of her probing with the tip of the knife, she looked up. "I found it. I felt the knife scrape against something."

"Okay, pull it out," I said.

"That's usually not the best idea," Jack said. "The victim is more likely to bleed out with the bullet gone."

"This isn't a human being, Jack," I snarled at him. "This is a vampire. *The* vampire, and if we can get the fucking silver out of him, then he can heal. Becks, get the bullet out."

She nodded, then looked up at me again, stricken. "I don't have anything to pull it out with."

"Use this." Pravesh's cultured voice accompanied an outstretched hand holding a multitool. I looked at her, definitely the worse for wear after being shot in the leg but holding together pretty well. I raised an eyebrow at her.

"What? You carry two guns and three knives everywhere you go. I carry a Leatherman. Which one of us is stranger?" she asked.

"Says the snake woman," I muttered, then gave her a sideways smile. "Thanks."

Becks unfolded the needle nose pliers and wedged them into the wound, her face a rictus as she imagined the pain she was putting Luke through. I for one was really glad he seemed to be unconscious. After an interminable time of fishing around in Luke's chest, she pulled out a flattened silver bullet and dropped it onto the grass.

"Jesus," she said. "That was awful." She looked up and around at us. "I know, worse for Luke. Just gimme a second."

"I can do this if you would like," Pravesh said. "I am not as... emotionally invested."

All of Luke's suspicions flashed back in an instant, and I immediately snapped, "No. She's got this."

Pravesh gave me a puzzled look, as did most everyone else. Flynn looked up at me, her face a wreck of sweat and tears and blood spatter. "Harker, are you sure?"

"I'm sure."

"But it was me he was protecting," she protested. "Shaw was trying to kill me, and Luke stepped in front of the bullets." I could see the guilt on her face, and it broke my heart, but I had to stay firm. I was almost certain that Pravesh was not a mole, but almost wasn't certain enough to let her dig around in Luke's chest with a silver bullet.

"And he'd do it again tomorrow," I said. "Because that's what we do —we take the bullets so our loved ones don't have to. Now get these chunks of silver out of his chest so he *can* stand between us and certain death the next time."

Melodramatic, but it worked. Becks turned back to the prone vampire and examined the next wound. "I think this one may be deeper, but it's in softer tissue. The last one looks like it may have hit a rib, and I think it's pretty close to the surface. It should be easier. So, I'll do the harder one now. You...might not want to watch this. It's going to be incredibly gross."

She turned back to her patient and took a deep breath. Then she sliced his shirt completely open, instead of trying to work through a small tear in it like with the last slug. Apparently she'd decided that as long as the silver was gone, Luke could heal from almost anything, because she made a long horizontal slash across his abdomen, wide enough to get her entire hand in.

She was right, of course. I'd seen Luke grow back an entire hand once, so coming back from some meatball surgery in the middle of a football field would be painful, but I was willing to bet he'd be more upset about bleeding onto his expensive Italian shoes. Even I winced as Becks closed her eyes and shoved her hand into his abdomen and just started feeling around for the bullet. I was one of the few people actually watching, so almost no one but me saw her eyes go wide.

Flynn looked up at me, a grin splitting her face. "I got it!" She pulled her hand out, and sure enough, there was the second bullet. She dropped it onto the grass and turned back to Luke, then froze.

"That is...incredibly uncomfortable, young lady," Luke said, his voice thin and reedy.

"Holy shit," I muttered. "You're *awake?*"

"Not by choice, I assure you, Quincy. But it is frightfully hard to sleep with someone's fingers tickling your gallbladder. By the way, my dear, the next time you go traipsing around in someone's abdomen, please trim your fingernails first."

"I'm so sorry," Flynn said, rocking back on her heels. "I thought you were unconscious. We thought you were dying. I never would have—"

"My dear child, I *was* dying. Now, thanks to your ministrations, I am not. I am still very weak, so if you would please remove the final bullet, I can inquire as to the willingness of some of these fine officers to aid me in my healing."

Flynn nodded, tears in her eyes, then said, "Um…could you close your eyes again? I don't think I can cut you with you looking at me."

"If I could move my hand, I'd do it and tell jokes the whole time," I said, drawing a frown from my uncle.

"It is a good thing for you I am injured, Quincy. Otherwise I would be forced to slap you for that."

"You get back to standing, and we'll spar again, Uncle," I said. "Promise."

"I shall hold you to that." He looked at Flynn, then closed his eyes. "Please proceed, my dear."

She leaned down again, and this time all eyes were on her as she worked. I guess that's my excuse. I was so intent on paying attention to Luke and Becks, that I wasn't alert for threats. I mean, we'd fought our way through a mob of monsters, cops, and federal agents, knocked out a shitty police major, and killed a succubus with her own tail, that last while our heaviest hitter was lying on the ground near death. We'd been through enough for one night, right? I could take two minutes to just watch my fiancée save my uncle's life without somebody trying to destroy everything I loved, right?

Wrong.

The first hint I had that anything was wrong was hearing Jo say, "What the—?"

I turned to see Jack with his sword cane drawn, silvered blade gleaming and tears rolling down his face. He looked me in the eye and said, "I'm sorry. But My Master promised to make it all right again…"

Then he raised his sword and drove it forward, straight for Flynn's unguarded back.

The angle he had would go straight through Becks and into Luke, pinning both of them to the ground and possibly piercing both their hearts. I dove for them, but my wounds from the fight with Shaw were too much, and I sprawled to the grass on my belly, taking Glory down with me. I heard Pravesh shout something, but with her bum leg, there was no way she could reach Jack in time. I bounced off the turf just in time to see Luke fling Becks to one side, clear of Jack's blade and safely away from all of us. The blade flashed down, and the world held its breath.

As Cassandra Skyler Harrison flung herself in front of the sword and took the thrust meant for Flynn and Luke. She wrapped both hands around the blade and yanked it with her as she leapt between it and Luke, who struggled to move after spending so much strength to fling Becks to safety. Cassie pulled the sword, and Jack, along with her, and when she hit the ground, Jack overbalanced and fell forward, driving the blade all the way through Cassie as he did.

Time froze as we watched Cassie fall, as we watched the blade pin her to the ground, as we watched the blood begin to pool underneath her. Then time thawed, and as Luke and Jo screamed in unison, the light fled from Cassie's eyes.

41

Everything was silent, and everything screamed. Time froze for an instant as I watched Cassie die, less than ten feet away from me and too far to save. One fat tear rolled from the corner of her right eye as she breathed, "Alex," her late husband's name a whisper in the too-silent night. Then she was gone, and everything slammed into full-speed life again with the clarity and clamor of a car crash.

I pushed myself up off the turf and sprang for Jack, who knelt on the grass with his hands on his knees, staring at the body where our friend used to live. I tackled him around the shoulders, driving him to the turf, and rolled him over. All my injuries were forgotten, rage burning through every cell as I slammed my fist into his face.

"What the fuck, Jack? Are you a fucking traitor? What are you doing? What? Why? Who made you... Why her...?" I felt a hand on my wrist, yanked free, then felt another, stronger grip. I couldn't keep hitting him, even though I wanted nothing more than to smear his face all across the field. I looked up to see Becks standing a few feet away, with Glory right above me holding my fist suspended in the air.

"Stop it, Q."

"Let me go."

"Stop."

"Go help Cassie! Get her some of Luke's…" My words trailed off as Glory's face registered. "No…" The word felt very small and yet it filled every square inch of me. I felt the empty, the anguish, the rage, the sorrow, all of it boiled up in me like a volcano, and I shot off my feet to grab Glory by the shoulders.

"Help her!" I pointed at Cassie's body, lying face-up on the grass, both hands splayed out to her sides. "Save her." It wasn't an order. It wasn't a request. It was me begging, not just her, but God Himself, to save my friend, and suddenly it was a hundred years ago again and I was back in England looking at my brothers' wasted forms in their filthy beds, fourteen and twenty years old and destined to never grow a day older. Suddenly I stood in their sickroom and I was looking up at the ceiling bargaining with someone, some*thing* I didn't even think I believed in, to no avail.

Then I blinked, and I was standing on a blood-stained high school football field littered with dead bodies and injured beings and shell casings, staring into the eyes of the angel who had done the impossible so many times, who had reached down into the fire and yanked me back to the light more times than I could count, and I was watching her heart break for me.

Glory stood there, tears rolling down her face, shaking her head. "She's gone, Q. I watched her soul walk into the light. She's gone. I'm sorry, I can't bring her back."

I stood, staring into those deep blue eyes, knowing that she'd never lied to me in all the time I'd known her. She might not have told me everything I thought I needed to know, but she'd never lied. And there was no way she was lying now. I tried to turn back to Watson, but Glory held me in an iron grip.

"Your family needs you now," she said. She took half a step to the side, forcing me to look at Flynn, down on one knee with her hair spilling down over her face as her shoulders shook with sobs. I saw Jo, sitting cross-legged on the grass, her face blank, completely in shock, with Pravesh's arms wrapped around her shoulders. I saw Luke writhing on the grass in fury and pain, clawing at his injured shoulder where a silver bullet was still lodged in his pectoral muscle. Broken, every one of them. At least as broken as me, maybe more. Nothing would fix this, but one thing might at least pick up the pieces.

I looked Glory in the face and said, "I'm not going to hurt him, but we have to know why. We have to know what he was trying to do."

She peered deep in my eyes, and I let her in. I let her see it all, my rage, my pain, my knowledge that nothing I did was going to bring Cassie back, but if I could save the rest of them, she wouldn't have sacrificed herself for nothing. Glory nodded and let me go.

I turned back to Watson, who lay curled up in the fetal position on the grass. "Sit up," I said, my voice cold and hard as a gravestone in midwinter.

"I'm so sorry." His moans were pitiful, and his words, coming from the shattered mess of his face, were almost incomprehensible.

"I don't give a fuck," I snapped. "Sit the fuck up before I rip your arms off and beat you to death with them. The only thing keeping you alive right now is what you know, so start talking, and it better be useful."

Jack wiped his eyes, smeared the blood around on his face a little, and managed to drag himself up to his knees before he looked up at me. His face was a horror show. I had literally beaten him into a nearly unrecognizable mass of broken facial bones and bloody pulp. I stared at him, a kaleidoscope of bruises and agony, and felt not an iota or remorse. He killed my friend. He was lucky Glory was there to stop me, or I would have literally beaten him to death. Even so, he probably had a fractured skull. I looked down at my hands and saw for the first time that all the knuckles were split, one clear to the bone, and my hands were swollen almost into paddles from the beating. I didn't feel it. Nothing outside hurt, and everything inside was too damned cold.

Jack looked up at me and opened his mouth. I held up a mangled finger, and he closed his mouth. "I only give a fuck about two things, Jack. You tell me those two things, and I won't rip your goddamn head off. You lie to me, and they will never find all the pieces. You understand me?"

He nodded.

"Why? Why her? Why *Cassie?*"

His shoulders shook as he fought back sobs, then he turned to the side and retched, emptying the contents of his stomach and vomiting up blood all over the grass. He spit out more blood, then turned to look up at me. "It wasn't supposed to be her. It was never supposed to *be* Cassie. It was supposed to be Luke. And if I couldn't get Luke, then Flynn. When she started pulling the bullets out of his chest, I thought I might be able to kill them both, then he couldn't be angry because of all this." He waved his hand out at the football field.

"Who is he?" I asked, my voice shaking with fury. Not only did he murder my friend, he killed her trying to kill the two people I love most in the world. This motherfucker was *not* walking off this field tonight, Glory or no Glory. Jack didn't answer, so I leaned over. "Who?!?" I yelled in his face from inches away.

Watson cringed, flinching away from me. "I don't know! I never saw his face, never spoke to him in person! Almost everything was on encrypted phones, or through Shaw. She was his right hand; she was the one..."

"The one what?" I asked. Nothing. "Goddammit, Jack, if you make me repeat myself every fucking time, I swear to God—"

"The one who said she could fix it!" Jack cried. His voice was so pitiful, and when he looked up at me through that ruined face, his eyes were so full of remorse and anguish that I almost started to forgive him. Then I felt Becks' presence in the back of my soul, knew that he wanted to take that away from me, and forgiveness died on the vine.

"What was she going to fix?" Something hit me as one hand drifted down to the knee right above his prosthetic. "Did she say she could give you your leg back? Did you just fucking kill Cassie so you wouldn't have to wear a prosthetic leg? You selfish mother—"

"No!" The word was muffled, but I could tell what he was trying to shout. "That's not it. I mean, yes, I'd get my leg back, *too*. But that wasn't what I wanted. I wanted her to fix it *all*. Make it so it never happened. So we never hit that fucking IED. So Tolley, and Hayes, and

Bartalone didn't end up strewn across the goddamn desert. Yes, I wanted my leg back, but I wanted *them* back more. I did all this to save their lives. They were my men, Harker, and they died. I was on the fucking radio instead of looking ahead for threats, and I didn't see the car where they planted the bomb. They died, and it was my fucking fault. So, if I could kill a four-hundred-year-old parasite to bring back three good men, I was okay with that." He glared up at me, defiance bright in the one eye he could open around the swelling.

I shoved aside the fact that the "parasite" in question was my closest relative and oldest friend. For a second. "This mystery man claimed he could erase the explosion?"

"Yes! That's what it was all about! I just wanted to save my men!"

"And get your leg back."

He looked down and away, not answering.

"You've been rubbing your fucking knee ever since you sat up, you prick," I said. "You can tell yourself this was all to save your men, but you got tired of your fucking prosthetic and were willing to kill Luke or Becks to grow a new leg like a fucking starfish!"

"Yes!" he shouted. "You're goddamn right I'm tired of this thing! I'm tired of it hurting, I'm tired of it not bending right and making me walk like a drunken sailor on shore leave. I'm tired of it chafing. I'm tired of meeting a woman, and before I can take off my pants, I have to take off my fucking leg! I want my fucking leg back, Harker! Is that so fucking bad?"

"You were going to kill my fiancée to get your fucking leg back, you traitorous piece of shit. So yeah, it's that fucking bad. Now who is he? Who was Shaw's Master?"

"I told you, I don't know! I swear to God—"

"Don't you fucking bring Him into this," Glory said. "He doesn't abide this shit any better than Harker does, and I should know. I was around for the Old Testament."

"You don't know anything?" I asked. "Why Luke? Why Flynn? Why them?" I was pretty sure I knew the answer, but I wanted to hear this little prick say it.

"He said if I killed one of them, you'd go insane, and if I could somehow kill them both, there wouldn't be anyone left who could pull you back. He said that he wanted to take everything away from you before he killed you. Just like you did to him."

I looked at Glory, then Becks. They both shook their heads. Who the fuck could hate me that much? There were a lot of people who wanted me dead, but who wanted me to suffer like that? It didn't make sense. I looked down at Watson. "That's all you know?"

"I swear." He turned to Jo. "I'm so sorry. It wasn't supposed to be her. It was *never* going to be her. I loved Cassie!" A jet-black hand flashed in from beside me and laid a ringing slap on the side of Jack's face. I looked over and saw Faustus standing there, breathing heavy.

"Don't you fucking talk about love, you traitorous piece of shit," the demon said. "I'm a fucking *demon* and I have more honor than you! I learned betrayal in the pits of fucking Hell from Lucifer himself and I could never do the shit you've done. You lied to us, you lied to *me*!" Faustus stepped back, and I saw something I'd never seen in all my years. A tear spilled over the demon's eyelid and cascaded down his face. "You were my *friend*! My best friend. My *first* friend, you son of a bitch!" Faustus whirled around and stalked off. "I gotta go."

I looked down at the stunned Watson, leaning on his knees and one hand, the other pressed to his cheek. Then my gaze went to Jo, who had gotten to her feet and stood a few feet away, her father's hammer in her hand and salt tracks down her cheeks. "Your call, Jo. Pravesh can arrest him and make him disappear, or I can rip out his heart and leave him dead in a puddle of blood and shit surrounded by puddles of blood and shit."

"Or I can bash his goddamned head in with John Henry's hammer and deliver my own old-fashioned justice," she said, hefting the hammer as if testing its weight.

"Or that," I agreed. Glory took a step toward Jo, but it was my turn to put a hand on the angel's arm. "No. Let her decide."

Jo stepped up in front of Jack, and I got out of the way. I wasn't going to kill the bastard. I'd help Pravesh make damn sure he never drew another breath outside a cell, but I had enough blood on my hands for one night. And if he was dead, I couldn't visit him every few years to rearrange his face again.

"I should smash your fucking skull," Jo said, fury making her voice shake.

"You probably should," Jack replied.

"You killed my *mother*."

"I am so sorry."

"You think that helps? You think what you did can be forgiven?"

"No. But I am. Sorry."

Jo looked down at him, then slung her hammer over her left shoulder. "Yeah. You are. You're a sorry excuse for a human being, Jack Watson, and I hope you live a long time to think about that. A long time completely alone, without ever knowing the kind of friendship again that we gave you, that *she* gave you." Jo turned to me. "I'm not going to kill him."

"I figured."

"We're the good guys, Harker."

"Most days."

"Then I'm not gonna kill the son of a bitch. Because we're the good guys, and that's not what we do."

"Okay," I said, and held out my arms. Jo fell into them, her body wracked with giant sobs, and I felt Glory's hand in the center of my back, holding me up just like always.

Then I heard the rustle of grass and cloth, and a slight groan, and as Jo stepped back, I turned to see Luke struggling to his feet. Red-tinged tears stained both cheeks, and his right hand was covered in blood and clutching something too small for me to make out.

"You. Killed. My. Renfield." He gasped out the words, as if his lungs couldn't hold enough air yet, like he hadn't started healing from his gunshot wounds. He raised his hand and flicked something in Jack's direction, and when it struck the kneeling man, he fell back, a hole appearing in his right shoulder.

"What the fuck?" I muttered, but I knew what it was. It was a bullet. It was the silver bullet Luke had dug out of his own shoulder as he lay on the grass writhing in pain and grief.

Luke staggered over to where Jack lay on the turf, then he fell upon the traitor and fastened his teeth to his neck. Jack's feet kicked once, twice, then fell still. Luke remained latched onto Jack's throat for several more seconds before he stood and turned back to face us, leaving Jack twitching on the field, not dead, but definitely heavily drained. Jo, Flynn, Pravesh, and I stood in a loose semicircle, with Glory behind us, helping to hold me up.

Luke's face was a horror show, his lips and lower jaw covered in blood. I'd seen Luke feed many times, but never with the feral light in his eyes that shone there now. This wasn't my uncle, Lucas Card. This was fucking *Dracula*. He crossed the distance between us in a blur of motion, completely restored after partially draining Jack, and looked Jo in the eye.

"I loved your mother."

"I know."

"She loved me."

"I know."

"She remained faithful to your father, and I respected that."

"I know."

"Good. But there are two things that you were very wrong about, Joanna Rebecca Skyler Harrison."

"What's that?" Jo asked, her voice quiet as she looked into Luke's eyes.

He reached down between them and took her great-grandfather's hammer. Without breaking eye contact, he twisted the handle until the wood began to crack. With one fluid motion, he snapped the head off the huge sledge, leaving a splintered mass at one end.

Luke turned away, hammer handle in hand, and took three long steps over to where Watson lay struggling to roll over. Luke looked down at him, said something too quiet for even me to hear, and drove the improvised spear into Jack's chest. Then he hoisted the dying man up on the handle, raising him high above his head and grinned up as Jack's traitorous blood poured down upon his face. He stood there, smiling up into the crimson rain, until Jack's body slid down the handle, its weight pulling the stick through itself. Then Luke tossed the corpse aside like so much garbage, to land with a wet *thunk* on the ground.

Luke walked back over to where we stood, frozen. "You were wrong, my dear. I am not a 'good guy,' and this is *exactly* what I do." Then he blurred into motion and disappeared into the night.

I looked at my friends, looked at Jack's impaled body, then looked up to the heavens. "God help us all," I said. "The big bad...is back."

THE END...For Now

ABOUT THE AUTHOR

John G. Hartness is a teller of tales, a righter of wrong, defender of ladies' virtues, and some people call him Maurice, for he speaks of the pompatus of love. He is also the best-selling author of EPIC-Award-winning series *The Black Knight Chronicles* from Bell Bridge Books, a comedic urban fantasy series that answers the eternal question "Why aren't there more fat vampires?" In July of 2016. John was honored with the Manly Wade Wellman Award by the NC Speculative Fiction Foundation for Best Novel by a North Carolina writer in 2015 for the first Quincy Harker novella, *Raising Hell.*

In 2016, John teamed up with a pair of other publishing industry ne'er-do-wells and founded Falstaff Books, a publishing company dedicated to pushing the boundaries of literature and entertainment.

In his copious free time John enjoys long walks on the beach, rescuing kittens from trees and getting caught in the rain. An avid *Magic: the Gathering* player, John is strong in his nerd-fu and has sometimes been referred to as "the Kevin Smith of Charlotte, NC." And not just for his girth.

Find out more about John online
www.johnhartness.com

ALSO BY JOHN G. HARTNESS

THE BLACK KNIGHT CHRONICLES

The Black Knight Chronicles - Omnibus Edition

The Black Knight Chronicles Continues - Omnibus #2

All Knight Long - Black Knight Chronicles #7

BUBBA THE MONSTER HUNTER

Scattered, Smothered, & Chunked - Bubba the Monster Hunter Season One

Grits, Guns, & Glory - Bubba Season Two

Wine, Women, & Song - Bubba Season Three

Monsters, Magic, & Mayhem - Bubba Season Four

Born to Be Wild

Shinepunk: A Beauregard the Monster Hunter Collection

QUINCY HARKER, DEMON HUNTER

Year One: A Quincy Harker, Demon Hunter Collection

The Cambion Cycle - Quincy Harker, Year Two

Damnation - Quincy Harker Year Three

Salvation - Quincy Harker Year Four

Carl Perkins' Cadillac - A Quincy Harker, Demon Hunter Novel

Histories: A Quincy Harker, Demon Hunter Collection

SHINGLES

Zombies Ate My Homework: Shingles Book 5

Slow Ride: Shingles Book 12

Carnival of Psychos: Shingles Book 19

Jingle My Balls: Shingles Book 24

FRIENDS OF FALSTAFF

Thank You to All our Falstaff Books Patrons, who get extra digital content each month! To be featured here and see what other great rewards we offer, go to www.patreon.com/falstaffbooks.

PATRONS

Dino Hicks
John Hooks
John Kilgallon
Larissa Lichty
Travis & Casey Schilling
Staci-Leigh Santore
Sheryl R. Hayes
Scott Norris
Samuel Montgomery-Blinn
Junkle